Kim Westwood was born in Sydney, Australia, and spent several years of her childhood in New Zealand. In 2002 her short story 'The Oracle' won an Aurealis Award. Since then, her stories have been chosen for Year's Best anthologies in Australia and the US, and for ABC radio broadcast. She is the recipient of a prestigious Varuna Writer's Fellowship for her first novel, the critically acclaimed *The Daughters of Moab*.

KIM WESTWOOD

THE COURIER'S NEW BICYCLE

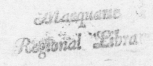

HARPER
Voyager

Harper*Voyager*
An imprint of HarperCollins*Publishers*

First published in Australia in 2011
by HarperCollins*Publishers* Australia Pty Limited
ABN 36 009 913 517
harpercollins.com.au

HarperCollins*Publishers*
Level 13, 201 Elizabeth Street, Sydney NSW 2000, Australia
31 View Road, Glenfield, Auckland 0627, New Zealand
A 53, Sector 57, Noida, UP, India
77–85 Fulham Palace Road, London W6 8JB, United Kingdom
2 Bloor Street East, 20th Floor, Toronto, Ontario M4W 1A8, Canada
10 East 53rd Street, New York, NY 10022, USA

National Library of Australia Cataloguing-in-Publication entry

Westwood, Kim.
    The courier's new bicycle / Kim Westwood.
    ISBN 978 0 7322 8988 1 (pbk.)
A823.4

Cover design by Darren Holt, HarperCollins Design Studio
Cover images by shutterstock.com
Typeset in Bembo 11/16pt by Letter Spaced
Printed and bound in Australia by Griffin Press
50gsm Bulky News used by HarperCollins*Publishers* is a natural, recyclable
product made from wood grown in sustainable plantation forests. The
manufacturing processes conform to the environmental regulations in the
country of origin, New Zealand.

6 5 4 3 2 1   11 12 13 14

For Brenda

You can change the story. You are the story.

Jeanette Winterson

The.PowerBook

I

'Eve's Delight?'

The shop assistant on door duty with the atomiser sprays indiscriminately. It's too late to veer; I hunch over the bike's handlebars straight through the cloud of cologne.

'Gives your hormones a lift,' the woman spruiks.

Yeah, right. Up my nose and down my throat. Makes me cough. I swear and dodge a pedestrian, then cycle off the pavement to snug in beside a slow-moving tram.

I don't want a dose of Eve's Delight. I already have another woman's scent on my skin. Last night Inez faced me, too close for conversation. 'So kiss me,' she said. I responded as only the unpractised do: immediately.

I lean for a left turn, and nearly collect a scooter rider. We both make rude signs. Scooters are the latest scourge of the road now the petrol guzzlers are gone, banned from Melbourne's CBD. These ecotech replacements are zippy, erratic and ridden by thrillseekers aged nine to ninety.

Northeast of the city grid, Dingle Street is a crowded Fitzroy thoroughfare lined with dilapidated shopfronts separated by the occasional service alley. Here there are more scooters and some motorised three-wheelers towing small covered buggies. Halfway along, the Good Bean café squeezes between an Asian grocery and a laundromat. On a busy day when all the washer-dryers are going full bore, the café vibrates. It can give a gender transgressive a bit of a thrill if they're sitting astride their barstool right.

I wheel the bike through the door and rest it against the inside glass, nodding to the proprietor, who lifts a finger in reply. Sitting at the end of the bar, his hand permanently attached to a demitasse of the Good Bean, Frank oversees all comings and goings, his boxer-faced features set in a permanent droop. He's one of the few I trust with my most treasured possession: an aging road racer, sought after by thieves in a city nobbled by fuel shortages.

The café is narrow but deep-backed. The barista's shiny work station and metal counter take up one wall, a line of formica tables the other, lampshades hanging low over the tables like card players' lights.

'Salisbury!'

Gail strides my way in executive black, her broad frame filling the space. Closer, a square jaw amplifies lush, colour-delineated lips below a patrician nose and plucked brows. The brows rise, amused, taking in my helmet-mussed hair and cycle jacket moulting its reflector strips. Her voice remodulates to speak of private things in public places.

'So glad you could extricate yourself from Inez's charms.'

I wince, feel the blush. News travels to my boss faster than telepathy.

Bussing my cheek, she murmurs, 'I have a little job for you.'

She leads me to a table and gestures me to sit. Frank brings our usual over himself.

'New Guinea blend,' he says gruffly then dabs the edge of Gail's saucer with his tea towel, betraying the soft spot I've long suspected he has for her.

She sips appreciatively. When Frank leaves, she says low-tone, 'I need something delivered to Cutters Lane.'

That lane runs like a deep vein through a section of the city called the Red Quarter, an enclave of bordellos, surrogacy organisations and fertility doctors.

'When?' I ask.

'Tonight. And there's something else.'

Now we get to it. Gail sells fertility hormones — 'kit', once legal, now banned — which makes me a midnight postie, a courier of secret packages … and sometimes, under sufferance, a snoop.

She frowns. 'Word is there's a new player on the field. Not one of us, so we need to find out if it's one of them.'

She means a distributor of kit sourced from animals in the out-of-town hormone farms — a barbarous practice Gail has no truck with.

She waits for a café-goer to pass. 'I've heard they're operating out of Fishermans Bend. If they're rookies, they'll

3

be easy to spot. Take a quick nose around the area tomorrow, starting with the old hormone factories at the end of Barrow Road. Nothing fancy, just casual daytime stuff. See what you can see.'

I sigh inwardly. I'm to scope out rookie players. And if they catch me looking?

I check sideways to the patrons seated at the bar, then back to where my coffee wisps a genetically altered steam. Frank buys his beans from an associate of Gail's, an importer of illegal GM produce.

'I'm a bit short of friends,' I say casually to the cup.

'Fixed.' She slides a hand into the breast pocket of her expensive suit then palms across two blister strips of tiny blue-filled capsules. 'The ones with a yellow stripe are a new recipe,' she warns. 'Come by my office later for your parcel.'

Outside, dusk smudges the air between buildings, the streetlights blinking on, coral pink. Under the halo of the closest, a Saturday prayer meeting is hands high for a miracle. Of course, there's really only one they're after these days. And with the current government's B2N — Back to Nature — laws prohibiting 'unnatural practices', including gene therapy and hormone replacement, a miracle is all they have left to hope for.

The huddle comprises two men and three women in sackcloth penance shawls. I glide past, eyes front, the bike's chain ticking quietly around greased cogs. 'Good luck,' I murmur.

Further down the street I pass another lot. Dusk always brings them out like moths.

I turn the corner and push in among a slow line of solar-electric vehicles, the streets no less congested but strangely quiet since the phasing out of the old engines. Personally, I prefer leg power. Always have. But I never intended a life of skulking in the city's alleyways, one foot on the pedal, ready to bolt.

No one could have predicted what the flu pandemic ten years ago would bring, the vaccine dispensed Australia-wide messing badly with human endocrinology. The effects of endocrine disruption from everyday chemicals had been creeping up for decades. The vaccine, cut with an untried adjuvant to make it go further, was simply one straw too many, pushing what were already primed physiologies into auto-immune overdrive. As fertility plummeted, people scrambled for restoratives like adulterers for clothes, and entrepreneurs like Gail positioned themselves to exploit the opportunity. Her legitimate hormone-distribution business was forced underground when, five years later, Nation First won the elections and closed down all surrogacy organisations, then told the public to cast aside the Devil's help, place their trust in God and pray for the return of their fertility.

A tram clangs a warning up ahead, its front light a bright star below the umber-streaked sky. With Gail not expecting me until eleven, I head first for home.

My flat is in an unrenovated row of terraces in Fitzroy, opposite an overflowing public housing high-rise. A creaky old wattle provides shelter at the front, while in the enclosed courtyard accessed from the laneway at the back a pebble path meanders like a dry creek bed between stands of native grass and bonsai dunes — xeriscapes *de rigueur* now due to the permanent water restrictions. Call me ungrateful, but I pine for English green: lush rolling lawns and a few water-sucking willows.

I stash the bike temporarily beneath paint-peeled eaves, put the key in the back door and push on old wood. Hinges squeal complaint; I leave them that way deliberately. My pauper's version of an intruder alarm.

Nitro waits for me on his kitty couch, his fur glowing a muted purple the equivalent of six watts. Eight years ago I picked him from a mewling litter a variety of colours, ears tagged by wattage, shortly before glow-in-the-dark enhancements — animal or otherwise — were banned. Now he's one of the few left in the wake of the Unnatural Practices Act, and wanted by the Animal Patrol.

He pads across the carpet to rub against my leg. I always expect some of the colour to come off, but happily it stays with the cat. I lean down to stroke along a flank, the thick fur a reassuring plush between my fingers. He mews plaintively and leads me to the galley kitchen. I splash some formula into his Benjamin Bunny saucer and watch him lap avidly, purring as he drinks, a miracle of feline survival.

I plug in sitting on a corner of the bath. A blue — unstriped — capsule goes in the dispenser then it's a quick subdermal shot, the portable unit delivering its contents

6

into the soft tissues and lymphatics using electricity as the carrier. A tingling sensation in my forearm and it's done.

Gail calls the stuff 'Courier's Friend', a special mix she distributes to her delivery team. It's an EPO concoction with a few feel-good extras thrown in. She likes to keep her messengers efficient and happy. As for me, I just like the occasional buzz.

I lean against the cool of the wall and watch a black juggernaut of cloud edge into frame through my bathroom window, its underbelly aflame. The effects of the capsule will trickle into my system across the next few hours, peaking around midnight. I return the dispenser to its niche behind a sliding section of bathroom wall, flush the empty capsule and step into the shower.

As I change into warmer cycling clothes, Nitro kneads the discards on the bedroom floor and I get a frisson of recollection. Here, less than twenty-four hours ago, Inez — my unrequited love interest of many months — undressed in front of me and led me to my bed.

I glance at the clock on the dresser. Time to fix myself some food before I go to Gail's. As for later … maybe I can persuade Inez back between the sheets.

My preferred route to Gail's office zigzags through back alleys into the old railway-workers' district of West Melbourne, its silent streets lined with ill-cared-for bungalows pressing ever closer to the earth. Here, windows are battened against the dark fingers of the night and fences give way to inky pools of unlit parkland. A dilapidated chain-link fence looms on my left; behind it the cutting drops steeply onto railway lines and freight yards. I breathe hard, shoulders working as I lean over the bars and push, guilty that a last-minute flurry of salacious text messages initiated by Inez has delayed me.

Four blocks out from Gail's, a boy in a muscle shirt and commando pants is stubbing his boot repeatedly against factory brick. I ease past his self-absorbed vehemence. Fertility issues aside, puberty is a treacherous passage chock-full of confusion and inexplicable bouts of self-hate and rage. Added to it now are the frustrations of the B2N prohibitions and temperance laws. So should I stop and give him a little blue capsule from my emergency stash? Guess not.

I come up off the seat for the last rise, pushing into the toeholds, enjoying the burn in my muscles and the surge of kit in my system. My physiology, made for sport, earned me the tag 'freak' at school; but now, when I choose to do it, that capacity combined with Gail's special recipes makes cycling lots of fun and me a useful employee, because in this job, bikes rule. I can get anywhere I want in the inner city, regardless of traffic regulations and curfews, and I can do it at speed.

Gail's business premises come into view: a two-storey warehouse occupying a prominent position on a corner, the Cute'n'Cuddly brand name writ large across the front. It's always been a source of amusement to me that my decidedly un-cute and non-cuddly employer's day job is trucking soft toys — wombats and wallabies, echidnas and cockatoos — out to a market hungrier than ever for comfort.

Closer, industrial windows and candy-striped brick make a patchwork of darkly reflective surfaces. I type on the keypad at the deliveries entrance and the heavy steel gate clicks open. Inside the enclosed yard to my right is a row of plain white delivery trucks sitting under carport cover; left is the main building with a recessed workers entrance and a pair of matching roller doors. Of the latter, one gives access to the warehouse at ground level while the other leads into the basement, which is a storage area ostensibly, and where Gail's 'alternative' business is conducted.

I lean the bike and press on the button that releases the catch for the door. Gail is waiting behind it in her office: the unmarked one with no windows that the Cute'n'Cuddly clientele never get to visit. There's no chair for visitors, no one else meant to be so comfortable as to want to sit in Gail's personal space — not even Gail it seems, who's perched on the edge of her desk, jabbing at the keys of a laptop.

She snicks the lid closed. 'You're late.'

Never one to belabour a point, she goes to a filing cabinet, opens the top drawer and hands over the parcel for delivery to Cutters Lane. As usual, it's neatly aesthetic and understated: brown paper wrapped with string. I wonder which of the 'cuddly' options tucked inside has been chosen to be the Trojan horse. A zip-up bilby, perhaps, or a chirruping galah?

'Number 137. Knock & drop,' she says, and shepherds me out the door.

The Red Quarter carefully minds its own business in a mid sector of Melbourne's CBD, its network of streets and alleyways home to a trade made perpetual pariah, each glowy pink entrance protected by a security grille and intercom.

This part of town is run by the Bordello Workers Union, a powerful cabal of madams who joined forces to buy up the real estate vacated during the flu pandemic, then successfully muscled out the local mafia and roving street pimps. The madams also took on the role of brokers for those working in the publicly disbanded surrogacy network after its members were 'outed' as Jezebels by Nation First and hounded mercilessly by the prayer groups. Any still prepared to meet the ongoing demand end up living here for their protection.

Mostly, those in the wider community partake of the services offered along Madams Row and leave the rest of the Red Quarter in peace, although occasionally a Neighbourhood Values Brigade gravitates further inside to bang on the iron grilles and shout of retribution. But even they don't venture down the numerous passages that have become home to an even more secret profession: the fertility specialists and gene doctors plying their illegal trade on the 'God-given' physiologies of their beleaguered clients.

The dual LEDs on my helmet and handlebars rattle forth a shaky light as I ride slowly over sheening cobbles, the gelid air glittering on lampposts and downpipes. I shiver, despite my windstop jacket and thermal layers. Those few still out are chins in scarves and hurrying to be somewhere else. No one wants to be seen in this part of town when they should be tucked up in their homes observing the strictures of a Sabbath morning.

Cutters Lane doglegs, too narrow for cars, deep inside the enclave. Keeping track of the numbers glinting on the doors, I round the final corner — and nearly pedal into a group gathered in the middle of the alley, their features hidden beneath sackcloth penance shawls.

Heads turn, invisible faces look. Sucking in my breath, I bite my lip and taste the sting of blood. So much for knock & drop.

Cursing, I veer down the nearest passage then haul on the handlebars as a cat streaks across my path. The bike slips on damp stone, nearly low-siding me, and my left pedal comes loose from its post, wrenching my ankle. I slew to a stop, my breath puffing through my balaclava in fast little clouds.

What's a prayer group doing here of all places, and at this time of night?

I'm examining the damaged pedal when two cowled figures appear behind me in the passageway, advancing deliberately. I yank it free and stuff it in my bag. Foot on the bare post, I ride on fast. Ahead, the passage rejoins Cutters Lane. I scoot out — and meet three more of them hurrying up.

A firecracker burst of adrenaline triggers in every muscle. I drop into racing position. No way am I going to be mobbed in the middle of the night by a bunch of hessian-wearing fanatics.

The leader makes a grab for my handlebars. I swing my elbow up hard under the cowl. It connects with bone and I hear the grunt. The others reverse-step, suddenly reticent. Speeding away along the lane, I cast a quick look behind. The five have already melted into the shadows.

Several alleys of overflowing bins and unlit entrances later, I'm back on Madams Row, and stop astride the bike to press the phonelink hooked in my ear. My conversation with Gail is a casual shorthand, in case Neighbourly Watch Central is listening down the line.

'Did you visit the rellies?' she asks.

'They were in the middle of a prayer meeting.'

Silence. 'How nice for them.'

'I can drop in on them again when I get back from my fishing trip.'

'Visit me after that.'

I press again to disconnect the link, then scan the street for movement, the sweat in my armpits chilling beneath the layers. I've never failed to make a delivery before. Parcel still in my bag, I exit the Red Quarter for the wide deserted avenues of the sleeping city.

2

The Glory Hole speakeasy is a door in a wall down Wickerslack Alley in the capillary-like heart of the city. The eye at the peephole withdraws and the lock snicks back. Rosie, the doorkeeper, complete with leather vest, two armfuls of tatts and a nose ring suitable for a bullock, secures my bike in the room behind her guard stool and drawls, 'When ya gonna get a *real* one, Sal?'

She's the proud owner of a shiny electric speedster — a Harley replica — parked out in the alley.

'When I win at church bingo,' I say, too polite to mention that Rosie's ecotech 'real bike' sounds more like a sewing machine than a Harley.

After a speedy detour home to stash the undelivered package, the adrenaline is still running like a train through me. I wait for my breath to slow and senses to adjust, then hand over my helmet and cycling jacket to the cloakroom attendant, a busty glamour puss with eyelashes to die for.

Marlene takes my stuff by her finger ends as if it pongs. It probably does.

Downstairs, the air is laced with an aromatic smoke — the GM kind that doesn't give you cancer ... or so its distributors claim. The room is large and the lighting dim; beneath the smoke I smell sweat and alcohol and kit. Ahead of me, broad-backed couches are grouped in protective huddles around the empty dance floor. It's too early yet for the abandon that will put its cluster of silver poles to inventive use.

This is my stamping ground, and Gail's. A smorgasbord of contraband is traded and variety of services swapped in its subterranean spaces, the entrepreneurial spirit flourishing among its denizens. Operating below the radar of Neighbourly Watch and outside the Morality provisions, it's also a neutral territory where the B2N laws hold no sway and all judgement over what constitutes as natural, gender-wise, has been permanently suspended. Meanwhile, people elsewhere feel they've lost their raison d'être with their fertility, and are busy shoring up their masculinity and femininity as if to force an uncrossable distance between two non-intersecting camps. Having always manifested the indicators of both and felt like I belonged to neither, where does that leave me? A lean and lanky girlboy, a polymorphous mix: unsettling to some, and downright blasphemous to the Nation Firsts.

As I make for the bar, someone lunges across it at Trin Li, the bartender, who steps adroitly back.

'What's up with Verne?' a voice asks beside me and I jump.

'Oestro flux,' another replies from the cushioned depths of a couch.

The lunger is persuaded back to her table, but Trin has seen it all before. Shirtsleeves up and muscles flexing, he begins to polish glasses, mesmerising those seated in front of him.

I mouth *Inez?* and he nods me to the curtained alcoves at the far edge of the room.

I move along the alcoves, peering past thick brocade to tasselled lamps and socialising groups or coupling bodies, my mumbled apologies hardly noticed.

The fourth curtain nets success. I'm pulled in, greeted by an arm around my waist and three fingers on my lips. Then my new girlfriend is teasing my mouth open with her tongue while her companions look on, amused.

My pulse jerks into allegro.

'You've had a shot of Friend,' she murmurs.

The unmistakeable musk of her begins a slow cascade in me. I pull back, and regard grey almond eyes that reflect the lamplight. I may present to others as confusingly androgynous, but Inez is unmistakeably 'femme rising': skin dusted cinnamon, her scented curves and hollows a subtle Koori-Irish mix.

'Staying long?' she asks.

'Long enough to make sure I didn't imagine last night,' I say self-consciously, aware the others are listening.

'And then?' She takes her fingers from where they've been playing with the zip on my jersey front.

'More,' I breathe, the shimmy of pleasure vibrating in my bones.

We leave the alcove and head across the room of reclining figures, couples bent close over candlelit tables, a raucous trio at the bar. Marlene sees me coming and holds out my cycling jacket as if its presence has befouled her racks. I take the offending item, then my cycle helmet, reminded to attach some new reflector strips.

'You'd think Gail could afford to supply her favourite messenger with some new equipment every once in a while,' she says disapprovingly, her lashes sparkling, heavy with sequins.

A haughty cisgender hetero, Marlene can out-drag the drag artists. I smile weakly and follow my girlfriend to the door.

Inez is eyes closed, curled beside me in my bed. I reach out a hand to caress. She murmurs, half in dream. I cup a breast and kiss, and she brings her arms around me to tuck closer. The flame of last night's lovemaking rekindles. She lifts her hips to me and sighs. I turn her over, sliding one hand into her from behind, then hold her as her body gives to my fingers. Her surrender is in slow waves, skin slick on skin, both of us dragged along the rip together. Tumbled to shore, she smiles deliciously.

It's late morning, and the sky through my bedroom

window has turned wren-blue between scudding clouds, only a slight coolness left in the air from the zero-degree night. Plummeting temperatures have brought autumnal tinges to the city's trees, but this afternoon there'll be enough bite in the sun to remind of summer. I pull on a pair of baggy cycle shorts and a tee, then murmur to Inez snoozing in my bed like a voluptuous Lord Leighton *Iphigenia*, and go organise some supplies for my bike pack. The failed delivery sits in the fridge compartment labelled FISH. Tonight I hope to get it to its destination.

My bike leans in the hallway, its broken pedal gaffered on. I open the front door and wheel it out. The honeyeaters are busy in the wattle tree, but beyond that the street is Sunday calm in the enforced tradition of a Nation First Sabbath.

I could pick up a van from Cute'n'Cuddly for the snoop trip to Fishermans Bend, but decide to ride by my friend Albee's all-terrain bike shop instead and prevail upon his generosity.

Bike Heaven's unassuming single-storey building is tucked between SEC — solar–electric conversion — car yards in the shadow of the South Melbourne freeway. Albee, his broad tanned face lit by a smile, unlocks the security screen at the side.

'Salisbury!'

He's one of the few apart from Gail to call me by my full name. For most people it's too long, or too perplexing, to say. For them it's Sal, but at school it had been Sally — Sally Forth: my parents' travel-inspired creativity paid for by me many times.

I wheel my bike inside and lean it against the big front counter that extends the width of the service area. Behind it, several aisles of floor-to-ceiling shelves lead to a workshop space and a back door out to a pocket-sized concrete yard. Few know about the other door down the far left aisle, beyond which is the tiny studio space that my bicycle-mad friend calls home.

Albee ignores the Sabbath, and never has a rest day. His relaxed air comes from the contentment of doing what he loves best and is extremely good at, which is fixing bikes or bargain hunting for their various parts. We've known each other thirteen years, and met at a youth refuge when both of us were sixteen and scared as hell, living in a community that considered itself tolerant to difference but taunted us as perverts and spat at us in the street.

Albee, short, broad and very strong, opted for gender realignment surgery on his twenty-first birthday. I asked him if it had always been in his heart to do. He'd taken a while to reply, then said that for him it was less about the 'equipment' than the place to rest in. The hate had got to him — that, and the constant vigilance it took to stay safe. People call it sex change, but for Albee it was simply confirmation of what he already knew: he hadn't become male, he'd always been male.

Compared to that, the way for me has always been

muddy. Growing up I confused everyone, including myself. I was ostracised, blamed for not looking or behaving as clearly girl or boy. How could I explain that it felt like I was elements of both, inextricably mixed? I ran from the questions, but more waited around every corner. When people began to express their confusion as anger, I learned to run fast. For some, this seeming indecision between parts is a thing to fix. Over time I've come to view it as a freedom, albeit a dangerous one, there being no place for who I am in my own society.

Albee draws me along an aisle, its metal shelves cluttered with bits of bike and unlabelled boxes. Try as I might, I can see no pattern to the arrangement.

'I know I've got one of those SP-55s here somewhere,' he muses, shifting bits. Out comes a red plastic tray full of pedals. He grins. 'There's hope yet for that old treadly of yours.'

I follow him to the workshop space.

'Got time for coffee?' he asks.

'Afterwards, maybe. I'm on a mission for Gail.'

He nods, knowing better than to ask.

I lean against his workbench. 'Actually, I was hoping to borrow some alternative transport for the afternoon.'

'The panel van, or one of these?' He lays a loving hand on the knobbly-tyred BMX bike clamped to the bench, a row like it on ceiling hooks at the back wall.

The other option is parked outside. Albee collects his finds in a compliance-converted 1970s Holden Sandman — a 'shaggin' wagon', complete with lurid airbrushed pictures on the side. He did the artwork himself, and is inordinately proud of the lifelike detail of the peleton speeding past what looks to be an erupting volcano. It's the last thing I could go snooping in.

'Think I'll take a two-wheeled favourite.'

'Excellent choice,' he says, lifting one off its hook.

He puts the replacement pedal on the workbench along with a few other items picked up in the aisles, including a spick-looking mini pump and some reflector strips. 'I'll sort out your racer while you're gone,' he tells me. 'We can transfer your strap-ons to the mountain bike.'

He begins to detach the material and Velcro toeholds from my pedals: snug for maximum pulling power, and easy to get in and out of, no need for cleats or impossible-to-walk-in shoes.

'How much do I owe you?' I ask.

He treats me to a guileless look. 'What's the latest and greatest from Gail?' Albee is partial to my Courier's Friend mixes.

'Some tried'n'true, and a new recipe if you're game.'

He laughs. 'Shop's always too quiet on a Sunday. I could do with a diversion.'

I hand over a yellow-striped capsule still in its foil blister. 'It carries a warning,' I say, and Albee's eyes crinkle handsomely.

'You know I like those the best.'

*

Knobbly tread whirring, I ride through Port Melbourne to the tunnel under the freeway and into the Fishermans Bend industrial area. I'm no happier today than yesterday about snooping here, and at the top of Reserve Road near the abandoned karting complex, Albee's custom-built bike seems to brake of its own accord.

Broken glass glitters in the bitumen; a burnt-out truck sits on its wheel hubs in a vacant lot. I wait uneasily, watching for movement in the street ahead, but even the roving scavengers in their overladen jalopies are doing something else this afternoon.

Fishermans Bend is an urban wasteland hugged to the south bank of the Yarra as it sweeps towards the sea. Its messy conglomeration of defunct business parks and industrial estates had been marked for a makeover, but with the crisis of confidence that accompanied the flu pandemic many of the companies went bust. Now the wide streets are lined with tilting warehouses that have run out of the energy to stand up straight but aren't yet bothered to lie down flat. These days, people come here for one of three reasons: to scavenge, drag race, or trade sex for kit.

The day is much warmer now, and still. The nose-wrinkling smells of old industry taint the air. To my left, the grasslands of the nature park are a heat-flattened ecru, no autumn rains yet to coax them back to life. The picnic area consists of a commemorative plaque, a picnic table and a bashed-in tidy bin. I take the loop path through it and cycle past the Ponds: two noxious-smelling artificial lakes growing bacteria like giant petri dishes. Scattered about them are the park benches and picnic nooks used by the cruisers and bruisers in their nightly swapping of sex and suss kit. The Ponds are also the place for payback, which is why they're dredged every once in a while by the police forensic squads.

Further along, the track meanders in yet more unpleasant terrain — sand and scrub mixed with the stink of effluent — before arriving beneath the rising span of the Angels Gate Bridge, the most recent casualty of Melbourne City Council's renaming spree in the push for a more pious-sounding city. A cable-stayed girder design, its single concrete arm stretches eight hundred and fifty metres across the water in a feat of engineering that lost lives and broke hearts to complete. I ride into its shadow and between pylons, then out to where the cycle path meets the west-most end of Barrow Road. Here, set back from the cul-de-sac, are the pillaged buildings of the Ethical Hormones group, or EHg: Gail's feeder company. Next up the road is what's left of NatureCure, and further, BioSyn Solutions, each currently operating out of better-hidden premises.

During the post-pandemic fertility nosedive, this trio did a booming trade while other industries struggled. Now the steel structures gape where glass should be, and roofing dangles precariously. It's hard to believe this was once where busy manufacturers distilled their sought-after products.

When the hormone replacement business was a legitimate industry, the kit was made to order and distributed through pharmacies. The government of the day had given the researchers and pharmaceutical companies *carte blanche* to do what they could to help restore 'normal function' to the population; but in reality, help was only for those who could afford the premiums. For the rest, there were poor substitutes got over the internet or on the street.

Human physiology, however, is complex and fickle at the best of times — which clearly these were not — and five years on, the failure of the researchers opened the door to a number of lobby groups touting for change. With public opinion divided over the government-instigated surrogacy schemes and a relaxed immigration policy to reinvigorate population growth (an open door as long as fertility could be proved), the next general election brought out everyone from radical therapy proponents to social purity wowsers. It was a version of the latter, the Nation First party, that won, and their first act was to slam the immigration door and close down the surrogacy organisations. That their campaign was funded by an evangelical group called Saviour Nation was a fact largely underplayed — and underestimated — at the polling booths. But once they'd been voted into power, a raft of Saviour Nation's worship leaders were handed key political posts.

The first attack on the Fishermans Bend hormone manufacturers came soon after: a mob in a frenzy of NF-inspired retribution. That public ransacking set the tone in the community, and built dread in those of us who found ourselves on the wrong side of the morality fence. Sex and gender nonconformists of all kinds were made pariahs for our 'unnatural' ways and treated as a biblical plague, while those who worked in the hormone industry were routinely terrorised. When the B2N laws came into effect, the company owners were forced to ditch a thriving trade and go underground.

I shudder. The place is full of ghosts, even in daylight.

Further up Barrow Road, the newer buildings give way to older, dirtier industry and sagging fences, the rubbish accumulated like tatting in the chain-link. In some, only the concrete slabs remain, overgrown by thistles and tussocky grass, the structures above having already taken the plunge and gone to debris. I take a right, intending to dogleg back to Reserve and past Wolf Road where the drag racers meet, then on to the underpass. But as my body begins to release its tension and my breath quickens for home, something catches my eye: the last building on the street, with a sawtooth roofline and a brick chimney, and a flag of orange roadworks plastic hanging in a ground-floor window.

It's bright — too bright — against the gloom and fust, the marching dereliction.

I force myself to ride through gates that have graunched part-open, crossing the car park to a pair of industrial-height doors, chained and padlocked, rusted each to the other. I crane up. Announced in relief on the lintel is FERGUSON'S PAINTS. Beside, in a cobwebbed window, the orange flag dangles like a salmon lure. I try to argue away its significance, but it's deliberate and I know it. 'In here' it's saying, brash and dangerous.

I ease past the front façade and make my way along the service road at the side before dismounting, then peer around the back wall. A padlocked roller door is first, set high with a concrete sill. There's another door, which I'm relieved is also locked. Unfortunately, the window beside it shows a finger's gap between the sash and frame. I sigh, not cut out for foot-slog sleuthing. The stress gives me gastric.

One shove on the sash and the window lifts, wood screeching on wood. I tense, thinking of my makeshift alarm at home, then clamber through.

First is an empty room, which opens onto a short corridor then the two-storey factory space. The roof is a series of forty-five-degree corrugations inset with vertical rows of multi-paned windows, the steel girders below it crisscrossed with a sprinkler system and air extraction pipes. A wide gantry makes a mezzanine level on which sit a row of tanks. Their plastic gravity feeds dangle above the factory fill line, their ductwork combining into a single flue to meet the brick chimney outside.

I stop to listen. Nothing but iron ticking in the heat and sparrows scuffling in the eaves.

Jutting above the corridor behind me is what looks to be an office, got to by a set of metal steps. I eye them dubiously; but the other set by the front entrance look worse, missing vital bits.

I walk over. The whole structure rocks, no longer firmly bolted to the concrete. A snoop could have an accident here and it would be a while before their boss came looking. I sigh again, then climb the steps to the door at the top.

If not the materials of a hormone-packaging operation, I'd expected office bric-a-brac behind the door. Instead is what looks to be a love nest. The light filtering through the roofline reveals a mattress and blanket beside a couple of half-burnt candles fixed to the floor with dripped wax. There's some clothing dumped in a corner, while the sliding door at the back of the room opens to a scurf-edged toilet and washbasin.

I return to the office, where the only bona fide piece of office furniture is a filing cabinet. In the top drawer I find a few empty jars, a stack of porn mags and some rat droppings. I think of my bike outside and want to leave. Chastising myself for such lily-livered sleuthing, I go to the mattress and gingerly lift the blanket.

No body parts. Excellent.

A sour smell wafts up, and I recoil. As I drop the blanket, a movement in the pile of clothes startles me. It's the owner of the droppings. We scrutinise each other.

'Cosy?' I ask.

Its reply is to scurry around the skirting, so I inspect its bed — which turns out to be a penitent's sackcloth shawl. Something tiny glints. I lean closer. A sequin is embedded in the rough weave.

Staring at it, I can't help a rush of sympathy for those

26

who meet here — that emotion quickly flipping into anger at the bunch of compliant acolytes the population has become. Do they even remember there was a *before*, when the church didn't control the state, and street corners weren't for prayer groups, but for newspaper vendors and fruit stalls?

I make my way to the door. I've seen enough and am keen to go. While I may decry the laws that force tawdry trysts in industrial estates, that doesn't mean I want to bump into the people who've made this their special place. Not now. And not later, either.

3

It's nostril-squeezing cold and my finger ends hurt in their cycle gloves. My senses are zinging, but it's not just the wind chill and slippery road surface. At every corner I feather the brakes, scanning for the unexpected and ready to pedal like hell. It crosses my mind that there are surely better things to do in the middle of the night than this — just not as exciting.

Face it, Sal: on the bike you're an adrenaline junkie.

Glancing up, I can see a few stars beyond close-kissing eaves. Stars are one of the nicer things that have been returned to the city by the transport changes and power shortages, but right now not even the alley cats are out to appreciate them.

I lean into another elbow bend. What streetlights there are don't work this deep in the Red Quarter, but outside Number 137 a lamp is shining — the kind that used to advertise dentists and doctors to passers-by. That lone bulb is a welcome glow in the darkness. It'll give the prayer groups and muggers no anonymity.

Bike propped against a railing, I lift the flap on my courier bag and remove the parcel then sprint with it up the three steps to the door. As I reach for the buzzer beside the metal grille, I hear the tiny inset camera above me swivel. They've probably been waiting.

The grille clicks open. I pass my delivery to unseen hands through the mail slot in the door, then leap gratefully back down the steps, all three in one go.

I have no idea who I've just delivered Gail's expensive products to, and I don't care. Beyond the knowledge that I'm in fertility doctor territory, my mind is an information blank, and what's done behind these doors for the city's desperate inhabitants is nothing I ever want to know. Genderbent and happy, that's me. And now my duty has been done, my rent will be paid.

The subtle warmth beginning to leach from limbs to fingers is mainly my parasympathetics kicking in, but there's something else there too. It's the satisfaction of having played my small part in a greater insurgency; just one of the termite team munching into the behemoth structures of a regime that would have us all thinking the damaged fertility of a nation is punishment for our sins, and that praying for forgiveness — and preying on transgressors — will bring about our only reprieve.

I ride out of Cutters Lane feeling more relaxed despite the cold. Time to report to the termite queen.

★

I wish I could say I'm comfortable visiting my suave and sophisticated boss at her home; but I'm not. South Yarra and Toorak are still where most of the old wealth sits — the land alone worth a mint, not to mention the heritage mansions. Gail has always blended in well with the hoity-toity.

The route along the south edge of the Yarra beside the Botanic Gardens is one of my favourites, but this time of night the view across the water to the CBD is eerie. The power-saving measures put in place to force frugality means the city blocks are subject to rolling blackouts, the streets only minimally lit. I bump along a weed-infested cycle path that reflects the general downturn to Melbourne life, as if the whole city is suffering from the sort of depression that makes it hard to get out of bed each morning.

Toorak was divided into 'estates' and gated several years ago, the residents not trusting in simpler measures to keep the riffraff out. 'Checkpoint Charlie' is a guard box in the centre of the road. It has a window, an intercom and a bored and burly member of SOS — Service One Security — inside.

Straddling my bike, I punch in some numbers on the keypad then stare into the identity-check lens. The LED goes green and the gate slides open.

Beyond it, the street curves gently, my cycle lights picking out low stone walls and high hedges looming black in a grey-toned darkness. By day, grand houses can be glimpsed set well back in manicured grounds. But even old money can't bring the rain. The gardens are sad reminders of their former glory, many of the original lush-leaved plants replaced by hardier specimens, and the lawns a dull, parched version of green. At least here they haven't yet resorted to the solutions of the more downmarket suburbs: faux grass — the bright emerald kind — or concrete.

I enter Salmon Close and catch the scent of jasmine still in bloom. To my right, pencil pines spear uniformly to the sky. Left, a thicket of hardenbergia hides a garden gate, and a tall brush fence makes an impenetrable barrier. I make for the end of the close, where an electric three-wheeler sits by the kerb. Built for inner-city use, these vehicles are really motorised tricycles with rain bonnets, and so gutless that a scooter rider can easily drag them off at the traffic lights.

I repeat the number on the keypad outside Number 5, and the metal gates swing slowly open.

Gail's residence smacks of old colonial behind its square-trimmed photinia hedge and imposing entrance. The house is two-storey villa style, a driveway leading to grand, curving steps and the modern addition of a glass portico. The French windows set along the front open onto gently sloping lawn — real grass, thanks to the majestic oaks each side of the drive that provide summer shade.

I lean my bike against the last in a line of chest-height terracotta urns that flank the drive. This one has large handles and a spout meant to channel water into the empty fishpond.

As I unclip the phonelink from my ear and take off my helmet, a sparkling apparition emerges from the house. Marlene makes her way down Gail's front steps as theatrically as a Hollywood starlet stepping into the bulb-popping glare of the media. A fur stole wraps her shoulders above strapless lamé — some poor dead possum, or a whole furry family of them, stitched together for her comfort.

Gail appears in the portico. The two had a brief dalliance a while ago. For Marlene, it was an interesting sideways shimmy from her usual voracious pursuit of men, and with Gail's reputation for casual one-nighters being the stuff of legend, I assumed it was over between them. But it's none of my business who my boss decides to take to her bed.

As Marlene steps by, high heels crunching on gravel, she casts me a cursory, dismissive glance. As tall as her, I meet her eye to eye, but feel like one of the minions put there to wave or bow, or strew rose petals at her feet. Having missed all those opportunities, I lean against the urn and do nothing.

Sometimes Marlene really shits me.

Gail comes out to stand on the top step. She has a kind of classical Grecian beauty that I always feel a bit in awe of, a presence both lush and commanding. She motions to me. I lock the bike to an urn handle — you can never be too careful — and mooch up the path, the ill-dressed country cousin, courier bag trailing. I can't help hoping that Marlene is freezing her tits off right now.

Inside is a lot warmer. I strip off my wind jacket and a couple of thermal layers while Gail takes my dirt-streaked bag and puts it on a chair. One thing I'll say about my host, designer-neat as she is, she's not prissy about the upholstery.

'I heard the knock & drop was successful.'

'No prayer groups tonight,' I reply. Then add, 'the first time was an ambush.'

Her expression hardens. 'More and more of them in places they don't belong — and now this. Something's going on, and I want to know what it is.'

When Gail wants to know, she finds out. I just hope it's not me she chooses to play detective. Last night's attack really creeped me out. It's an occupational hazard, couriers getting mugged for their deliveries — but not by prayer groups.

Her gaze bores through me, unseeing, then belatedly refocuses. 'Tea?'

'Sure,' I say, a bit relieved, and follow her into the kitchen, an area about three times the size of my flat.

She's silent awhile, her movements from cupboard to sink a smooth, concise automatic: kettle on, cups and saucers out, the teapot warmed and tea spooned in. I watch, one hip against a benchtop, taking refuge in her assuredness and the doing of homely things. But I know she's thinking hard.

I remember back to when we met. She'd made me tea then, too. Not to dwell on the sordid details of seven years ago, but I'd just had a few fingers broken. The person who did the breaking had taken exception to my appearance and chose a very painful way to show me. I was working for a cleaning company at the time. It was one in a series of casual jobs to make ends meet while I tried to figure out what the hell else to do with my life. Among their select client list (the properties of the well-to-do) was Gail's house. She came home unexpectedly and found me crying like a baby over a vase I'd managed to drop because splinted and bandaged hands don't work properly. She helped me pick up the pieces — Ming Dynasty for all I knew — then sat me down and gave me tea, and, after a relatively painless interrogation, offered me better-paid work. My bank balance calculated in cents not dollars, I didn't have to think. I took it. Later I heard she found the guy who did the breaking and had him relocated. Much later I heard it was to somewhere underwater. Certain things are best never to know for sure. My fingers work fine now, thanks to sessions with the physio (billed to Cute'n'Cuddly), but I won't be taking up petit point or bead threading in the foreseeable future.

We sit in Gail's orderly living room, me on her large white couch, spooning in sugars, and her folded elegantly into an armchair.

'Number 137 has been warned they're a mark, and I've revised the schedule for all C&C couriers, starting now,' she says. 'Even if yours was a freak event, everyone needs to take extra precautions on their delivery routes until we know what we're dealing with. I'll enquire around the other Ethicals — see if they've had any similar incidents with the prayer groups. Now tell me about your fishing trip.'

'Nothing there to catch,' I reply. 'All I found was a love nest inside a paint factory off Barrow Road.'

Gail's well-shaped eyebrows rise, then fall into a frown. 'We're missing something,' she mutters.

I look at her. Two mornings ago this was about a casual recce.

'What makes you think they're setting up shop in that area?'

'A little birdie told me.'

Gail doesn't divulge her sources. As one of them, I know it's safer that way for all of us. I take a slow sip of tea, savouring the sweet liquid, letting its warmth course deliciously down my gullet. My boss makes a mighty fine brew. Imported contraband, I assume.

Gail refolds her legs. 'Something more serious may be happening out at Fishermans Bend,' she says after a bit. 'There's a murmur the opposition is moving into town. There's no sign yet of their product on the street, but I'm getting a bad feeling about this. Stay vigilant.'

The Ethicals and Non-ethicals have waged war since day one of the pandemic. Early on, Gail formed an exclusive business relationship with EHg, one of a handful of companies, including NatureCure and BioSyn, that guaranteed their customers a free-from-cruelty plant-derived mix. That, of course, was when the compounding was done in pristine facilities, each company operating under licence and subject to regular Good Manufacturing Practice inspections.

After Nation First won power, things went downhill fast. Quick to respond to the forced closures and sudden dearth of supply brought about by the B2N laws, the unregulated industry spawned the return of a number of internationally outlawed practices, including harvesting hormones from live and dead animals, and milking oestrogen 'the old way' from pregnant mares. These practices are the domain of the hormone farms, ugly windowless complexes housing abject animals that will never again see open ground. Much of what's produced there is snake oil; but not all of it. The products from the CEO — conjugated equine oestrogen — farms are loaded with impurities, but also high yield and effective because pregnant mares make very good oestrogen factories. Meanwhile, their doomed foals get slaughtered for endocrinal supplements. So now hormonal help can be bought in a variety of forms, like any other illegal drug, coming to the buyer straight from the mare's bladder or the dead foal's pituitary. Poor bloody horses.

Gail's never dealt in the stuff — she's kept her ethics and her association with EHg. But the rest of the world want their hormones on tap, including the two-faced Nation First politicians. It means only token effort has been made to shut down the thriving black market industry that operates outside city limits, its well-connected and carefully anonymous owners protected from prosecution by an endless series of parliamentary filibusters. Complicating the situation is Neighbourly Watch, the community arm of Nation First, which runs extortion rackets, squeezing distributors and farms alike for hush money. If one of the Non-ethicals is trying to forge new territory, you can bet NW will be interested. Either way, it's a provocative act to set up where the Ethicals used to be — and a warning they have their eyes on the inner city.

'Take me through Fishermans Bend,' Gail says abruptly. 'Everything you saw and heard and smelled.'

4

I sleep late. Monday being my day off, I do nothing except a load of washing.

Lunchtime, I realise the light on my answerphone is blinking. It's my younger sister, Helen, asking me to meet her this afternoon at the Neighbourly Arms, a tavern in the business sector of the CBD. No 'how have you been?' preamble and no goodbye, just a terse message and a hang-up.

It's the only contact she's initiated in five years. A handful of years before, in that first rush of fear when infertility became linked to Divine punishment and the necessity to atone, my family had scrambled to be 'saved'. I'd declined the offer to join them. Then Helen married the enemy.

I stare at the phone, and can't suppress the tiny voice inside that whispers hope of reconciliation.

I arrive at Lord Place on foot. Being something of a bastion for things traditional, its various clubs and bars are popular with the Nation Firsts, and weeknights the area is awash with political wheeler-dealers and Neighbourly Watch officials. Hypocritically, the Neighbourly Arms is the only city establishment with an exemption on Blue Laws days — the local slang term for the city's reinstated Sunday bans on alcohol, trading and fun in general. For Helen to ask me here is unkind but not surprising: it ensures she's the one on safe ground.

Located halfway down the bluestone square, the shuttered cottage exterior of the tavern makes it look like a tacky reconstruction; in fact, it's one of the oldest buildings in the city. Helen's sipping a glass of something through a straw at one of the outside tables, a wine keg with stools around it. Perched on a stool, she tugs self-consciously at the hem of her skirt.

I don't bother going to get a drink; I have a feeling this is going to be quick. I seat myself across the keg from her.

Neat as a pin in matching pastels, she eyes my sneakers, black slouch jeans and hoody, and gets an irked tilt to her mouth.

'You look well,' she says. (An improvement on last time's 'Get out of my life'.)

'You too,' I lie. To me, she looks strained and pasty.

'It's Mum and Dad's thirtieth wedding anniversary on Wednesday. Just in case you were planning to put in a surprise appearance, I'm here to say don't.'

In goes the barb. *Pierce my heart.*

She produces a card with pearly bells and glitter on

it, and hands me a pen. 'They just want to know you're alive.'

I'm seeing in tunnel vision, the pen a long way away. My hand reaches out and does the writing: *Much love on your special day, Salisbury.* It hands back the pen.

This is what leaving home at sixteen and coming out as a gender transgressive did to my family relations. At first, my parents hoped for contrition and atonement; then, when they abandoned their Presbyterian traditions for the Saviour Nation church, they wanted me to have my 'difference' baptised out of me.

Helen puts the card in its envelope and slips it into her handbag, then manoeuvres delicately off her keg stool.

'So that's it for another five years?' I ask.

She doesn't answer. Her eyes drift from mine to the tavern entrance. I follow her gaze, and see someone standing there watching us. Her NF politician husband, Michael, shoehorned into power by his Saviour Nation flock.

My sister always knew the kind of life she wanted was marrying and making lots of babies in suburban bliss. When the pandemic hit, she was just seventeen — and facing the prospect of premature ovarian failure and infertility. A year later, she took up with Michael Bannister, the prayer leader of the local church, and two of her three desires were quickly granted. But without the hoped-for babies, I can't help wondering if suburbia became more a prison for her than a paradise.

Michael turns to a companion, suited and heavyset in the shadows behind him, and speaks briefly. As the other disappears inside, he detaches from the doorjamb and walks over. His perusal of me is expressionless.

'You done?' he asks Helen.

'Yes,' she says to a spot on the pavement, and he steers her away with a proprietary arm.

I can't shout. I can't cry. In Lord Place no one makes a scene — no one who doesn't want to be noticed, that is. I feel glances from the neighbouring kegs. I pull up my hoody and leave in the opposite direction.

More than anything right now — more than family reconciliation or my sister's love — I want Inez's arms wrapped tight around me.

The Animal Protection Vigilantes never meet in the same spot twice. This week it's a Salvation Army hall in Carlton, a suburb away from where I live. Nation First tolerates the Salvos because they shelter those in the community the NFs have no compassion for. How the Salvos cope with their massively increased workload, I don't know.

Inez and I go there together in her ute. It's a throwback to halcyon days: a lovingly restored anvil-grey FC Holden that she got from her dad. The car was the thing he did to ease the boredom and disappointment of retrenchment, but he never got to enjoy the fruits of his labour, being one of those taken early by the flu. Inez, thumbing her nose at the purists, had the engine converted in compliance with the city's strict new emission laws, and drives it in his memory.

She parks under a big elm a couple of streets from the hall. A block out, we don our prayer shawls and walk with carefully measured steps, as if already soliciting favours from our ungenerous Maker.

The APV is how Inez and I met. She joined our cell when she moved here from Sydney. For me it was lust at first sight, but she took a while to warm to me, and we worked together for nearly a year before the pilot light even went on for her.

The seven of us gather in the shuttered kitchen area at the back of the hall, more than the usual level of tension in the air. We're coming to the pointy end of an operation we've been planning for many weeks. This rescue is one of our most ambitious, and only countenanced because another APV cell contacted us to ask for our help. Three months ago, they were approached by a disaffected employee at Greengate Farm, fifty kilometres northeast of the city in the Yarra Valley. To all intents and purposes it's a dairy — there are cows, and it produces milk — but the employee gave up its dirty little secret. Deep inside its rambling set of buildings, where the dairy workers aren't allowed, is a series of connecting internal yards: a farm within a farm, for horses only.

Of course, all the workers there know about it, but need their jobs more than they need to rock a cruel and illegal boat. Our informant, Lars, a security guard, felt the same way — until he saw something he wasn't meant to on a CCTV screen. Something he couldn't forget. Something nobody should do to any creature. He handed the farm's details to the other cell and offered to stay on to help with the raid. It was too big for that group to manage alone, so they appealed to us.

'What's the latest?' Brigid asks.

The prayer shawl discarded, her shoulders look tense in her sleeveless top, her hands shoved defensively in her jean pockets. She's been against trusting a third party from the start. I must say I can't blame her — it adds an extra layer of worry none of us wants. But it's thanks to Lars that Inez has come prepared today.

We gather round as she unfolds a map-sized sheet of the farm's layout and spreads it across a benchtop. A technician with Southern Electric by day, Inez is relied on by the group for her expertise in disarming things like CCTV and alarms. She earned her stripes back when she worked as a systems analyst for Defence intelligence, fighting computer hackers. Now she's joined their ranks.

'Look and memorise, folks,' she says. 'This is our route in and out.'

I watch her strong brown fingers trace the lines and shapes and think of where else they've been recently — then force my attention back to what she's saying.

'The latest batch of stuff from Lars has this week's entry codes and passwords, plus the digital surveillance footage I requested,' she tells us. 'The footage I'll loop and doctor for time and date. When I hack in, that's what'll feed to the surveillance monitors. We'll be invisible to the cameras.'

While we have every reason to trust Inez's hacking expertise, the interior of the farm where the horses are kept is run on a semi-automated system, and it's made everyone jittery, especially Brigid.

'What if the system comes back online while we're still in there and triggers a lockdown?' she asks.

'I've a special patch for that kind of fail-safe. It won't happen,' Inez replies. She looks at the rest of us. 'An hour before we arrive, I'll start running the pirate program. By the time we get there, the "ghost" machine will have insinuated itself into the farm's computer system. I'll be able to control all the security functions from my palm computer.' She glances reassuringly at Brigid. 'One key press will disable the movement sensors and automated alarms; the next will swap the CCTV with the dummy substitute; the last will spring the doors. And then, my friends, we'll be in like Flynn.'

My pulse does a little flip. I love her when she talks dirty.

She gets out a set of photos next, and we study the grainy shots, hurriedly snapped: our route through the dairy to the internal yards, and the exit where the other cell will be waiting for us with the horse trucks.

'Lars has risked a lot giving us all this,' she reminds us. 'We need to move fast.'

Lydia, beside me, nods vigorously. The rest of us scrutinise the layout, trying to feel confident. Only Nagid seems relaxed. A newcomer to our group but seasoned campaigner with Greenpeace, he's seen all kinds of direct action.

'Anything more to know about the caretaker?' he asks.

Inez shakes her head.

We've learnt from Lars that the farm's owners have become complacent, thinking themselves safely connected to the powers that be, and reduced the security detail on the overnight shifts to a grand total of one. The only other person onsite at night is the caretaker, Russ Stefanovic, in a cottage half a kilometre from the dairy. On Friday evenings he goes to the pub for his weekly binge session.

I look around the group. 'Lars is doing the Friday shift this week. We give the thumbs up to the other cell and the job's on.'

'Say again about the security cameras?' Brigid presses Inez.

'They'll be effectively blind while the monitors in the security office are streaming doctored video. Anybody watching will see only a loop of old, uneventful footage. No one — not even Lars — will be able to tell there's been a swap-over from their system to the ghost. He'll stay put in the monitoring room and do none of his usual yard checks or perimeter inspections. Once the horses are loaded, I'll beep him to get out of there.' She pauses. 'Our usual onscreen greeting will come up at the 5 am change of shift.'

It's become customary for each APV cell to leave its calling card after a raid: a message claiming responsibility, framed by a picture of happy horses galloping in a grassy paddock. It's just one small satisfaction in an ocean of injustice. The farm owners can fume all they want, but they can't make public the rustling or their outrage. Well-connected they may be, what they're doing is still illegal and they could be charged under the Unnatural Practices Act.

'Do you think we can manage twenty-one horses?'

Brigid asks the question for all of us. Greengate isn't the largest of the hormone farms, but has more horses than we've ever tackled in one go.

'Absolutely,' says Inez, refolding schematics.

'Then let's do it!' Lydia thumps the table and we all jump.

Lydia's our token extremist, her fearlessness having saved and risked us in almost equal measure. Lately, she's made us more than the usual amount of nervous, and reeling in her enthusiasm has fallen to me. Inez tells me it's because I'm the only one who knows which wires to snip to defuse her. I'd hate to disillusion anyone by confessing that I guess.

I start to say something cautionary, but Brigid beats me to it rather less tactfully.

'Let's not lose our heads and smash anything on this job,' she says to the bench, and Lydia looks suitably shamefaced.

The rescue before last, our extremist impulsively trashed a piece of equipment containing something volatile in the farm's laboratory, the fumes from it dense enough to trigger the optical fire sensor and set off the sprinkler system. Luckily, Inez had already disabled the fire alarm; but we all got a soaking. Far worse, the concrete surfaces turned slippery and we only just got ourselves and the terrified horses out unscathed. It was not one of our finest moments. In fact, it was the closest we'd all come to a one-way trip to an NF detention facility, and even Lydia realises she stepped way over the line that night.

Despite that, the rescue turned out a win, the animals placed in the care of a Mount Macedon horse sanctuary. Unfortunately, even a win feels like a pyrrhic victory these days. The level of demand is so high that when one hormone farm drops out of production, the others just collect its business.

'Shall we move on?' Max, our resident vet, breaks the uncomfortable silence.

Inez's answers have satisfied Brigid for now, and the rest of us are keen to focus again on the job ahead. None of us wants to rehash the mistakes of the past. I push aside a niggling anxiety about Brigid and Lydia being able to work effectively together, and look enquiringly at James.

'All set,' he says, and grins.

At eight o'clock on Friday, when Russ Stefanovic makes his usual pilgrimage to the pub ten kilometres away, James will be there, a larrikin companion, ready to ply the man with beers and Rohypnol. Meanwhile, three large animal transports modified to take seven horses each will roll up to Greengate Farm. Once we get the horses in their variously weakened states unstrapped from the equipment and out of the stalls, it will be over to the members of the other cell to transport them to the sanctuary. There is, however, one crucial APV member we haven't yet confirmed.

'Cicada?' I ask.

'Waiting for our call,' Max replies.

Cicada is the closest thing we have to a horse whisperer. He moves between cells raid by raid, his almost supernatural skills in high demand. He's also the most taciturn person I've ever met, his communications tuned almost entirely to those with four legs not two. An ex-stockman, his nickname derives from his almost complete silence when among humans. Max is the only one who can divine meaning from his barely audible grunts, which makes him a handy interpreter.

The final element slotted into place, I look around the circle of faces. We're as ready as we'll ever be.

Inez zips the folded schematics into the lining of her jacket and we finish with a run-through of equipment before the group begins to disperse. The next time we gather will be Friday night for the trip to the dairy, our hopes for success placed in the lap of Epona, the horse goddess.

Dropped off in the city by Inez, I hurry down Wickerslack Alley's steep pavement. The door to the speakeasy is where the alley doglegs before turning into Daisy Lane on the way back up. There could hardly be a less salubrious entranceway — which suits the Glory Hole and its diverse clientele just fine.

I bypass Marlene in her hidey-hole and pick the alcove closest to the bar to wait in for Gail. The text message I got as I was leaving the Salvos' hall had brooked no dissent, something definitely up.

Rosie opens the door again. Several perfectly executed strides around the furniture and my boss is at my alcove.

A couple of mineral waters appear magically on a tray at her elbow, compliments of Trin, one of her satisfied Ethical Hormones customers.

Gail nods thanks to the bar and sits down, but before she can haul across the privacy curtain, we have visitors: Mojo Meg, a rival of Gail's, flanked as usual by two goliaths. Standing demurely between them, Meg seems delicate, almost birdlike — but don't let that fool you. She's the doppelgänger of my food technology teacher at high school who marked all our many misdemeanours in her little black book — the wrong utensils used at table, the bowls caught mid-lick, the food chewed too loudly — her thinly veiled contempt the unbalancer that made me more than once leave the tea towel burning half in the oven door.

Meg conducts both business and pleasure from a permanently reserved corner of the speakeasy. Her po-faced minders are light on conversation and heavy on hardware. Why they get to keep their toys when the rest of us have to hand ours in to the cloakroom attendant is down to Meg, who's always been an exception to the Glory Hole's rules because she owns it. I look at the thuggish duo and wonder if they know their job has turned them into clichés. The closest to me outstrips her boss by a good half-metre, her dimples turned to jowls from too much time spent scowling. The other is shorter, wider and could probably ease up now on the angry pills.

'Gail,' says Meg, bead-eyed, sweet-voiced.

'Meg,' says Gail, the air around us already chilled to one cube short of an ice cocktail.

'How's business?'

'Booming.'

Gail is the epitome of suave, nothing showing beneath that smooth professional veneer; but Meg never indulges in chitchat without a purpose.

'Heard otherwise.' She glances my way, then back. 'If you're thinking to downsize your operation, I'm always hunting for new recruits. Can't have good workers put out on the street.'

I look at her in surprise. How she can be so brazen is a sign of her and Gail's equal standing, and the level of rivalry between them. I don't know what's going on, but if Meg wants the pleasure of stalk and capture, poaching something of value from a competitor, she won't get it from this worker.

Not one to waste energy, Gail smiles her most pleasant smile and refrains from answering.

Meg is unfazed. 'Leave you in peace then.' One finger flicks a signal to her minders, who shepherd her away as if she's made of something breakable.

I sip my drink and wait while Gail maintains a brooding silence.

'Oh no,' she says suddenly.

I look up. Marlene has left her nook and is a bright battleship, full steam our way. She berths spectacularly at our table, and gives me the usual dismissive once-over before turning to her real target.

49

'Sweetie,' she says, 'I hope you'll be home later, because I left my very favourite earrings at your place the other night.'

Her body language is sultry and persuasive, every part of her playing the mating game.

'I'll give them to gate security and you can pick them up anytime,' Gail says.

Marlene recoils as if stung. She gathers herself up, a diamanté puff adder, and I make like a mouse against the fluffy boudoir cushions, transfixed by such flamboyance and ferocity combined. Cleopatra eyes flash; carmine nails gleam like talons on the hand splayed against the brocade. I hold my breath. But she turns without another word and steams off between the tables, back to her coat-check domain.

'Hell hath no fury …' Gail murmurs, and I think maybe I was right after all about her having ended what was a casual fuck.

I try to say something vaguely platitudinous and she makes a wry face.

'Marlene's just jealous.'

My look asks the question.

'Of you,' she adds.

'What — of the couriering?' I can't believe Marlene would have any aspirations in that direction.

Gail treats me to her patient, parental expression. 'She thinks you're my next conquest in the bed department.'

'But that's ridiculous.'

'Tell *her*.'

She reaches up to yank the sash holding back the curtain and we're enveloped in a musty aromatic dark. The lamp on the table glows like a still, red heart. She lays a delivery satchel beside it and finally reveals the emotion she's kept in tight abeyance since her arrival. Seeing a usually equilibrious Gail deeply angry is an experience I don't get often — and don't want to. But I know her too well to think it's to do with Marlene, or anything I've done.

She takes a fast, angry gulp of her drink, untouched till now. 'Someone's putting bogus kit out on the street stamped with the Ethical Hormone group's logo. People are buying it thinking it's the good stuff selling at cut price.'

I'm confused. 'Are we talking about the new player?'

Gail takes another swallow and sets the glass down. 'I'd lay bets on it. If they're short-termers, they'll be trying to make a fast buck off EHg's reputation before disappearing into the sewer hole they crawled out of. It's that or a tactic thought up by one of the opposition to discredit us.'

So that's what Meg was referring to.

Gail opens the satchel. 'One of my regulars just gave me this.'

She draws out a polystyrene ovoid. Where the two halves join at its midriff is a blue wax seal, the EHg trademark pressed into it. The seal already broken, Gail twists and separates the halves then lifts an ampoule from one of the neat holes in the polystyrene.

I look at the tiny vial. The liquid is cloudy and I think I can see sediment.

'You'd have to be desperate —'

'Sniff!' she commands.

I snap the top off the ampoule then bring it obediently to my nose. The smell is unmistakeable. It doesn't matter what form the stuff takes — pill, patch or rub-on, troche, implant or injectable — it always reeks of animal.

It's not just a matter of pride to Gail that she's never been affiliated with the hormone farms; her customers buy from her on the surety. As sole distributor for EHg, and anti-animal cruelty to the bone, she's rankled by this blatant fraud making a mockery of those long-held values. Her every bone also being an entrepreneurial one, she knows how bad this could be for business.

I wedge the ampoule back in its slot then match up the two halves of the polyshell. The seal is a crude job, the EHg logo burred and indistinct. There's no way C&C would do such a botch job.

Gail speaks in an angry undertone. 'The buyer, Savannah Rose, is a long-standing customer of mine. Some guy tried to sell her this outside her place of business. She paid him for it so she could show it to me and ask if I'd stooped to selling my stuff on the street. Then she opened it. She thought I'd crossed over to the Dark Side.' Gail turns her fierce gaze on me. 'She owns the Shangri-La on Madams Row. I'll set up a meeting for you. I also want you to go back to Fishermans Bend — with Anwar this time.'

Anwar is Gail's distribution manager, and one of her most trusted friends.

Gail shifts forward in her seat. 'There'll be more where this came from. The question is, how much more? EHg already has its scouts out, ready to whisk the stuff off the street as soon as it lands. Meanwhile, we need to find out where they've set up shop — and my information says Barrow Road.' She flicks a short, unvarnished fingernail against the shell on the table. 'If that doesn't net us anything, we'll search every factory and warehouse at Fishermans Bend.'

My heart sinks. Several large blocks, several large buildings to a block. 'That's a lot of buildings.'

'I know,' she replies. 'But if we don't find the tail of this monster and twist it *hard*, business will be going belly up very soon.'

And going with it will be my cosy flat, its impossible-to-replace privacy, even its spiky desert landscaping, all beyond the means of someone unemployed. Gone will be the safe place for my cat, and my ability to feed and protect the both of us. Demoralised, I think of Meg's not-so-subtle job offer, then feel instantly guilty. My boss's rival had accidentally tapped into my weakest spot: fear of Nitro being taken away by the pet exterminators.

Gail refixes the curtain sash, and I follow her out of the alcove.

'There's an APV excursion Friday, but I could start surveillance with Anwar tonight if you want,' I tell her.

'I want,' she says.

5

Evenings, Madams Row glimmers, a bastion of sin, the ruby-studded thoroughfare a ward against the moral privations of the city. Reds and pinks soften brick and cobble and wash a diffuse light onto the pavements, while business shingles promise all kinds of comfort, a seeker's hidden pleasures. I'm not reticent to admit at times I've been that seeker, loneliness and unrequited love a potent mix for any transgressive.

The area has undergone a transformation since the madams took it over; but there are no pimps or bouncers outside chaser-lit doors, and no jiggling body parts and garish signs advertising *Girls Girls Girls.* Instead, the precinct's sensibilities are tuned to those of a different century — how it might have been, for instance, inside the walled pleasure quarters of the Oiran — and its business owners are as respected in their modern-day realm as the Athenian hetaerae were. (Fair to say, this is a fanciful connection to a past more mythological than historical, but it's one I like to conjure, and ironic that it's taken a pandemic and a splinter of the Christian Right to provide the circumstances of change.)

Those working in the sex and escort industry have ever been at the mercy of pimps and 'benefactors', but here it's the madams who hold the reins of power. Politically astute, they've wrought a secret agreement with Melbourne City Council to register their businesses as 'guesthouses', and stay in operation as long as they never admit to what they really do. This succeeds thanks to the variety of services they offer those challenged by infertility and impotence, while their contributions to the municipal coffers provide enough of a prop-up for the city's struggling economy that even the moral crusaders among the people's elected representatives have hesitated to curtail such a large and reliable source of income. Just don't mention it to the wowsers.

I walk slowly, savouring the atmosphere. This is the time of lull, the transit into night, and it's my favourite, even though a slight tinge of melancholy accompanies the gradual cloaking of daytime preoccupations. For me, the twilight will always carry an alluring air of freedom.

The Shangri-La is a three-storey building halfway down the Row, its shingle expertly swaged metal, lit from within. A crimson door and welcome mat hide in the recesses of a tiled portico, the lanky geraniums in the window boxes each side stretching for a rare glimpse of sun. The door's security grille, shut fast in the off hours, has been swung wide, the bordello open for business. The brass knocker on the door is two entwined bodies. I grasp their various parts and bang.

Rudolph Valentino opens the door — or, at least, someone who looks very like him. He seems to know already who I am, and graciously ushers me in. Steering me away from the client parlour to my right, he takes me left into a reception area. Minimalist and assured, it could be the lobby of a boutique hotel. A Rothko print graces one wall: two wads of colour slit midway by a third.

I'm gestured to a voluminous couch beside a low table, its vase of oriental lilies wafting a pungent — and expensive — sweetness into the air. As I stare at the Rothko, imagining a distant sea in the midway strip, Savannah Rose arrives through a door behind the reception desk.

Her name had thrown me off track. I'd expected a blonde prairie girl, but stretching her many-braceleted arm towards me is a sultry, aristocratic Egyptian.

'Gail sends her regards,' I tell her as we shake hands.

'Gail is always welcome at the Shangri-La,' she replies, and smiles a glorious smile.

Briefly I wonder how welcome, how often. If I were Gail, it would be as often as possible.

Savannah and Rudolph exchange a look of tacit understanding, then she leads me out of the room past the Rothko. I pause just long enough to realise it's not a print, and stare in new amaze at my hostess's seductively clad back.

We enter another ground-floor room decked out in more opulent style. It reminds me of a Moroccan salon with its gilt-edged mirrors and lights caged in metal filigree, the plush ceiling-to-floor drapes in a rather visceral shade of red no doubt hiding what would be disillusioning views. Against one wall is a wooden cabinet with a carved latticework front, its shelves arranged with tantalising items: leather, silicon, metal. I glance over them, feeling too constrained to look properly; but they remain in my peripheral vision, beckoning.

Savannah gestures to two day couches set on a small riser against adjacent walls, their ornately carved ends meeting rather intimately in the corner. Naked bodies again. As we settle into velvet cushions, they release the scent of cinnamon and orange. Fabrics swirl rich colour, and I feel mildly opiated.

The beautiful man from reception brings us drinks on a tray, setting them down on the low table between us. I watch his smooth departure. Rudolph, eat your heart out.

'Travis makes a mean mint julep,' Savannah says as I pick up my drink.

The glass is frosty cold, and its contents taste so good I want to slurp them down. Savannah, on the other hand, sips with seamless etiquette, taking the opportunity to observe me over her glass. I hope I'm measuring up, but feel awkward being treated as visiting royalty when I'm dressed like the paid assassin: head to toe in basic black for the all-night stake-out with Anwar.

I place my glass back on the coaster protecting the table's polished inlay, and launch straight in. 'Tell me about the guy selling on your doorstep.'

Savannah leans back into the cushions and sighs. Her bracelets clink softly.

'He was a string bean with bling who stank of cheap aftershave — the sort who used to pimp in this area before we saw them off. He was also wired. A tic in one eye and lots of unpleasant teeth-grinding. Whatever was running through his system made him pretty careless, and he wasn't trying to hide his wares. In fact, he was waving the stuff around, showing it off.'

The whole thing sounds like a taunt, a message sent to the heart of Gail's distribution territory that she's being set up for a fall. And why wouldn't a competitor want to knock EHg and its sole distributor off a coveted perch?

My thoughts swing to Mojo Meg and the exchange I'd witnessed in the speakeasy. But as battle-hardened and ruthless as Meg is, this kind of attack is anathema to the moral code she shares with all the businesses that satellite around the Glory Hole and its diverse clientele. To shoot a chink in the armour of one Ethical ultimately weakens them all, and they know it, especially when there are others in the game courting very different friends: bent NF politicians in bed with the hormone farms, Neighbourly Watch racketeers 'protecting' the Non-ethicals for a cut of their profits, and an army of parasitic dealers flogging a cocktail of addictives in their hormone mixes.

Savannah continues. 'First I was incensed someone could hawk their wares so brazenly right outside my door, then worried when I saw the logo on the polyshells. I paid the asking price so I could take one to Gail and find out what was going on. The guy seemed so blasé, as if he knew someone had his back …' She muses awhile, then says, 'Those slimy lowlifes don't usually feel so safe in here.'

I know what she's referring to. These days the madams are a formidable force with their own systems of protection. The first is a private security firm, aptly dubbed the 'Red Quarter militia' for its uncompromising efficiency. The second is an impressive visitors list that includes a bevy of NF politicians and Neighbourly Watch card-carriers — and, no doubt, a correspondingly impressive collection of incriminating photos kept in a vault somewhere as surety against their clients' unendearing capacity to turn with the political tide.

I listen as she describes breaking open the polyshell. By then she'd decided it was stolen goods. Of course, on the first whiff she knew it to be entirely animal … She lapses into silence.

I wonder how much kit the street seller had managed to foist on the unsuspecting before he got to the Shangri-La. Clearly he was an expendable, and by now will have taken his reward and bored back into the understoreys of this sorry city to ingest it, plenty of others to do his employer's dirty work for a handful of pills or bag of powder. But with four other Ethicals distributing in the city area, why did they go for EHg? Was it a chanced-upon opportunity, or a more personal link none of us has sussed yet?

Savannah leads me down a central hallway — all doors politely closed — to the front entrance. I resist the urge to make a quick detour through reception to visit the Rothko one more time. I've never been within kissing distance of an original.

'Give my greetings to Gail,' she says, adding, 'You'd be welcome here too, anytime …' Her demeanour is cool and professional, but her eyes are smouldery, inviting.

The heat rises in me, just a little, before something starts up a frantic internal flapping of hands against the dangers of the flame. If I were unattached, I'd be more than charmed: I'd be *tempted*. But right now I'm a one-girl genderbender, and that girl happens to be Savannah's well-paid electrician.

'I'm honoured,' I say, and step out the red door.

My agreed pick-up with Anwar is at the bottom of Benedict Street, opposite the Southern Cross train station renamed Station of the Cross. He swings open the van's passenger door and I lever myself up inside. Glancing across, I see he's dressed in his usual: a neatly pressed suit. He looks like an office worker going to his daily nine-to-five, whereas I look more like a cat burglar in my black joggers, black pants and zip-up jacket. For the second time this evening — but for an entirely different reason — I feel style challenged, even if it's due to a lifelong resolution to never wear anything I can't run like hell in.

Unlike the spruce white Cute'n'Cuddly delivery vehicles, this van is rusty and battered, as if on its last few clunking kilometres before a final parking space in the wrecker's yard. But that's just for show. Behind the blistered patina of cheaply tinted windows it's fitted out for comfort, and the nice new SEC motor under its mouldering bonnet whirrs as quietly as a beetle's wings.

We negotiate the nightmare of detours that's the perpetually unfinished roadworks at the end of Saviour Street then cross the river into Port Melbourne. At the city end of Barrow Road, Anwar pulls onto the verge and kills the lights, and we sit there while the van's engine flutters silkily, its clever hybrid design a reminder of human ingenuity amid so many mistakes.

The streetscape ahead is a chiaroscuro of shadowy recesses and glimmering surfaces lit by moon, nothing stirring above the layers of industrial dirt. I remind myself it's early yet for Fishermans Bend. Nothing happens here till after midnight.

We ease into gear and inch forward, tyres crackling on broken glass.

The industrial park is set out on an unfinished grid, many of its streets petering into dead ends, waiting for the extensions and development that never came. Several roads lead left off Barrow as it heads towards the Angels Gate Bridge. We do a slow crawl to the cul-de-sac then park with our backs to the water and wait, our eyes fixed on the wreckage across the road that was once one of the swishest drug factories in town.

I scan the misshapen buildings doubtfully. 'Gail's sure they're doing business around here …' I let the sentence hang.

'She is,' says Anwar.

My eyes are drawn to the plastic Donald Duck figure stuck on the dashboard, its head bobbing gently on a spring. Surely it's a piece of frivolousness not reflective of Anwar's restrained style. But then, what do I really know of him?

I breach the silence again. 'Where'd you get the van from?'

'The confiscated vehicles compound on Atonement Street.'

I shoot a look sideways. Last I heard, the compound and the police headquarters next to it had been torched by two of their own on a steroids rampage.

'They had a fire sale,' he says, deadpan. It's the closest thing to a joke I've ever heard from him.

Anwar is small and unprepossessing, with an almost surreal equanimity. That level of calm is, ironically, disconcerting to be around at first; but I've shared overnight vigils with him before and have become used to the lack of chit-chat, the long silences. No chance of any personal intimacies accidentally escaping here. What little I know of his life has been pieced together from other sources, the scars on his arms enough to silence questions out of mere curiosity.

The child of asylum seekers, at twelve years old he saw the rest of his family drown in international waters just off the Lucky Country. The residue of grief that must be there he covers well. He was put in a detention centre until the government of the day finally conceded to the human rights lobbyists and let the survivors of the sunken fishing vessel become Australian citizens instead of keeping them in a stateless limbo. Still, Anwar could have gone into adulthood an angry man, or broken-spirited and weighted with a victim's despair; instead he developed a stepped-back relationship with the world, an invisible buffer against the vicissitudes of life.

The only person this reticence doesn't apply to is Gail. As long as I've known them, she and Anwar have been close, no one else she trusts more. That trust is clearly mutual.

I push back in my seat to unbend my too-long legs and place my feet on the dash beside Donald. Anwar fishes in a duffle bag and passes me his thermos. Hot chocolate. I'm grateful — and mildly guilty that I hadn't organised anything to share with him for the long haul.

'Moon's close to full,' he observes.

'All trades tonight,' I agree.

With no artificial light of any sort, Fishermans Bend is a preferred location to barter contraband. In moonlight it also becomes a playground for the drag racers, who command the wide empty streets with their illegal souped-up rides, racing each other without lights on. I think of Ferguson's paint factory, and wonder if its upstairs office will be visited tonight.

After several minutes, no movement in the shadows opposite, Anwar puts on his overcoat and I pocket my can of mace. We lock the van and walk carefully over to the EHg building. Behind us, choppy planes of ink-black water shine like freshly poured tar, and waves slop under the lone wooden pier, nudging at its mooring bollards. A regular ferry service used to stop here, and in happier times there'd be a row of hopefuls casting their lines into the not-so-clean waters of the bay. Unfortunately, the seafood caught in the Yarra Basin lost its appeal once it was discovered that the mercury levels in the fish had reached percentages high enough for folk to start filling their own thermometers.

Anwar leads and I follow, our torch beams flicking across the broken architecture. I'm glad not to be searching here alone.

We enter the rear of the building, passing glass-divided labs with aisles of benchtops and shattered sinks, then the powder-preparation rooms, their ransacked containment cabinets all doors open. Beyond that is office space, the equipment long gone and nothing of interest.

It's the same at NatureCure, so we move on to BioSyn. There we find three people sprawled semicomatose in a corner and rudely give ourselves permission to rifle through their stash. But it's not any stuff marked with EHg's logo, just some brandless feel-good-then-die crap laced with God-knows-what gut-rotting, brain-sizzling impurities. We hand it back and leave them moaning incoherencies in their grotty corner.

On our return recce of Barrow Road and the business parks behind it, we stop several times to peer through windows and try locked doors, and once to investigate a movement between buildings that turns out to be two people grinding their pelvises into each other against a wall. We even swing by the paint factory, shining a light on its front entrance to check for the flag — not up. There's nothing anywhere to suggest the presence of a packaging operation or distribution site.

Our last stop is the Ponds on Reserve Road. Several vehicles are already in the picnic parking area, none of them what you'd call flash, so ours fits right in. I grab a blanket from the back of the van. Not exactly the height of sartorial elegance, but who cares on a park bench? Time to sit and see what's on offer.

The moon rides the zenith, and the place fills with flitting shadows. Night creatures — some animal, some not — move between the windbreaks and flurry disconcertingly in the sedges. Forget the wildlife; the cruisers and bruisers are here for sex and kit, both willing to trade what they have for the other. I grip Anwar's arm unashamedly and pray that no one comes at us with a knife.

Across the next bum-freezing hour we get a number of propositions — a few drug-related, a few carnal, and a few quite difficult to picture — but no offers of EHg-labelled kit. We return to the van then head up Reserve Road to the T-intersection with Barrow, swinging right into the driveway of Enzo's Auto Wreckers.

The sign is a gleeful mechanic wielding a giant hammer above a ramshackle car. It hangs precariously by one corner.

Behind it is a workshop space and burnt-out office, and, in the adjacent paddock, hundreds of compressed metal carcasses stacked like mini high-rises.

Anwar wheels one-eighty degrees then backs into the workshop and turns off the ignition. We'll wait here for the moonlight parade. To park in plain view between now and dawn would invite someone to pinch the only things that look worth having off the van. Its tyres.

A warning rumble, slowly growing, and the first arrivals burble past: all kinds of retooled, recycled and refitted machines, none of them with a hope in hell of conforming to the latest emission limits. They crawl in from Port Melbourne and the city, the drivers finding their way here through the back streets, risking the notice of the emissions patrols and any citizen affronted enough by their shameless flouting of the laws to report them. That challenge, of course, is part of the game, and once they get here it's a dangerous, high-octane game. The drag racers are a law unto themselves, and this is their playground.

The Bend is busy tonight, and it's not just transmogrified petrol guzzlers and revheads. There are shadowy others arriving the lo-tech way: by scooter or bicycle, or on foot.

We watch them pass. The plan is to wander down to where the racers and onlookers will have assembled on their favourite stretch of cut-up tarmac, and ask around the groups. It isn't exactly my idea of safe snooping, but this is a close-knit crowd who'd notice anyone new in their play area, especially if they were doing something as foolish as trying to sell kit out of a car boot.

Not that the racing fraternity would care. Notoriously single-minded in their sporting pursuits, they don't get their kicks from the substances bartered most nights at Fishermans Bend. To them, using chemical help is equivalent to cheating. Their passion is for the growl of illegal engines, the squeal of stolen tyres and the thrill of the chase, all stops out, down a bumpy and potholed stretch of wasteland road. The fastest and most fearless are treated as demigods, their supporters clamouring to be chosen as passengers.

'When was the last police bust?' I ask Anwar, who always knows these things.

'Thursday week ago.'

'So they're not due again for a couple of weeks?'

'About that.'

We lock the van and close the garage tilt-a-door, then join the shadowy throng heading up Reserve Road.

Nation First may think it has conquered the opinions of the suburbs and suppressed dissension in the inner city, but it's given up the battle out on this stretch of urban wasteland crouched between the shells of industry and the wide slick waters of the Yarra. Here, a section of the city's underbelly is gloriously revealed and the architects of prohibition only have themselves to blame, pushing individuals to ever more inventive expressions of subversion and resistance.

The cops know that if they take away the option of Fishermans Bend (as they were forced to do with the nightly 'cruise parade' along Lygon Street a few years back) the racers will only regroup in a less convenient spot, so they've opted for a pragmatic solution. As long as the activities are contained in an isolated area away from the rest of the city's inhabitants, and the racers do nobody but themselves any harm, the police patrols are happy to turn a blind eye. Their bosses, however, still need to show a nervous public some encouraging statistics, and so the 'stings' happen once a month, as rehearsed as a play. A line of paddy wagons wail out of the CBD, lights flashing, but with the word already gone out, the racers simply don't show. The cops arrive to nothing but old rubber burns in the road. They haul a few wasted souls out of the shadows and pick up a bit of contraband from a once-round of the Ponds, then make their report, satisfying the community's need to believe they're out all hours keeping folk safe in their beds.

We arrive at the racetrack start, a giant roundabout at the junction of Reserve and Wharf. The rivals are already parked around the circle, their spectators gathered in the middle on makeshift risers to watch the duels and cheer on their favourites. Anwar and I survey the moonlit scene, each souped-up ride attracting its own knot of torch-carrying groupies.

The energy here is primal, supercharged: the pungent smells of rubber and exhaust cutting through the cold night air, and the crowd getting off on their own potent mix of adrenaline and hormones. I can understand the attraction, even though engines aren't my thing — they're far more

Inez's passion. If she didn't cherish every perfect part of her restored '58 FC, she'd probably be down here on the full moon burning rubber with the best of them.

On first look, the drag-racing fraternity is an eclectic mix of dress codes. The racers themselves favour motocross clothing stitched with a multitude of defunct brand names, while their groupies appear to divide along rather old-fashioned lines — the butch and the femme; although it would be a mistake to assume only one sex is being represented within those categories. Briefly I wonder where I'd fit in, until I catch sight of the 'ghetto' set in baggy clothes with caps and hoodies.

Anwar and I agree to approach the groups separately. I'm a bit sorry, because to witness this unassuming and neatly suited man at work is quite something: his natural equanimity, matched with genuine interest, manages to persuade even the most reticent to divulge what they know. It's a gift, and I keep hoping some of it will eventually rub off on me.

He heads to the group gathered at a piece of grotesquery that could once have been a Volkswagen Beetle but now looks more like its mutilated offspring, while I make for the closest knot of spectator femmes.

Aware of my approach, they tacitly ignore me until I'm in their midst. I introduce myself, and they eye me with a mix of suspicion and curiosity. I can see they're wondering how to categorise me. I feel the irony: always the 'other', even here.

The first to introduce herself is 'Tits'. I'm not sure I've heard right. I keep my eyes on hers.

'Titania,' she explains. 'Like in Shakespeare. And that's my boyfriend, Squid, over there, who your friend's talkin to right now.'

Following Titania's lead, the rest offer limp hands to hold briefly, the baubles on their fingers like beads on abacuses. The friendliest of them totters expertly on a pair of platform shoes. Goth in her use of lipstick and eyeliner, she has safety pins stuck through each eyebrow, her nose, her bottom lip. I get the feeling the trail doesn't end there. She tells me her name is Lola.

I explain what Anwar and I are looking for, and one by one they shake spiked and lacquered hairdos.

'Talk to my boyfriend, Skinny,' says Lola. 'He knows everything about everything.'

She points across the road to a figure getting out of a matt-black speedster, most of its engine sitting on its bonnet. A truly brave act would be to drive *that* through suburbia. As for his name, this is no urban-slang irony. Skinny really is skinny. He swaggers over and horizontals his index and middle fingers at me in a drag-racer's salute.

I ask him what I asked the group, and he replies emphatically. 'No way, bro, not here. And I'd know, cos I shittin well own these bad streets.'

Skinny blows smoke out of more orifices than his car's rear end, but he's likeable with it. Beneath the macho veneer, I detect a brittleness that makes me sure his girlfriend is the stronger, emotionally, of the pair.

Lola gives his hand a little squeeze. 'Got a hello for your

best babe?' she asks, and he tips her back with a flourish and kisses her the old-fashioned movie way. I have to hide my smile. Skinny is a romantic underneath.

'You got a name, Andy Pandy?' he asks me.

I thought I'd heard all the variations there were on androgynous, but not that one.

'Salisbury — Sal,' I reply.

'Well, Sal, anytime you want to park your Andy Pandy arse beside me in Black Beauty here' — he points to his mean machine — 'you just come on by.'

'Thanks for the offer,' I say, sure I'll never be taking him up on it.

Skinny's race number comes up, and Lola takes the ride with him. Tits lends me her milk crate and I perch on it at the edge of the roundabout, craning along Wolf Road.

It's exciting being in the makeshift grandstand with the screeching, hooting crowd. Flashlights laser in all directions as Skinny and his rival rev their motors at each other then burn their way down the churned-up bitumen, the twin clouds of exhaust followed by the rubber-tearing sound of brakes at the far end. Skinny comes back triumphant and treats Lola to another romantic kiss, the rest of us witness to true love right here at the Bend. Anwar quietly suggests we leave, and I nod. I've learnt zip for Gail, but am almost ready to take part in a duel myself — behind the wheel and hand on the gearstick, that is.

6

Friday night, and the Animal Protection Vigilantes are heading out of the city.

Reflectors flash by. I stare beyond the freeway safety barriers into a dim-lit skein of suburbs. Anwar and I have had four unproductive nights trawling the streets at Fishermans Bend; meanwhile, the bogus kit has made its appearance in several parts of the CBD and initiated talk everywhere of EHg's and Gail's demise. It's almost a relief to be out on a horse rescue.

Nagid drives our nondescript SEC hire van, soon exiting the freeway for the smaller roads that run northeast into the Yarra Valley. Here there's only light traffic, most people saving their energy consumption vouchers for cheaper daytime use. Our destination is a section of the valley just before the old bushfire line. It's 9 pm. All going to plan, the trip to Greengate Farm should take just under an hour.

Max sits up the front, his vet's bag on his lap, while Lydia and Brigid face Inez and me on the two bench seats in the back. The six of us are uniform in black clothing and steel-capped boots. Our backpacks contain work gloves and balaclavas, head and wrist torches, and the lightweight halters we'll use on the horses. These last are a flat nylon weave: strong but very soft. We share the responsibility of the tools, Lydia carrying the heavy stuff tonight.

Brigid wordlessly passes around the sugar cubes and we stuff a handful each in our pockets. Experience has taught us it's the little things that can decide the difference between a smooth rescue and a rout.

The suburban sprawl gives way to reserve land. At Crystal Brook, Cicada emerges last minute from the shadows of a bus shelter beside the road and we nearly miss him. He hauls on the side door and climbs in beside Inez, barely a nod to any of us. The only one not in black, he's wearing scuffed brown riding boots under grey King Gees, and a chequered flanny and wool jumper already smelling of the stable yard.

Cicada won't go near the city unless it's for an animal emergency. He's made his home somewhere outside it, no one knows exactly where. From what I've heard, it's a bivvy bag under the stars. I feel a little envious of his apparent indifference to the usual human niceties. But I imagine it's a double-edged sword, both freedom and loneliness in it.

Half an hour later we're on a narrow, badly cambered secondary road, and conversation falters, the magnitude of what we're about to do weighing on us. The silence deepens. We are in shutdown, emotions plugged and thoughts suspended, everything narrowed to the immediate: sitting, breathing, watching.

The land outside is limned by moon. A sign glimmers on the left, an uninspired combination of a cow and a green gate. We kill the lights then drive across the cattle grid, stopping so Lydia can get out and cover the numberplates, front and back. If it all goes pear-shaped, we don't want to be traced via something as simple as rego.

Two hundred metres beyond the cattle grid is the caretaker's cottage, all dark. A couple of dogs set up a frantic barking on the ends of their chains, but there's no light or movement from the house. This, we assume, is because its occupant is at the pub as usual, and James is keeping him company there. While Cicada communes with the dogs, we double-check. No one wants to resort to the contingency plan, which consists of six balaclavas, a length of rope, and tying Russ Stefanovic to one of his kitchen chairs.

We return to the van. Moonlight stipples paddocks cropped back to nothing, the stony ground transformed into a patchwork of silvery greys. The dark hulks of dairy cows loom both sides of the unfenced track. A couple wander into the beam of our headlights and stop, their heads turned towards us, benignly looking. Nagid brakes hard. The last thing we need is a vet emergency of our own making.

The cows move off slowly. It looks like Greengate uses Jerseys for their milkers. I've always felt sorry for any farm animal having to endure the harsh realities of Australia's heat-stripped terrain, and somehow it seems wrong to have cows from Jersey grazing in anything other than lush, undulating fields protected by copses.

Chill air blows in as Max rolls down his window to listen. There's the occasional lowing of an adult, but no calves. They'd have been taken off their mothers' teats on day one and sent to slaughter.

The track climbs gently. We summit the rise. Beyond it, the land drops away to river flats and the dairy hunkered in its protected valley, invisible from the road. A single floodlight illuminates the empty car park at the front. We pull up outside the pool of light, Inez busy at her palm computer. If her hacking program hasn't worked, or something's happened with Lars, then shortly we'll be walking within sensor range of a back-to-base alarm and bank of floods, our arrival recorded for posterity.

She lifts her head to the rest of us. I give her an enquiring look and she responds with a decisive tap on the pad. Balaclavas and gloves go on. From now we'll hold to silence as much as possible.

The dairy is a large hangar-like space beneath a slanted corrugated-iron roof. To the left is the administration area and visitors entrance; to the right are the yards and races that funnel into the milking shed. Even from here the smell of shit and milk is strong.

I step into the illuminated area, testing. No alarm. No bright lights.

We hurry together across the car park, our breaths puffing out little white clouds, then huddle around the entrance for the moment of truth. Ignoring the number pad below the doorhandle, I push and hear the snib release. The door swings open. High five for Inez.

Head and wrist torches flick on in succession, a corridor illumed. Shed-side, the wall is half glass to give a view of the milking operation from a nice clean distance. A couple of energy-saver lights cast a ghoulish glow on the race that leads to the carousel-style milking parlour and its monitoring equipment. The cows' lactation rate boosted with growth hormones, the animals soon learn to take themselves to the milking shed to relieve the bursting pain in their udders. It's short-term gain for the dairy and agony for the cows, their lifespan reduced from twenty to about three years.

We begin our check of every room, in case anyone's decided to stay at work to cook the books or cosy up with a special friend instead of going home. I adjust the rope looped across my shoulder, the same contingency plan for them as for the caretaker.

The first door says OFFICE. The room has a desk piled high with papers, and an overflowing waste bin. The shredder has documents waiting in the slot. I pick up the slim sheaf and fold it into my jacket to look at later. It might be interesting to see what information Greengate wants destroyed.

Next is a kitting-up area for the workers, a row of white plastic aprons and overpants hanging on hooks with gumboots lined up in neat pairs beneath, ready for the early-morning shift. Above a box of papery mob caps is a sign: DON'T FORGET YOUR HEADWEAR!

We pass the workers' kitchen and eating area with its plastic tables and plastic chairs and ubiquitous sink-top urn. After that are toilets and a storeroom.

Last on the right is a door marked PRIVATE. This is the control room where Lars will be ignoring his hijacked surveillance monitors and shirking his scheduled checks for the night. Inez messages off a quick enquiry. On the reply, Max puts his head around the door for confirmation. Then we move on.

The corridor elbows left, ending in a fire exit. Before that, on the right, is another door, NO UNAUTHORISED PERSONNEL writ large. Unlike the others, this one has no handle, just a touchpad on the wall.

I look around. The CCTV lens is positioned on a cornice behind us.

Inez goes to the touchpad and punches in the code supplied by Lars.

Nothing.

She frowns. We hold our collective breath as she does it again. This time there's the sound of the mechanism unlatching, and she shrugs. We're through to the horses' secret enclosure.

First is a rectangular yard with a low Laserlite roof, corrugated-iron walls and no windows. This is the cleaning and inspection yard, its concrete floor bevelled to gutters at the edge for easy hosing. It would be boiling hot in summer, and is freezing now. A row of feed bins attach to the wall opposite; beside them are stacks of plastic jerry cans and a tap with a hose. Left is a double-door fire exit. This, we know from the schematics, is the horses' only way out, making the whole place a fire trap as well as a torture chamber.

The internal door clicks behind us. I glance up, straight into the dead eye of a CCTV lens, and silently thank the APV's lucky stars for Inez's techno wizardry. We pull off our balaclavas and pocket them, then get the halters from our packs and loop them to our belts. I hand two to Cicada.

A strong smell emanates from an opening, far right. As Inez, Brigid, Lydia and Nagid busy themselves in the yard area, Cicada, Max and I move to what waits beyond. The smell gets stronger. Breathing through my mouth, I steel myself; there will be nothing clean or kind about this production line.

There are three rows of stalls with two aisles between, seven horses to a row. A tube snakes from each stall to a collection can on the ground behind. We enter the first aisle. Face in to the wall and haunches to us, the animals are effectively blinkered, but they sense our presence and shift nervously, ears twitching. Dung is piled high in the stalls, and the stench of manure and piss and sickness is terrible.

I inspect a jerry can. Its scummy plastic is one-third full. But it's where the tubing attaches at the other end I'm more worried about.

Every mare is confined in a space hardly bigger than her body. A harness arrangement attaches to a cage-like structure above and loops down around her haunches. This keeps the UCD — urine collection device — in place. She's haltered and tied in front as well, with just enough length to allow her to reach feed and water troughs, the latter being almost always empty, the water meted out in miserly doses to keep the oestrogen saturation in the urine high.

Cicada leads the way to the first stall. He slips inside the gate and works his way along the mare's flank to her withers. She brings up her head and rolls her eyes, but he soothes with his hands and calms with his voice, murmuring the sorts of things that only he and horses understand.

On his nod, Max and I move in beside her to begin the task of disconnecting the UCD. We've done this on over a dozen occasions together and have a system. First I snip the plastic line to the collection can, then Max releases the buckle straps our side of the urine bag and slips a hand between the mare's legs to ease away the rubber perineal seal. This is supposed to stop faeces mixing with the urine, but the seal is perished and probably hasn't worked for months. It will, however, have chafed her skin into weeping, scabby sores. I wait, ready with the anaesthetising antiseptic pads.

The bag drops down and swings against the far rails, a sodden mess. We bring our wrist torches up to inspect the damage. The mare's urethra is pustular and swollen, the urine-soaked skin around it smelly and infected, while the insides of both haunches are red raw from where the UCD has rubbed day after day, week after terrible week.

Max motions and I pass across a hand-sized pad. He presses it to her vulva and we ready for her to try to kick. We wait a count of sixty, then he hands it back and I give him two more, these for her inside legs. Another count of sixty before the used pads go in a disposal bag, and we're ready to try to move her.

We open the stall gate as Cicada continues his wordless conversation with the mare. While we've been working, he's replaced her filthy halter with a clean one. We're lucky the first one wasn't embedded in her skin.

We start to back her out. This is a critical moment. If she goes down onto the concrete, she'll be almost impossible to get up again. Persuaded into the aisle, she's shaky but still standing, and we can lead her slowly to where the rest of the team is waiting with fresh water and hay.

We proceed like this, one horse at a time, until we have seven in the yard. They are meek and listless; their haunches show no muscle, their coats no sheen. The soft clop of overgrown hooves on concrete is followed by a thirsty slurping in the buckets. Apart from suffering what must be constant pain, each is badly dehydrated due to the miserly water regime. We can only hope they all make it to the sanctuary.

Max's mobile beeps softly. The other cell has arrived.

We open the double doors. Cold air drags in — and a sight to warm it: three transports waiting silently, ramps down.

Six figures detach from the shadows. They extend hands to the horses first, allowing them time to smell the scents on their hands and clothes from the outside world, and then they turn to us. Briefly, cold hands clasp hello. None of us has ever met, or is likely to. It's safer that way.

They glove up, and together we lead the mares out of the shed. Most have trouble walking on stiff, sore legs and stumble; some need a person each side as well as at the front; but none resist the ramps up into the truck. We've noticed this phenomenon before. It's as if their wills are so broken, they don't care where they're being led. It breaks my heart to see, even if it simplifies the loading. Call me overly anthropomorphic, but what I prefer to believe is that the horses somehow know — whether by smell or aura or something else — that we're not the farm workers here to inflict more hurt, but instead have come to help, and that the ramps into the trucks are their escape from pain and sickness and death.

Max and Cicada and I return to the stalls and begin on the second row of mares. When we're done, we move on to the third.

Five hours after starting, we're at the last stall. In it is a white Appaloosa, her head down, her breathing loud and ragged. The collection can behind her is completely empty: a bad sign. Cicada moves slowly along her flank, then looks back at us and shakes his head. This mare is nearly dead in her harness. Sorrow sits like a stone in my chest.

'She'll drop when we release her,' Max murmurs.

The others are finished in the inspection yard, and join us in the stable area. The sight of the Appaloosa elicits gasps. Whatever we've seen on previous raids, it doesn't inure us to the next cruelty.

No animal should suffer the last moments of its life tethered and alone. They busy themselves pulling hay from the feed bins to make a soft bed around her as Max prepares the hypodermic and gives it to Cicada. Then we ready ourselves on the harness straps.

Cicada gently rubs along one bony cheek to lay a hand on her withers. I catch a glimpse of something beyond his perpetually shuttered expression, and for a fleeting moment have a window through to his own injured soul. It's too raw and intimate and I have to look away.

He slides the needle in and the mare's legs buckle, her weight bearing down on the straps. We slip then release our hold and she drops where she is, barely more than skin and bones. There will be no proper burial for her; only an end, finally, to her suffering.

There's one thing left to do.

Cicada stays with the downed mare while the rest of us yank the plastic lines off the urine containers and carry them back to the inspection yard for emptying.

At the end of the third row, past the Appaloosa's stall, is an unmarked door that we've studiously avoided until now. We know from Lars that this is the laboratory where the mares' urine is concentrated into its end products, ready for transport. Those evil bastards would have walked through the horse yards and past the Appaloosa every day to get to their place of work. Lydia lingers at the door. I know that look. I draw her away before she goes for the crowbar. *No*, I gesture firmly, and she doesn't try to counter me.

I return to the Appaloosa mare, Cicada still crouched there cradling her head. Reaching through the stall bars, I stroke her coarse mane and say my goodbyes.

Outside, the trucks are loaded and waiting, their huge shapes delineated by the glow of their parking lights. Each has been refitted to take seven horses. We planned on twenty-one in all, but now there will be only twenty.

When the double doors have been swung closed, Inez sends the signal to Lars. Cicada, with a brief nod to us, jumps in the cab of the lead transport, and we watch as they roll forward onto the track and begin the slow climb out of the valley.

When their tail-lights have disappeared over the rise, we pile into the van and follow. No one speaks. Inez, beside me, reaches for my hand. Opposite us, Brigid leans on Max's shoulder, her eyes closed, while Lydia, in the front seat beside Nagid, stares fixedly out the window. We pass the cottage, its metal roof sheening the light of the moon. The dogs yip half-heartedly. They would have smelt the horses as they went by in the trucks — and perhaps they sense something extraordinary is going on. No freedom in it for them, they fall silent at the ends of their chains.

7

My place with Inez, under the doona. I move aside the floppy purple plush that's Nitro nestled on my pillow to go make coffee and toast for my girl, a déshabillé vision of loveliness in my bed.

Dawn, we'd cuddled each other to sleep, cocooned in the knowledge that Greengate Farm would be waking to find Lars and the horses gone, the warning beep of its security system bringing up the APV message on all the monitors. Now we devour brunch, then shower, comparing bruises from the raid, before deciding on a stroll to the Good Bean — my Saturday tradition.

We lounge in the sun at one of Frank's tiny outside tables, sipping more coffee as we envisage our rescuees delivered into the care of the sanctuary workers, their illnesses and injuries being tended to at last by experts. The deeper stuff — the effects of so much suffering — will take a lot longer to heal, but right now I feel like a kid with presents: another successful raid *and* basking in the miracle that is Inez.

An easy sensuality flows between us, hand casually brushing hand, foot resting on foot beneath the café table. Attraction vaulting over caution, there may as well be a neon light above us flashing, *Transgressors HERE!!!*

The talk drifts gradually into more serious territory, Inez hunching her singleted shoulders over a newspaper. The frown lines between her brows deepen. She jabs a finger at a headline. 'The government says they're winning the war on infertility and the fight against perverts.' She makes a face. 'They're using the endocrine disruptor stuff against us again. Another NF-owned scientist is saying she's proved a link between exposure to pesticides and sexual deviance.'

The argument against transgressives is replayed across a dozen different scenarios, all with one aim: to prove that we, in our many variations, have been put together wrong.

The latest round began with whelks on boats. Shortly before the H5N1 virus mutated to transmit efficiently human to human, and its catastrophic antigen slashed the birth rate, a colony of female whelks was discovered to have penises. Scientists concluded the anomaly was caused by environmental contaminants — in this case, a component in the anti-corrosion paint used by the boat owners. They called the endocrine-disrupted creatures an 'imposex', and cited similar examples in the world's polluted water and landways: male alligators exposed to pesticide spills in the Florida lakes born with half-size sex organs; rodents in the grasslands downwind of heavy industry developing mutations in their DNA and passing them on to their young; frogs turning hermaphroditic in a logged and farmed Amazon … It hadn't taken long for the wowsers to pick up on the notion of imposexes multiplying everywhere in the ecosystem and apply it to the human community. By their reductionist logic, anyone who deviated from the 'standard' physiology or accepted behaviour for their gender was likely heading the same direction as the whelks. But it was the Nation Firsts who took this one crucial step further by connecting the phenomenon of endocrine disruption and adjuvant-induced infertility to the erosion of God's Law, blaming society's wanton and libertine ways for finally bringing Divine punishment down upon itself.

'Listen to this.' Now Inez is angry. 'Neighbourly Watch is advising prayer groups to "*seek out transgressors and lay on hands if necessary to help them cough up their demons*".' She tosses the paper onto the unoccupied table beside us. 'That's blatant permission for harassment and physical attack.'

I stroke the fine hairs on her forearm, not knowing what to say.

There's so much hypocrisy in the current fertility predicament. The preoccupation with appearance — plump and curvaceous for the women, muscular and 'well-hung' for the men — means the skills of the deregistered hormone doctors and cosmetic surgeons in the Red Quarter are increasingly being called on to help. How ironic that Inez, who's never had a day, pre- or post-pandemic, of being called — not even whispered to — by her ovaries, just happens to embody the current female ideal; meanwhile, I know only too well how I don't fit either category. Unsurprisingly, the androgynous look is out — *verboten* — helped by Nation First's decree that any deviation from the 'standard norm' is the work of the Devil, even though the 'norm' itself is no more than a construction.

Inez stiffens suddenly. I remove my hand from her arm and turn to where she's looking. Coming up our side of the street are five people in hessian shawls, chanting penitence. They monopolise the pavement, others detouring around them. The prayer groups have no manners now they think they're God's police.

My hand goes below the table onto Inez's thigh. I feel it tense as if she's about to spring up. 'Don't,' I murmur, squeezing gently.

Her anger radiates out as the prayer group arrives beside us. Silent now, they mark our presence. I concentrate on my cup as they stare down. I wonder if they're going to help us cough up our demons like in the newspaper report.

Before they get the chance, the Good Bean's glass door opens and Frank appears, solid and undeniable, hands on ample hips. He bustles over, placing his considerable bulk between them and us.

'Shoo,' he says loudly.

Put off, they move away. Out of Frank's territory their chant starts up again.

Inez's thigh muscle relaxes.

Frank gathers up our empty cups. 'Same again?' he asks.

We nod, and the Good Bean's door bangs behind him, rattling the glass.

I feel the passing of the rock meant for Frank's window. It's a woeful shot, and rolls beneath the adjacent table. I lean down to pick it up. A piece of paper is attached to it. I snap off the rubber band and read: *LEAVE THE DEVIL'S EMPLOY. SAVE YOURSELF WHILE YOU CAN.*

Not meant for Frank's window, after all.

'Bastards,' says Inez.

Crumpling the message, I put it in the empty ashtray. Now I'm angry. Lobbing rocks with warnings at transgressives is evangelism gone feral.

My girlfriend leans her forehead against mine, her breath damping my cheek. 'Don't let them spook you,' she murmurs. 'They write that to all God's good-looking queers.'

I slip my hand gratefully into hers, and slowly the sun reheats our day.

She tantalises me with coffee-flavoured lips. 'Wanna get a bunch of sci-fi movies and be couch potatoes this evening?'

'Can't,' I say soberly. 'I'm working all night.'

'I'll save you some chocolate then.'

Inez never prods for details, accepting that she remains in the dark when it comes to my work activities for Gail, just as Gail never asks about the APV, even though she bankrolls its activities via a monthly stipend from her company profits. Today, however, Inez has some information *I* want, being one very sought-after expert in the Red Quarter, the reward for having built the security systems for many of the businesses on Madams Row.

I nuzzle into her shoulder. 'Can you give me your impressions of Savannah Rose at the Shangri-La?'

She considers. 'Smart. Charming. No-nonsense.'

I notice she's used none of the adjectives that came to mind on my visit. 'What about attractive?'

'I suppose. She's not really my type.'

'Anything else it would be good to know?'

Inez considers some more. 'Never take her up on the offer of a game of chess. She's three times national champion.'

8

After uneventful snoop duty at Fishermans Bend, I sleep all Sunday and am back with Inez early evening, meeting Albee at the Glory Hole before the next overnighter with Anwar.

In her cloakroom nook, Marlene takes Inez's coat with gracious aplomb, and spends a little time flirting with Albee. Me, she just glowers at.

The three of us stand above the bar area, scanning for a free space. The speakeasy is always crowded on a Blue Laws day. I look sideways at my bicycle-fixing friend.

'You enjoyed that, didn't you.'

Inez grins on Albee's other side, and he looks sheepish. 'She has a certain something …'

'I'd agree with that,' I say. I don't divulge what something springs to mind, because it isn't nice.

We're lucky enough to secure an alcove, and Inez goes to get our drinks. Albee says, 'Back in a mo,' and wanders over Marlene's way to flirt some more. I make myself comfortable among the cushions on the padded bench seat, easing into the atmosphere of the place. I have to admit, while Anwar is everything I could wish for in a co-worker out on unpredictable ground, it's nice to be back on home turf in more talkative company.

I'm suddenly aware that I'm no longer alone in my alcove. Mojo Meg has slipped past the half-open curtain, and her two pit-bulls are blocking my view out.

'May I?' She motions to the seat beside me.

I nod, caught off-guard.

'Been watching you,' she begins, and already I'm unhappy with where this is going. Meg has a reputation for putting the hard word on the young folk. 'You're a good worker.'

I do a fast one-eighty in my head. Not about sex then …

'Your boss is likely going under with these latest troubles,' she says, cutting to the chase. 'It's almost impossible to drag back a customer's goodwill once it's lost, especially when there are others around to offer *guaranteed* product.'

I'm incensed on Gail's behalf, but say nothing, corralled as I am three against one. I wonder how much longer Inez will be, and wish I could telepath Albee to shift his rapt attention from Marlene's many attributes for just a moment to look my way.

Meg fixes on me, her eyes hard as buttons. 'Question is, do you want to go under with her?'

'You seem to know a lot about it,' I counter, and she smiles. The shape is not entirely successful. Must be an unpractised position for her mouth.

'It's my business to know,' she says. 'It's *all* our businesses to know. Gail's got herself an enemy, maybe a worm in the apple. If you jump ship now, you can save yourself. I can offer you good employ: bonuses, certain opportunities ...'

Blimey. Can't wait to hear.

Despite Meg's affiliation with BioPharm Industries netting her a large part of the distribution pie, I already know whose products out of BioPharm's and Ethical Hormones' I'd rather be delivering to the masses, the former rumoured to have rather less commitment to an entirely cruelty-free process.

She pats the cushion between us. 'Want you to know I sympathise with your situation,' her voice has gone all syrupy and persuasive, 'but loyalty shouldn't lead to a needless drowning.'

I glance up at her pit-bulls, playing with names. The speakeasy clientele — transgressives of all persuasions — give these two bully boys the cold shoulder. I decide on 'Crusher' for the short one, and 'Snarl' for the tall.

My self-invited visitor leans disconcertingly close. 'Speaking frankly, girl to girl, you're too valuable to be sacrificed, and this is the best offer you'll get.'

Now that just tears my heart out, Meg popping me in the category of 'girl' without so much as a by-your-leave. The gender slap vibrates in my bones. I bite back a fast retort, brought to tact by the presence of Crusher and Snarl and the thought of them hurting me in their big hands.

What she's said about Gail having an enemy so close really bothers me. She knows more than she's telling, while I've learnt nothing from my nights of surveillance at Fishermans Bend or my daytime enquiries. Somehow I've made it into Meg's good books. What if I can use it as leverage?

'I need some time to think about it,' I say, surprising myself.

'Offer closes soon,' she says crisply. 'Don't think so hard you break a blood vessel.'

Then she's gone and Inez is walking towards the booth, a quizzical look on her face.

I feel a bit ill, not sure whether I've just made a smart move or let Meg and her minders intimidate me. Too late, I wish I'd given a flat refusal, because even with no intention of taking up the offer, I'm tainted now by the expectation I can be bought.

I chuck the cushion Meg patted into the far corner of the alcove and shift along the bench seat to make room for Inez, then Albee returning from his tête-à-tête. Did I catch a tone of blame in Meg's voice? Surely she doesn't think EHg's troubles are the result of something Gail's done? I have to find out who's doing this to my boss, my *friend*, and stop it sliding her to destruction.

Inez waits for my explanation, Albee beside her sipping his drink.

'A business visit,' I say wryly.

'Anything you can talk about?' Albee asks.

I shake my head, and Inez, bless her, wraps her lovely arms around me in a hug.

Anwar and I have arranged to meet at the bottom of Benedict Street again — about fifteen minutes' walk from the Glory Hole. I check my watch when I get outside. Still three-quarters of an hour before he swings by. Mojo Meg's visit put such a dampener on my mood that I couldn't enjoy my remaining time with Inez and Albee.

Duffle coat firmly buttoned, I walk up Daisy Lane and turn left. The wind bites once I'm out of the protective dip of the alleyway, and I look up at clear sky. Another relentlessly dry summer has slowly given way to gentler days, but at night it feels like winter. I'm sure Melbourne evenings never used to get this cold this early. With each new season the temperature fluctuations have become harder to predict and more extreme.

The avenues that grid the city are wide and impersonal and feel unshielded in comparison to the smaller streets between. I stick west on Pilgrim Lane, which leads me directly to the financial sector ... such as it is. Half the buildings are empty, many businesses closed, while those remaining operate on a knife-edge between profit and insolvency. Of course, no matter how bad it gets, some professions will always be in demand. Plumbers and electricians, for instance.

The prayer meeting two lampposts ahead of me is out

rather late and huddled oddly, their heads bent over something on the ground. I hurry along the pavement towards them, my brain not yet able to interpret what it is.

The something moves, becomes a prostrate figure. Closer, it makes strange mewling noises. A trousered leg draws back and finds its mark. There's a muffled scream. 'Dirty little surry,' hisses one of the four silhouetted above, and instantly my brain decodes the image. The woman is curled on her side with the dark soles of her shoes towards me, and the group is kicking at her stomach ... her *pregnant* stomach; kicking the blasphemy out of her.

The realisation jolts an arc of current at my core. Adrenaline surges to my extremities and I start to run, then I'm barrelling my body's full force into them. Those half-turned are knocked aside like skittles. Faces register their surprise, legs still in the act of kicking.

I reach down to the woman and try to lift her, willing her to stand, but she flops back away from me like a rag doll. As I re-grip, hands grapple me, their efforts hampered by the prayer shawls. Arms rain ineffectual blows; I feel nothing except the sack weight of the woman, her ribs and breasts in my desperate clinch, her face a grimace, cheeks grubby with dirt and tears.

I reel up, snarling, and the group backs off, this uncoiled rage not what they'd bargained for.

'Get away from her, you monsters!' I roar as they bring their prayer shawls up over their heads to shadow their features.

The woman is still on the ground, bent double to protect her belly. I try to move her again, but she won't budge. I'm afraid the group is regathering to attack again, but when I look up, they're dispersing rapidly along the street, disowning their public thuggery.

The woman lets out a guttural groan. I press for Inez on my mobile and pray she'll answer.

She's still at the speakeasy. 'Five minutes,' she promises.

There's a metal bench under a shelter about fifty metres up the street. I speak slowly to the woman, telling her how it's just a little way, a few short steps. Her eyes are closed, her lips white. I'm afraid she's passed out, or worse.

A motorised scooter zips by on the other side of Pilgrim Lane and I wave frantically. Just when I think it's not going to stop, the rider performs a wide, fast wheelie, daring the ire of oncoming traffic. But there are no other vehicles, and no pedestrians; no witnesses but me to cruelty.

The rider slews to a halt beside us. He's painfully young. He looks at me, then the woman. His forehead crinkles in confusion below his black beanie.

'She's hurt,' I say carefully, so as not to spook him. 'It's very important to get her to that bench. Can you help me?'

I can see in his eyes that he's afraid to let go of his scooter in case it's some trick to filch his expensive ride.

'Look,' I say. 'She's hurt very badly. She needs us to do this for her. Someone will be coming very soon to collect her.'

Reluctantly he leans his scooter against the kerb and takes one side of the woman, and between us we get her the fifty metres to the shelter. When we have her slumped on the metal slats of the bench, I start to say thanks, but already he's running back and flipping the scooter upright with an expert foot. Then one leg is on the kickboard and the other pushing off as the little motor buzzes up the dark street, its rear light receding like an insect's warning eye.

I ring Anwar.

'I'll be by in the van,' he says.

'No, it's okay,' I reply. 'Inez'll be here any minute.'

He assures me he can do tonight's shift without me, and that he'll let Gail know what's happened.

As I ring off, Inez pulls up. She's out of her ute in a heartbeat, blanket in one hand. We drape it about the woman then shuffle her to the passenger door, manoeuvring her onto the bench seat between us.

We make the drive north up Temperance Street to the Women's Hospital in silence. Our passenger has stopped groaning and is eyes closed, probably gone into shock. She leans heavily against me. I look anxiously at her face. Mid-twenties, maybe, with dark skin and the tiny pockmarks of a hormonal adolescence on both cheeks. Her long black hair has been pulled out of its ponytail, the elastic still clinging to a lock. I detach it gently and place it over a knob on the dash.

I glance at Inez concentrating on the road, the question flapping like a loose sail in my mind. How had this woman's attackers known she was a working surrogate and not a 'happy families' fertile, or even an infertile who'd successfully turned to the Red Quarter clinics for help?

There are two people and a trolley waiting at Emergency when we pull up. In my call ahead, I'd said nothing of the circumstances, only that the victim of the attack was pregnant. Babies being at a premium these days, they pull out all stops to save them.

An orderly in blue helps us ease the woman from the ute. Laid on the trolley, she's tucked in then wheeled speedily through the automatic doors, and we're directed to the information desk to give our details.

We return to the ute. We couldn't even tell them the woman's name. I bundle up the blanket. There's blood on it, and on the car seat.

9

Inez and I drive back to the hospital at 8 am. Up in the lift to level four and the maternity wing, we tread squeaky linoleum to the visitors' waiting room. We describe who we're here to see, and are directed along a corridor by a sympathetic RN.

Nurses are often vociferous opponents of the current government's anti-surrogacy policy, being those most often landed with the sad results. They get to keep their jobs because they're in such short supply, the only trained staff left to fill the skills gap that opened when a raft of medicos working in the fertility clinics and gene-research centres were struck off the register and hospital payrolls. Not that this particular part of the hospital is busy these days, and at the far end it's imbued with an almost suffocating quiet. No babies here.

We stand at the door of the share room, looking in. A woman — not ours — is asleep under the covers in the first bed. The privacy curtains have been pulled around the second.

Inez calls a tentative 'Hello?'

On a low answer, I open a gap in the curtain and together we step into the sanitised white space. The woman in the bed is propped up by pillows. Her long hair, now neatly plaited, snakes past her breast over the hospital gown. One thin brown arm lies above the bedcovers, the contents of a drip bag feeding into it. She won't look at us, and it's clear it wasn't she who spoke. Her expression, and that on the face of the woman sitting beside her, tells it all.

Short and capable-looking, the latter rises from her seat and extends a hand. A firm, no-nonsense shake. I'm guessing sensible shoes too.

Inez and I say our names, and she nods. 'The nurse unit manager phoned me. I got your details from Admissions,' she says. 'I'm Tallis Dankner, from SANE.'

The Surrogate Advocacy, Networking and Emergency team works out of the Red Quarter, and is another of the madams' innovations.

She sits again. 'This is Roshani. She's doing fine, but she lost the baby.'

'We're so sorry,' I say, Inez silent beside me.

Tallis leans close to the semi-prone woman. 'Roshani?' Her voice is gentle, soothing. 'These are the people who helped you last night.'

No response. Roshani's focus stays on some invisible

point on the powder-blue bedspread. One slow tear leaks below a lash.

I find Inez's hand and we stand there miserably.

'We appreciate what you both did,' Tallis says, adjusting Roshani's hospital gown to cover a bare shoulder.

She nods towards the door. As we walk out together, she hands me a business card.

'I made a few enquiries. Your name came up connected to Gail Alvarez,' she says quietly.

Makes sense my boss would be well-known to SANE.

'I'm hoping you might pay a visit to my office in the next couple of days.'

'Absolutely,' I say, and look to Inez not included in the invitation. 'But I'm not sure I have anything useful to offer. I don't know how she got targeted like that.'

Tallis glances from us to the curtains obscuring her diminutive charge. Roshani had showed no sign of wanting to speak, and may not for a while. I suspect SANE's rep has seen this all too often before.

'Leave that with me,' she says. 'In the meantime, she'll be taken good care of.'

I don't doubt it. Surrogacy is big business, and SANE protects its own. But how they manage it amid the roving Neighbourhood Values Brigades and now attack prayer groups, I have no idea.

Outside my flat, Inez and I kiss a quick goodbye in the ute, aware of multiple eyes looking from the public high-rises.

We'll be seeing each other again in a few hours at the usual Monday APV meeting, which I expect to be a debrief on Friday's rescue and some discussion over what project we might tackle next.

Nitro greets me at the door, miaowing his disapproval at my many absences. I take him into the yard for a circumnavigation of the tundra before feeding him, then leave him stretched on his rather-too-ample side, washing his paws in a square of morning sun.

I wheel out my bike. Swinging a leg over the frame, I scoot from the back alley onto the main road, my sights set for Cute'n'Cuddly Pty Ltd. Along with a swag of rescheduled deliveries waiting to be couriered, I've some debriefing of my own to do. The ride, however, feels heavy, not the usual pleasure to be had in the smooth motion of muscles and steady pump of blood. I can't blame the day — perfect weather. It's my thoughts of Roshani weighing me down like a millstone, and bringing to the surface a renewed dread of things to come.

On my knock, Gail opens the door to her private office and ushers me through. She motions me to sit in the only chair — an unusual act in itself — then leans across the desk and looks at me intently, taking in the bags under my eyes and my lacklustre vibe.

'Anwar got caught up in a drag racers' dispute at Fishermans Bend last night and had all his tyres stolen,' she tells me. 'It took the rest of the night to negotiate them back, so I want one more go at surveillance there tonight. Are you up to it?'

I return her gaze. 'Can't let him have all the fun.'

It's a poor attempt at enthusiasm, but I would walk over broken bottles for her if she asked.

She smiles briefly. I can see concern in it, and relief. Below her tough-as-nails façade sometimes I think she cares for me as she would a kid brother or sister.

She busies herself a moment at an electric kettle, then a coffee plunger, two cups and ingredients appear out of a filing cabinet. We go through the deliveries. It's the regular drops to the usual places, and a relief to be concentrating on something comparatively mundane.

When we're done, she surprises me by saying, 'Let's check out the view from the roof.'

I've only been up once before, on my induction into the couriering business. To get there we have to go through her private quarters, the turret room where she sometimes sleeps if she's at the warehouse overnight. It's even more spartan than the office: just a camp bed and plain dresser, a single window looking south, and a fire-escape door.

We step outside and cross to the paint-peeled crenellations at the building's edge. I lean on the parapet, staring out. The day is gentle, almost balmy. A slight breeze frizzes the trees in the street below. South are the Melbourne rail yards; beyond them is Victoria Harbour and the Docklands. Further left, we'd be looking straight down the city grid if it weren't for a cluster of unfinished apartment towers blocking our view. There are no sounds of construction, and not likely to be anytime soon, the developers in receivership.

I watch a girl being walked by a scruffy dog, stopping obediently at every tree for it to cock its leg. The dog knows where it's going: a square of dirt a couple of blocks away euphemistically called a park. A popular spot for the homeless as well as dogs, it's all benches full at night.

'By the way,' Gail says casually, 'I heard something interesting from a colleague of mine in Drugs Watch.'

That organisation is an information hub set up by Nation First to keep tabs on doctors and dispensaries, every medicine prescribed and script dispensed logged with them.

Her voice lowers. 'On Saturday a doctor in the Yarra Valley reported a Rohypnol incident. The victim was a dairy worker. Nothing odd on the surface of it, but my colleague suspects the dairy's a front for a hormone farm, and so I'm thinking the incident has the hallmarks of an APV sting.'

Gail never asks about our forays. I glance at her, not sure what she wants.

'EHg have just finished trialling a new drug,' she murmurs. 'It's not traceable in the body like the benzodiazepines are. Tell Max to give me a call about it.' She angles me an encouraging look. 'For next time.'

Her attention diverts to the street below as a brown eco-lite slows and swings into C&C's entrance. I hear the electric gate grind back and the car drive in. I'm motioned to the turret door, our rooftop meeting over.

Back in her office, Gail hands me my pay packet. It's bulkier than usual: extra cash for the nights spent staking out Barrow Road.

'About last night's attack.' She holds the door open. 'Let me know if I can do anything.'

I know she means about Roshani's assailants, none of whom I think I'd recognise again.

'Will do,' I say. 'Thanks for the coffee.'

I collect my deliveries from the basement and wheel my bike through the secure yard. The eco-lite is parked in the visitors bay, someone waiting in the driver's seat. Two delivery hands are nearby, cleaning their already clean Cute'n'Cuddly van to an almost supernatural white. I nod hi to them, then I'm off into the day, my courier's bag packed full.

Despite the grimness of the night before, my spirits finally begin to lift. I have people — Gail, Inez and Albee, Max and Anwar — who care about me, and whom I can always call on for help. In this fucked-up world, I am not alone. I have *family*.

10

I have to run the gauntlet of a late-afternoon prayer offensive in Martyr Street en route to the APV meeting. It's a public show of faith, several dozen hands up and waving. Just up the road from them, I steer around a Neighbourhood Values Brigade spoiling for a fight outside a specialty grog shop, the owner probably dobbed in for Sabbath trading.

Despite these detours, I arrive early at my destination — the shuttered backroom of a tiny Fitzroy gelateria — and wait for the rest of the Animal Protection Vigilantes to arrive. As the others find their various spots among the packaging and equipment, I lean gingerly on a stack of boxes purporting to contain sugar cones, and can smell their sweetness through the cardboard. The Nation Firsts have put many pleasures on the 'forbidden' list, but thankfully they still allow their citizens the sin of ice cream.

Lydia clumps in, looking harried. Silently I hope this

isn't going to set the tone of the meeting. When she's settled, I close the door.

Max kicks off proceedings. 'I'd just like to say well done to everyone for such a smooth operation.'

It must be a nice change for Lydia that this time no one even looks at her.

'I spoke with the sanctuary owners this morning,' he continues. 'The horses are doing alright, considering. Not off the danger list, but we should feel lucky to have lost only one.'

A pall of silence settles momentarily on the group as we remember the Appaloosa mare. Uncharacteristically, it's Lydia who sniffs into her hanky.

'By the way, the news is all good from the foster farm that took our abattoir rescue foals a couple of weeks ago,' Max adds to brighten us. 'Apparently they're injury-free and blooming. There'll be no trouble rehoming them.'

The knackeries affiliated with the hormone farms make for very traumatic rescues. We'd heard one had taken delivery of ten CEO colts and fillies, all of them destined for the crusher the next day. It was in the drama of their rescue that something sparked between Inez and me, which then ignited into full flame — so I feel I owe a debt to the foals.

James gives his report next.

'Big Russ arrived at the pub bang on eight fifteen,' he says. 'I gave him time to knock back the first few beers, then walked in and sat down with him like I was an old mate, and everybody, including him, thought I was. The ruphy went in his drink at curfew. The pub's shutters came down and the conversation dived into the truly maudlin. When our friend toppled off his barstool, everybody assumed he'd drunk way too much, which he always does. We dossed him down in the ladies lounge — took four of us to shift him there. He's a lot to carry, most of it covered in tatts.'

'He must have felt like shit the next morning,' Brigid murmurs.

'Too right,' James replies. 'He'd have been comatose about six hours, then nursing a very bad headache.' He snorts. 'Apparently every Saturday, the dairy shift swings by the pub on their way to Greengate and load him, still drunk, into their vehicle.'

'Not much of a caretaker,' I say.

'What's he likely to remember?' Brigid asks.

'A blank — a blur at most. If any of his pub mates remind him, he'll be racking his brains over who the "old acquaintance" was that he got drunk with. As for the horse rustling, hopefully, he'll think it was just his bad luck it happened the same night.'

'About that,' I say. 'I just heard from Gail his Rohypnol incident was logged with Drugs Watch.'

The group turn to me, serious-faced.

'Russ must have got himself tested Saturday afternoon,' says Max.

'There was always a chance he'd twig,' Inez responds. 'This isn't the first time that drug's been used in a horse raid.'

'Maybe he thought you messed with him, James,' I joke.

'Not my type. All those tatts …'

'No more excursions to the Yarra Valley for you.' I make it flippant, but we all know the risk of recognition is greatest with him this time.

My thoughts turn to Lars. It had taken a lot of courage to stick it to Greengate's owners and do what he did. The alert will be out to find him, a suspected collaborator with the APV, but by now he should be winging his way to a new life somewhere else, a change of identity supplied by Gail's trusty relocation agent, Harry Tong. Apparently Lars was promised a beach house in monsoonal far north Queensland, where the vaccination vans hadn't made it to, and where, it's rumoured, the weather-hardy residents still beget with the best of them.

'So what's next?' Nagid asks, arms folded, one hip against a freezer chest.

'Something that involves scaling an industrial chimney or surfing a battleship's bow wave, so you can show us how,' James offers.

It's Max who makes the first real suggestion.

'I've heard from an old client of mine the battery hen farm that borders his property is going into production again. He says the stench is wafting over to his place already.'

We're all surprised. This means the government must be lifting the restrictions on factory farming.

'They wouldn't dare.' Brigid voices everyone's thoughts.

We all remember what happened when bird flu became a highly pathogenic new strain, transmissible human to human. The virus spread like wildfire through the poultry sheds first, and the factory then free-range farmers were ordered to destroy their stock — not just chickens and turkeys, but ducks and geese too. Even the carrier pigeons kept by racing enthusiasts and the caged budgies in suburban homes weren't exempt. Max was deeply affected, vets being called upon to supervise the gassing and decontamination of aviaries, dovecotes and chicken coops. And his loft of racing pigeons was his pride and joy.

The farmyard pyres burned and the wild bird colonies dwindled, their presence no longer viewed with pleasure but alarm and fearfulness. Nobody kept birds of any kind. Meanwhile, the health teams were mobilising across the country for the most comprehensive vaccination scheme in Australia's history. Auto-immune overload and mass endocrine disruption followed soon after.

'What short memories people have!' Inez exclaims. 'Everybody knows it was the conditions in those factories that created the problem in the first place.'

It transpired that the methods used to force faster growth and higher productivity had created a crucible for infection and disease, while the industry's slack regulatory codes, along with diabolical conditions in the hen sheds, had contributed to the virus being transmitted to the workers.

Max turns to Lydia. 'What does Animal Justice know about the factory bans being lifted?'

'I'm not really in touch with any of them ...'

Lydia has never explained why she left that organisation, but I get the feeling it was something personal. When the

Nation Firsts took power, the Animal Justice activists freshly arrived from overseas were speedily deported back there, and the local organisers — including Lydia — were jailed on blasphemy charges. They'd dared to argue it was human conceit to think we had a monopoly on the domain of the soul, and that if there were such a thing, then animals would have one too.

Max addresses the rest of us. 'There's a vet I know in one of the rebuilt settlements beyond the Yarra Valley bushfire line. His community mainly comprises small bio-organic holdings and hobby farms. As long as he gives the birds the all-clear first, I'd say the people there would be glad to take a crate or two each, no questions asked.'

For all the damage the vaccine did, at least it put an end to the panicked extermination of birds, rural households now allowed to keep certified virus-free chickens.

'How many sheds are we talking about, and what can we expect to find in them?' Nagid asks.

'They seem to be using only one shed in the row of five so far. But there could be thousands of debeaked pullets in there, jammed several to a cage. The ammonia levels will be toxic.'

I feel my jaw tighten. This shit is hard to listen to.

'It goes without saying,' Max continues, 'that the less time they spend in those conditions the more chance they'll have of living through the rescue. My ex-client says if we're planning anything unmentionable, we can do it via his place. His boundary fence runs right behind the row.'

'What about all the noise when we try to get them out?' Brigid asks. 'They'll squawk the place down —'

Lydia rounds on her. 'And you think that's a reason not to try to rescue them?'

Brigid stops, shocked.

I glance at Inez and Max. Lydia is getting more and more erratic, and we can't afford a loose cannon in our midst. Brigid, on the other hand, has the sort of constitution that suggests she burns calories through anxiety — which Lydia isn't helping any.

'I don't think Brigid meant that we *not* do it …' says Inez.

James steers the conversation back on track. 'Do you think your farmer friend could take some photos from his side of the fence?' he asks Max.

'Yep,' is the ebullient reply. I can tell Max has already taken this project on one hundred per cent.

'We're going to need cages for transport,' I say, 'and Brigid actually has a valid point about the noise.' I shoot a quick warning look at Lydia.

Nagid adds his thoughts. 'The battery farm won't be expecting opposition this soon. I doubt they'll have even bothered with an alarm system other than a smoke detector.'

'So …' Max eyes the six of us. 'Are we all agreed this is our next project?'

We assent variously, Brigid with a baleful glance Lydia's way.

Max, the logical choice to coordinate, hands out our

tasks for the next meeting: research, and sourcing rescue equipment. Only Lydia doesn't get something to do.

'You seem like you could do with a break for a bit,' he says to her matter-of-factly.

'I'm alright,' she mumbles, not looking at him. 'Just having a bad week. I'll be fine next meeting.'

'Well, that's when I'll give you something to do,' he says, gentler.

Proceedings winding up, I take the opportunity to draw her aside. 'What's going on, Lyd?'

'What do you mean?' Her eyes shift nervously from mine.

We're in a storage area beside the toilet cubicle. I shut the connecting door to the rest of the group.

'Come on,' I say. 'That was more than your usual enthusiastic response.'

She looks for a moment as if she might spin me some bullshit line, then shrugs. 'I did something I shouldn't have, and now I'm paying the price.'

She leans her head against the doorframe, and I wait as she struggles to get it out.

'I met someone I really liked. Do you know how long it is since that's happened to me?'

I don't say. I know how she feels.

'He's a Canadian geologist working for Austral-Uranium. He emigrated to Australia on the previous government's fertility initiative. Amazingly, he's still trying to find Ms Right to start a family with, and he thought I might be that person.'

The dam holding Lydia's big secret having burst, her words tumble out. 'I lied a little, said I ovulated every once in a while. I made it sound like conception was possible for me, when really I haven't had so much as a bleed for two years. I could picture us happy together, and didn't want to lose him to the next wide-hipped fertile who came sashaying around the corner. So I ten-timesed the dose of my usual hormones and took a pituitary stimulant on top of that. I figured a hormone hit might induce ovulation before he changed his mind.'

I don't voice my dismay. She could have done worse things to herself.

She continues bitterly. 'Everything seemed fine: I got soft and squishy in all the right places, like how I used to be. But then it hit me like a steam train and ramped me up like you wouldn't believe. I felt like I'd been taken over by a monster. I was getting upset at the tiniest thing, crying or shouting for no reason. He said I was too volatile to be anybody's fertility partner and called it quits. I was so angry with myself that I cold-turkeyed. I'd pretty much run out of money to get more kit anyway. So now I have oestro flux big-time.'

I try to say it as tactfully as I can. 'You didn't …?'

'Not a hope in Hades.' She sniffs.

'I'm very impressed that you held it together last Friday,' I tell her, and I mean it. Considering what she must have been going through, physically and psychologically, she did amazingly well on the raid. 'No one would've known.'

This elicits a sad smile. 'Thanks.'

'If you don't mind me asking, whose stuff did you use?'

'NatureCure's.'

An Ethical — something I'd assume with her; but desperation can do terrible things, even to an APV idealist. I make a mental note to talk to Gail about it after the meeting, then realise I forgot to tell her earlier in the day about my spur-of-the-moment manoeuvre with Mojo Meg. I make a second mental note.

'Lyd, I'll find out what you can take to help ease you through this,' I say, and she looks up tearfully.

'I'd appreciate that.'

Her whole body is drooped in defeat. This is not the gung-ho vigilante we've come to know and fret about.

'Just do me one favour,' I add. 'Apologise to Brigid for snapping at her. And whatever it is that sets you two off, sort it or shelve it. The group can't handle the tension.'

She nods, subdued for once.

I walk her back to the others. We set another location for next week, then people begin to filter outside and along the narrow walkway between the gelato shop and its neighbour.

A hand goes on my shoulder.

'Nitro is due for his shots,' Max says quietly. 'I've got some free time around twelve thirty Thursday, if you can bring him in.'

I make a quick calculation. Depending on what deliveries Gail needs me to do first, I can organise a Cute'n'Cuddly van over lunchtime and pick up the cat.

'Perfect,' I say.

'The appointments either side will be clear,' he adds. 'No pesky waiting-room conversations.'

'Thanks.'

I watch his solid frame depart. I can always trust him to think of everything.

When everyone else has left, Inez pulls the back door to. We emerge together onto the busy street and detour via the gelato counter. Inez decides on vanilla while I choose caramel swirl, my favourite.

'All the perverts are going for that one,' Phyllis, the owner, says, and winks.

I make a face at her, privileged with the information that when Phyllis goes home at night, it's to a tank full of glow-in-the dark seahorses and a five-watt orange ferret.

II

It's Anwar's and my final shift together at Fishermans Bend and the coldest night so far. The van heater keeps the windscreen from icing up and us from freezing, but outside, everything is growing white dendritic fronds. This time, at least, I've come prepared with a thermos of hot chocolate and a bag of raspberry muffins.

We munch hungrily. Having finished our round of the streets to check the flow of traffic and activity in factory yards, we're holding off for now on another stint at the Ponds. But it's funereally quiet: no mean machines rumbling by Enzo's, and the wraith-like figures of the cruisers and bruisers few and far between. It could be that the onshore southerly shivering in from the sea has kept everyone away, or maybe it's just that the denizens of the Bend need a night off occasionally.

'How did you persuade the racers to give back the van's tyres?' I ask.

'By appealing to their finer sensibilities.'

I look at him.

'I promised to deliver them something they want much more.'

'And that would be?'

'A set of racing fats off a stock car.'

I laugh. 'Can you?'

'They're in the back. We'll drive down after this and hand them over.'

I love the thought of my neatly attired co-worker making deals with a bunch of leather- and metal-clad street racers. Trust him to come up with a bargaining chip so coveted by the latter.

At midnight we make our delivery. There are only three vehicles on the roundabout, and no spectators. Clearly, tonight's affair is a private one. I should have predicted it would be Skinny and a rival lounging nonchalantly against their street machines, waiting to receive the goods. The pair in the third vehicle stare at us, but don't bother to get out. There's no sign of Lola or her friends.

Skinny turns his best cheeky smile on us. 'The offer of a ride still stands, Andy Pandy. Mr Suit can sit in the back if he wants.'

I have to laugh. His good-natured bantering is hard not to like. His rival, however, seems to think differently.

I help Anwar unload the tyres, rolling them onto the traffic island.

'So who gets the set?' I whisper.

'I believe they're going to duel it out.'

Skinny's competitor gets in her car. The third vehicle leaves down the racetrack, presumably to adjudicate at the finish line.

'Care to do the honours?' Skinny hands me a red-spotted kerchief.

Obediently I stand at the head of Wolf Road as they start their engines and proceed to rev the hell out of them. I raise the signal and wait a count of three, then let it drop. The roar is ear-splitting; I'm enveloped in a blast of exhaust. I bend to retrieve the kerchief and cough pure carbon monoxide.

As brakes screech down the road, Anwar shepherds me off the verge. 'Let's not wait for the result,' he says.

I suggest to him that he might like to take Skinny up on his offer sometime. He swings me an inscrutable look, then says, 'Show me the paint factory.'

The van left outside the gates, we scan the factory's front windows with our torches, then walk quickly down the side, hands stuffed in pockets and collars up against the chill, boots crunching on icy ground. At the rear of the building, I slide my fingers in the gap between the window and the sill and push up. Scraping through first, I turn to help Anwar, but he's already half in.

Ferguson's paint-making machinery sits in gloom and fust at the end of the corridor. I point out the office with my torch, but Anwar just nods and makes his way across the space to the far wall.

He stares up at the mixer tanks on the gantry. 'You looked in those?'

I say no, and feel remiss.

The metal stairs by the front entrance look worse than the office set, but are actually more securely attached. I climb, then work my way along the gantry to the first giant mixing bowl. I grip the handle on the lid. It's heavy but levers up, and I poke the torch beam inside the tub. The interior is thickly crusted and the colour hard to pick, but 'scurvy yellow' would be close.

'Paint,' I say down to Anwar, then try each along the row. Same result, different colours.

I descend the stairs and join him by the equipment. Here, the detritus makes sad piles on the concrete, the dust bunnies grown big enough to become dust hares. I scuff at a pile with the toe of my boot and something separates from the formless grey. I pick it up: innocuous, but recognisable anywhere. A piece of blue wax from an anti-tamper seal. I scuff again. More bits show up, all blue. I grab Anwar's arm.

He inspects the piece in my hand. 'It may have nothing to do with the current situation,' he says.

I look at him doubtfully. 'But so many?'

'Someone — your office lovebirds, for instance — might have been breaking open their personal stash here for years. And blue wax isn't used exclusively by EHg.'

I have to admit he has a point.

The polystyrene eggs are just one shape of a variety, the shells bought as blanks by distributors then filled with the manufacturer's products and sealed, the wax medallion at their join stamped with the maker's unique logo. Now we no longer live in a throwaway world, the distributors have a re-use system going. Buyers can return the old shells to receive a discount on their next expenditure, or they can be handed in for money, like bottles or cans — which is why you never see the whole thing lying around, just the remains of the tamper-proof seals.

Fingering a piece of wax, I watch Anwar inspect along the production line towards the conveyor belt and pallets at the loading dock. Suddenly he hauls on a handle and a piece of equipment rolls out.

'This is more convincing,' he remarks across the space.

I drop my find and go over.

It's a drill press, but the part that normally holds the drill bit has been converted to take a metal die. Beside it on the portable stand is a small camping stove and wax pot.

It's ridiculously simple. The polyshell sits in the concavity on the drill table, hot wax is poured from the pot into its indented seam, and then the swing arm brings the die down into the wax. With one piece of equipment and a few key ingredients, a small-time operation can do big damage to a company like EHg.

'Gail said it'd be on Barrow Road,' is all I can manage.

Anwar shrugs. Misinformation can happen to the best.

He fiddles with the drill chuck while I frown up at the office and wonder what the lovebirds thought when the others moved in below.

Anwar stops fiddling and holds up the die. It's imprinted with EHg's trademark. 'Sloppy of them, leaving this,' he says, and pockets it. 'Now let's see the office.'

We climb the stairs to the landing and I go for the door handle. It doesn't budge. Surprised, I train the torch beam below it, and find a shiny lock where the rusty one used to be. I stand there foolishly as a bad thought dawns. What if the orange flag in the window was never a signal for romance, but Gail's new player all along and I mistook the vital clue?

I glance at Anwar.

'I think we have a return date here,' he says solemnly, and my throat goes dry. I'm a wuss when it comes to confrontation. That's why I have runners' legs and a racing bike.

We're buzzed into Cute'n'Cuddly's delivery yard. Anwar parks the van beside a polished relative and we walk into the warehouse, Gail calling us to where, inventory in hand, she's sorting through a set of boxes stacked for delivery.

'It goes through phases,' she says, bending back the flaps of a box and brandishing a fluffy grey creature. 'Bilbies are the current favourites, but six months ago the market couldn't get enough of hairy-nosed wombats and growling koalas.' She puts the bilby back in the box and closes the flaps. 'In marketing parlance it's called "macro-charisma". Big furry animals will always win hearts and wallets over the tiny ones, such as insects, even if the latter are the true miracles of nature. Nobody wants to snuggle up to a weta or a dung beetle.'

I try to picture a Cute'n'Cuddly dung beetle. I fail.

We walk past production-line sorting tables and a forklift bay, back to Gail's unmarked office at the rear of the building. She heads for the roller chair behind her desk while Anwar and I both find something uncomfortable to lean against.

'I'm buying us some chairs for your birthday,' he informs her.

She smirks and makes a show of settling in her seat. 'Tell me what you found.'

Anwar produces the die and she sheds her easygoing air.

'I'll get the surveillance equipment installed as soon as it's light,' he says.

'We can monitor activity from here,' Gail replies. 'I'm not planning on jumping them, just getting the footage to identify them for others to deal with.'

I breathe a small sigh of relief. *Others*. Not me and Anwar.

Gail leans forward, intent. 'If we can catch them at it and expose them, things will begin to settle down.'

'What if there's a bigger player pulling their strings?' I ask.

'I'm looking into that.'

Gail has spies niched in the workings of Neighbourly Watch and Nation First. Anything she doesn't hear from them is usually picked up by the many eyes and ears of the underground network, which makes it all the more surprising she doesn't know who these people are yet.

She throws a glance at Anwar, deciding something.

'The vultures are beginning to circle,' she tells me. 'Yesterday I had an offer on the business. An anonymous party is willing to pay a minuscule cash sum for Cute'n'Cuddly before, as their go-between so charmingly put it, "the wheels fall off the gravy train". He put up some very persuasive arguments, but I declined.' She leans back. 'I'm not discounting the possibility he's part of whatever's causing our problem. Your discovery might help us with that.'

I don't want to spoil the best news we've had, but there's no getting out of what I have to tell her, so I launch straight in.

'I had a visit from Mojo Meg at the speakeasy on Sunday, and a direct offer to work for her. I'm sorry I didn't mention it yesterday morning. The attack on Roshani pushed it out of my mind —'

I stop in surprise. She's smiling broadly at me. Not the response I was expecting.

She laughs. 'I knew Meg was headhunting you even before she came to our table to tell me the market news.'

I must look shocked, because she laughs again. 'Salisbury, why are you always the last to know these things?'

'What do you mean?'

'Meg's had her beady eye on you for a while. Last week wasn't the first time she'd put out signals.'

'I thought it was just to get at you. To rub it in that there's someone trying to damage the business.'

'She wishes. Her entrepreneurial streak and her mean streak are one and the same. A flailing competitor makes her hungry as a shark. She's been looking for an opportunity to poach you and there'd be no better time than this.'

'Why me? There are plenty of other couriers available.'

Gail looks at me as if I'm stupid. 'Because you're a *first-rate* courier. And you should know in our game that's a valuable commodity.'

I shift uncomfortably, not looking at her. 'I didn't tell her no outright. I said I'd think about it.'

It's Gail's turn to look surprised.

I rush to explain. 'I'd never actually *do* it, but it seemed like she knew something we didn't, and I thought I might get her to divulge more.'

'That's a dangerous game.'

I'm downcast. 'It was an off-the-cuff thing — which I now have to weasel my way out of.'

I wait for her to castigate me for being so foolish, but instead she looks thoughtful. 'You know,' she says, 'it might actually be a good idea.'

'No!' I can't help the outburst. The thought of working for Meg for even a day is unbearable.

Gail picks up the die and weighs it in her hand. 'This proves they *were* at the paint factory, but not necessarily that they're coming back. In this business it doesn't take much to spook the customer into a mistrust of the product, and the pond scum we're dealing with have already done that. What if they have no more need of this?' She places the die on the desk. 'It puts us back at square one.'

I make a pathetic noise halfway between a groan and a whimper.

'Look, Salisbury, I don't think Meg is behind this, but your instincts were right: if anyone has any information worth knowing, it'll be her. She owns the compendium on other people's business. Can you keep her thinking you're interested for a few days?'

'I suppose …' It'll be like playing cat and mouse with a tiger.

'And if it came to it, would you be willing to work for her for a while? Business here will be on a downturn.'

It hurts me to even hear her say that.

'It'll look like I've deserted you.'

'Yes, it will.'

'Who'll know the truth?'

'The three people in this room — and only the three.' She eagle-eyes me. 'Not best friends or girlfriends. Not even the cat.'

I'm so transparent. My thoughts had leapt instantly to Inez.

In my heart, I know Gail's right. If Meg smelled a rat, who knows how she'd retaliate? She'd have no qualms about leaning on Inez if she suspected me of anything, and I can't let that happen.

Anwar, silent all this while, nods at me: a small gesture telling me I can count on him in this, no matter where it goes. I'd like to say it makes me feel better, but it doesn't.

My boss ignores my dismay and carries on. 'In tough financial times, people have to find any means they can to keep their heads above water, and with demand for EHg's products in a tailspin, everyone'll see it as a move of necessity on your part.'

I grimace at her using the same drowning allusion as Meg.

'But —'

'It may not even need to happen,' she cuts in. 'If it does, it'll only be for a short time — say, incommunicado for a week. Then we'll have another talk.' She watches me sympathetically.

I feel wretched. *But Inez won't see it that way*, is what I'm thinking. Going off to work for Mojo Meg without so much as an explanation will seem like the worst kind of betrayal. I'd better pray the surveillance at Ferguson's nets us a result or my new girlfriend will very quickly come to hate me.

Gail gets up from her chair, our powwow over. Hangdog, I follow her to the door. Anwar stays put, some heavy conversation to be had after I'm gone.

Out in the yard she motions to my bike left here earlier. 'You going to be okay on that?'

I nod. It'll be a relief to ride and feel the burn.

Last thing, she presses a troche pack into my hand. 'Tell your friend Lydia this is a month's supply of hormones.

If she takes them *exactly* as directed, it'll smoothe out the oestro flux, but she should consider seeing a Red Quarter specialist and becoming a regular client.'

'Thanks,' I say. 'I'll make sure she knows.' At least after tonight one of us is going to be a much happier human being.

I seek out Inez. Her place is in Richmond, a semidetached cottage a few minutes' ride from mine. She inspects me through the spyhole then unlatches the chain and deadlock. The door opens. She's standing there in just a tee-shirt. I get a sudden urge to fuck her wildly, insanely.

'You alright?' she asks.

'Just here for a hug,' I reply, but it comes out so forlorn.

She takes my hand and pulls me inside, the bike left across her front step.

The door barely closed, we are kissing in the hallway. The press of her lips on mine is electric; hunger surges from somewhere deep. She grabs the waistband of my jeans, drawing our bodies closer.

The tee-shirt is too big for her. I drag it off one shoulder to get to a breast, and kiss fervently, the flavour and texture of nipple like no other.

I have her up against the wall. 'Make me come,' she says.

My hand dives, searching for the wet. She's not wearing knickers. A wellspring meets me. I drive the heel of my palm against her mound and slip a finger into her.

She moans. Her pelvic muscles grip and release, that

action an incendiary in me. We rock in sync, faster and faster motion. She comes in shudders, and we collapse together on the floor.

She looks askance at me from beneath mussed hair. 'You seem … different,' she murmurs.

I don't know what to say. 'Work stuff,' I manage, feeling duplicitous.

She's watching my face, her brow creased. Like everyone, she knows Gail's troubles are also mine.

'What's your boss got you doing for her now?'

I can't meet her gaze, the truth impossible to tell.

'Go,' she says. 'Sleep. You look like you need it.'

'Love you,' I whisper. And then I'm walking out her door.

12

Even in daylight, SANE's precinct is well-hidden inside the Red Quarter. It takes several wrong turns through the alleyways to work out the instructions written on the back of the business card Tallis Dankner had handed me at the hospital. Eventually I find the faded lettering of the *Padstow & Flint, Haberdashers* wall, and the doorway hacked in more recent times through its brick.

I remember the mass exodus from this part of town in the first days of the pandemic — mainly yuppies who'd recently bought here. They fled to the countryside in the hope that putting a bit more space around them might act as protection from the virus spreading like wildfire in the close confines of the CBD. It didn't. But it left those parts of the inner city that had been declared plague zones as unpopulated as they'd ever been, and ripe for takeovers. Those who stayed behind the barricades blocking off their streets had no money to do anything else, but as prices plummeted and more and more properties were offered up for hurried sale, others stepped in who were less afraid. This is how a syndicate of madams was able to buy up the real estate on the main thoroughfares of what is now the Red Quarter, and how the surrogacy organisations and medical professionals who'd been made pariahs were able to move into its backstreets. With that shift in demographic, something of the personality of 'old Melbourne' was returned to its centre. A reversal of fortunes, I have to say, I've never been sorry about.

I buzz and look up into the lens, and hear the lock release.

Behind is a passage leading to a courtyard and internal-facing set of buildings. I wonder who lived here in Padstow & Flint's day. Light bathes the worn flagstones and archway relief. A figure sits, mug in hand, on a bench seat beside a gnarly ficus. I cross to an open door where the sign in the stairwell points up. Leaving my bike at the bottom of the stairs, I climb three flights to the top floor.

The emergency team coordinator's office is refreshingly light and airy, the morning sun slicing through open skylights onto wide, scuffed boards.

'Glad you could make it,' Tallis says, and rescues me an armchair from under a pile of papers.

I don't tell her how I nearly didn't, having slept through my alarm. The memory of the fast and furious sex in Inez's hallway — and my just as speedy departure — lingers in my body, a mix of emotions.

Tallis offers tea or coffee, but I demur, breakfast and no secrets from my girlfriend what I really need. Together we drag the armchair over to another positioned beside the windows looking onto the courtyard.

'How's Roshani doing?' I ask.

'Extremely well,' Tallis replies, and plonks herself down, motioning me to join her. 'She was discharged from hospital late yesterday and is recovering here now.'

A twenty-four-hour turnaround. 'That was quick.'

'They never keep them long. They're short-staffed and know we have some expertise.'

Both chairs are low and easy-backed, designed for comfortable conversation, but my host is anything but comfortable right now. She leans forward, elbows on knees, fiddling with a pen.

'She's told me what happened Sunday night.'

I'm impressed: Tallis has done wonders in such a short time. I remember she mentioned she'd been a midwife until the Nation Firsts confiscated her licence. I'm betting it's some of that talent she's brought forth to persuade the traumatised young woman from behind her veil of silence.

Tallis continues. 'Roshani was visiting her brother. He lives in a squat in the financial district. It's been a regular thing, dinner at his place every Sunday — something *not* okayed by us or SADA, the Surrogates and Donors Agency. She says she followed the personal safety protocols and is sure nobody saw her leave the Red Quarter. Apparently they converged on her from different directions on Pilgrim

Lane. She didn't realise what was happening until it was too late.'

My spirits sink. I'd hoped it was an unhappy coincidence — wrong place, wrong time — but it sounds planned.

'Has the brother been told?'

'We sent someone around early yesterday morning. He'd been worried sick.'

'So he knows the circumstances of her pregnancy? Is he trustworthy?'

'That's open to conjecture. Normally SADA would vet every contact, but Roshani did this secretly.'

'Which squat is he in?'

'The Tea House.'

A Melbourne icon. Originally a warehouse then offices, it was converted into boutique apartments by a Singapore hotel syndicate that went bust because of bird flu. Its six storeys of red brick are marooned at the bottommost corner of the financial district between the Saviour Street Bridge and the half-finished high-rises that totter like giant pins on the foreshores of the Docklands, all restoration and development there stalled for nigh on a decade.

Along with other older-style buildings in the financial district, the Tea House was gradually taken over by a new breed of squatter: savvy and sophisticated refugees from the business sector after it took a nosedive in the pandemic. Many of them, playing a cavalier game with the money market, had accumulated extraordinary wealth that was just as extraordinarily wiped out. They forfeited everything, including their homes. The government couldn't help them or anybody else, being in ten different kinds of strife itself. In desperation, the business professionals (brokers and bankers among them) formed 'guilds', each group targeting a vacated building in their old work district to take up squatters rights in. The Tea House has been run these past years by the Stockbrokers' Guild, its strict membership rules and security measures put in place as bastion against the successive waves of itinerants prowling the city for premises of their own.

So now I know what Roshani's brother *used* to do —

Tallis interrupts my train of thought. 'The question we're all asking here is how the attackers knew Roshani was a surrogate … and whether they have information on others.'

'How would that happen?'

'Roshani or her brother letting something slip to the wrong person.'

Bad.

'Or a leak somewhere within the surrogacy organisations.'

Worse.

Tallis's strong, square features have creased in worry. She pushes up both shirtsleeves and grips her forearms in an unconscious action of anxiety. I can see those capable arms supporting women in the throes of birthing agony and delivering wrinkly, squalling babies out into the world.

'We were wondering whether you might do some digging on our behalf,' she says, her deft use of the plural reminding me of the raft of invisible worried others.

'You know I'm a bike courier not a private detective, right?'

'Yes.' She smiles. 'But Gail speaks very highly of you ...'

'Ahh,' I say. Never underestimate a SANE worker's capacity to network. I feel her eyes on me, patient and remorseless, and can't refuse.

'I guess I could pay the brother a visit,' I offer.

'That'd be wonderful. We'll introduce you as an independent whom we've hired to help find Roshani's attackers. Not everyone is a fan of what we do here. He might find it easier to talk to someone from the "outside", so to speak.'

Or he might not.

I realise I know very little about how the surrogacy organisations operate and what measures they take to protect their own.

'It might help me get my head around the situation if you can take me through your protocols; for instance, how you go about shielding the identities of your workers,' I say, and Tallis is happy to comply, leaning back at last in her chair.

'There are strict protections in place for the surrogacy arrangements,' she starts, 'all of which are brokered by the madams and SADA. Surrogates take no direct part in any of the negotiations, and never meet those they've contracted to give birth for, and vice versa. Their anonymity is zealously protected, as with all donors, regardless of what service they're supplying. On acceptance, each donor is given an alias. From then on, this is how they're referred to in all discussions and on all written agreements and medical reports.'

I think of Roshani — which I guess isn't her real name.

'So how do potential donors and surrogates put up their hands for the various jobs? And how do you choose?'

'They apply through SADA, and are vetted before interview like any other worker in any other job. Of course, the difference is that what we do here is illegal, so there are a few more hoops to be jumped through before they even get a look-in. The successful applicants are contracted to the relevant fertility organisations under SADA's umbrella. But it's only the surrogates who are sponsored to live in the Red Quarter, which they do for the duration of their pregnancy. That way we can take care of their health requirements and safety — usually.' Tallis looks pained. 'The only other people in the loop are the Red Quarter doctors who do the monitoring and procedures.'

'Could any of them be turned?' I ask.

'Unlikely, since it means putting their own heads on the chopping block.'

From everything Tallis has said it seems to me the weakest links in the chain of secrecy are the surrogates themselves.

'I take it the successful applicants know each other?'

'They share living spaces and provide support for one another.'

A thought strikes me. 'Do you ever have any trouble when it comes to handing over the newborns?'

'I won't say never — and we have contingencies for that — but on the whole these women come to it as professionals, and are paid accordingly.'

Which makes them supremely well-adjusted with it. I can't help wondering what they think of the brave new world those paid-for babies are being born into.

'What about the recipients of the surrogacy arrangements?'

'They're handled by the brokers — the madams — who liaise with SADA and the fertility clinics on their behalf. The two parties in the arrangement are kept completely separate the whole way through.'

'And the recipients of Roshani's baby?'

'They'll be contacted by the broker and told the hard news. A no-liability clause protecting SADA and its workers is built into the contract they signed; after all, we're dealing with an event that can bring a multitude of unforeseen complications. In time, they'll have the opportunity of a new arrangement.'

Sounds hard-nosed, but this is business. I say my thanks and push up out of my chair, then turn to Tallis at the door. 'It might be worth finding out whether Roshani made any enemies among her fellow surrogates.'

She nods sombrely. 'I'll look into it, and let you know as soon as we've contacted her brother.'

Downstairs, the person with the mug is gone from the bench seat. I wheel my bike out into the bluestone alley. At my back, the signage barely tints the brick; ahead, close-hugging walls shade the cobbles and shuttered windows are latched behind rusting metal bars, the layers of grime on the walls making unreadable hieroglyphics of the paintwork. Hunkered beyond them are the surgeries and procedure rooms of the fertility doctors and cosmetic surgeons, nothing to advertise their existence apart from numbered buzzers beside bolted entrances. In SADA's protected territory, there are no real names. Here, there are no names at all.

I fasten my helmet strap and zip up my cycling vest. Tallis has given me a lot of food for thought, most of it bitter and unpalatable.

13

No work on for Gail, I use the rest of the day to catch up on sleep. Late afternoon I take the bike out for a spin and make my delivery to Lydia, three suburbs away.

Riding back home, I worry. I've had plenty of time to ponder how I might tackle the subject of Roshani with her brother, Braheem, but I'm not confident he'll welcome a stranger's intrusion, even if it's to help find his sister's attackers. I don't much like the idea of meeting him in his home either, because the squats are usually heavily monitored, and it's likely that among the Tea House's unemployed stockbroker residents there are Neighbourly Watch snitches. I haven't yet ruled out Braheem as one of these — pity Roshani if that turns out to be the case.

Tallis's call comes as I'm entering my laneway: Braheem's invited me around tonight. SANE's emergency team coordinator is a fast worker.

I shower hurriedly then catch a tram to the Tea House.

On Temperance, we roll past a guy scratching up a piece of gum from the pavement. I glance back and see him putting it in his mouth. These are tough times; who knows what scion of the community he might have been five years ago?

The entrance to the squat is on Saviour Street. 'Scapegoat' would probably be more apt, or 'Persecution'. The front door is overhung by a jutting lintel. It's small protection against the weather, which is already beginning to chill, an eddying wind whipping up the rubbish in the street and sending it swirling a few metres before just as quickly dropping it. Cap low and collar up, I look for Braheem on the door list, and press the buzzer. He responds immediately, as if he'd been waiting, finger on the intercom button.

The door clicks open. 'Down in two secs,' he says.

I walk in and immediately see the camera positioned on a cornice. Resisting the instinct to hunch, I stroll deliberately to the sign-in desk.

The visitors register is laid open, a warning propped beside it on a stand: *All visitors must sign in and remain in the foyer until met by a resident. No firearms permitted. No hawkers.* Not exactly reassuring.

The way the squats are run as closed communities with their own sets of laws gives outsiders the impression of crossing into another country. All this foyer needs is a couple of border guards and an X-ray machine.

At the far end is an elevator, stairs beside. The highly

polished floor I assume was added by the defunct hotel group. Braheem arrives down the stairwell, two steps at a time. Dressed in jeans and untucked shirt, he looks both casual and professional. He's very obviously Roshani's brother. His frame, like hers, is delicately compact, and he has the same deep-set eyes, with an alert intelligence about him that makes me want to step up my game before play has even begun.

He extends his right hand. The handshake is firm and brief.

'Braheem Rani.'

'Sam Brown.'

'You'll have to supply your particulars, I'm afraid.' He points to the place on the page. I notice there aren't any other entries for the day. Given the atmosphere of the place, I'm not surprised.

I pause, the pseudonym I'm about to write solid but uninspiring. If I tack an 'e' onto the surname, it'll suggest a dash of creativity. I follow it with the address of the burnt-down Atonement Street Police Station. *Go check*, I dare the invisible eyes.

Braheem takes the pen. 'I have to vouch for you. If anything goes wrong — you burgle the place or shoot someone — I cop it.'

He attempts a smile, and I realise that he's a bundle of nervous energy beneath that urbane veneer.

'I promise I'll behave. After all, we're on *Candid Camera*,' I say to break the awkward moment.

He grimaces apologetically. 'We have a Residents Committee modelled on the Stasi. Although these days it's more of a front because nobody can be bothered policing the incomings and outgoings of the building like they used to. As you can see, it's not exactly Southern Cross Station' — I note the deliberate use of the old name — 'especially now the other crowd have set up a stock exchange in the Olderfleet building.'

That's news to me. The Olderfleet is a fine example of Gothic Revival architecture, and a well-known lawyers' squat. Their guild must have entered into some sort of arrangement with the stockbrokers and bankers.

'The latest craze,' Braheem tells me as we walk towards the stairs, 'is to speculate on climate change. Not the commodities but the events, like rain and temperature. Investments in Rain are down, but it's a bear market for Solar Flares. Even though the exchange is just a local venture, with walk-ins off the street doing most of the buying and selling, it still does a brisk trade. My friends track the weather patterns like they did the old indexes. They say the stress makes them feel alive again.'

Old habits are hard to break.

'And you?' I ask. 'You're not keen to get back into it?'

'I've got plenty of other stresses making me feel alive.'

As we walk up four flights of stairs — the lift not operational — we maintain a polite silence, neither willing to speak in the reverberant stairwell, as if it might funnel our words through the rest of the building.

Inside his apartment it's a different story.

The door closed, he turns to me, clearly upset. 'Tell me how she is.'

I'm taken aback. 'I haven't seen her since she got out of hospital, but I hear she's doing really well and will make a full recovery.'

I just tacked on that last bit — a kind of white lie. But I *hope* she will, and Tallis never said she *wouldn't*, which adds up to almost the same thing.

Instantly he looks less agonised. 'I'm sorry. It's been terrible, the waiting. I haven't been told yet when I'll be able to see her.'

'I'm sure it'll be very soon,' I reassure. Another little white lie. Really, I have no idea.

He leads me into a cluttered living room, two sash windows looking north up Saviour.

'Make yourself comfortable,' he says. 'Would you like tea?'

'Please,' I say, and he disappears into the kitchen off the lounge area.

I sit one end of a battered couch with brown and orange flower patterns reminiscent of the body-painting sixties: love, peace and STDs. Opposite is a bookshelf loaded to groaning, an unframed print tacked to the wall above. It's a pastoral scene, and a personal favourite of mine: the ploughman and his horse oblivious to the winged man plunging headfirst into the bay beyond.

Braheem pops his head around the corner. 'Sorry I couldn't see you earlier. I run a stall at the Queen Vic

Markets, and with so many shops closing down we've extended our hours to cope with the demand. I'm there every day, but I always knock off before sunset. It's one of my rules. The rest of them think I'm crazy losing the evening trade.'

I'm wondering whether it's something religious, or just wanting his dinner early, when he comes out again with a tray holding two teacups and a teapot and answers my question.

'The truth is, I don't feel safe any more being out at night. I prefer to be home by dark.'

So it's not just Roshani with reason to be scared. Or is it *because of* Roshani?

'If you don't mind me asking, what do you sell?' None of my business, but I'm curious.

'I have a small jewellery stall. I used to trade stocks and shares. Now I sell fake Asian trinkets.' He gives a wry smile. 'My mongoose-tooth fertility charms are winners.'

I'm beginning to like him so I hope he doesn't mean real mongoose teeth.

He catches my look. 'They're sheep's teeth. This will probably sound macabre to you, but every couple of weeks I take a train out of the city and poke around in the sheep paddocks looking for carcasses. The farmers don't care. They call me "the mad Paki" even though I'm Indian, but they all know the meaning of subsistence living. I pick up whole jawbones, or partials with the teeth still in them, and bring them back here to extract. I have a little lapidary wheel and polish them up. Then I glue a metal cap on them and attach some leather thong. Sometimes I paint them.'

He begins to pour our tea. I note with approval that it's real, the leaves caught in a strainer.

'Does anybody ever mention that they look like sheep's teeth?'

'No. We're living in an age where the willing suspension of disbelief is everything.'

My mind flicks to the mass baptisms of the past several years, and the rise of the prayer groups.

He motions me to help myself to milk and sugar, then goes over to the window and looks down. I see sadness welling in him.

'I don't condone what my sister does for a living,' he says softly, 'but these are hard times and we all have to find a way to earn a crust. As for those prayer-vigil predators …' His voice gets an edge. '*They* are the monsters, not her.'

His vehemence surprises me. I realise I'd carried in a few unhelpful preconceptions about Roshani's ex-stockbroker brother, one being that he wouldn't be so emotionally open.

I have to broach the subject of her visits. 'Who knows she comes here every week?'

'Lots of people. I sign her in. We wave at the camera. They all know she's my sister.'

The question is forming on my lips when he turns to face me.

'Four months ago, Geeta told me she'd been accepted as a surrogate.'

I file Roshani's real name away for future reference.

'It seems stupid now,' he goes on, 'but we didn't think her employers would approve her Sunday visits here, so we decided the best thing was to keep them quiet. She was going to stop soon anyway because her pregnancy was about to show.'

He turns back to the window.

'You're wondering how she stayed a fertile. She was in India with our parents during the vaccination drives. I was fourteen, and not interested in a trip to see the rellies, none of whom I remembered. I just wanted to be here with my school mates, and so I was billeted with family friends — which meant I got the flu shot along with everyone else. My sister and my parents contracted the virus while they were still over there. I thought they were going to die. They were away for several months, unable to come home until the country quarantines had been lifted.'

'That must have been very tough on you.'

He doesn't answer immediately. After a bit, he says, 'I want to thank you for what you did for Geeta that night. Without you there to stop them, who knows how far they would have gone.'

So this is what has earned his confidence in me. Tallis must have told him.

I say the next thing as gently as possible. 'Have you confided in anyone — another family member, a friend or workmate, anyone at all — about the real circumstances of her pregnancy?'

'No one. I know how to keep the family's secrets.'

He's adamant, and I feel improper picking so callously at a recent wound.

Downing the dregs of his tea, he comes over to pour some more. 'It's a cruel irony, isn't it, that here people are crying out for the children they can no longer have, while over there is a burgeoning population still getting rid of girls as they would vermin.'

He's surprising me again with his emotion. I sit back on his flower-power couch and let him talk.

'In India they had no government initiatives for mass vaccination. How could they? The virus ran its course and you lived or you died. Many died; others developed immunity. That immunity, they're saying now, is being passed across the placental barrier, the antibodies in the mother present in their newborns.' His eyes darken. 'It's the girl–child killings and widow suttees that are our pandemic. Many people are standing up against such practices, campaigning for education, new laws and punishments, but these things you can't change overnight, or even across generations.'

I can't help thinking of the increased public bullying of transgressives here. Communally held prejudices are like monsters waiting to be given air: all they need is the imprimatur of authority — or its blind eye.

Braheem sighs. 'Our parents came here to get away from all that and give Geeta and me the chance for a different life: school, university, work, raising our own kids — girls too — in a society that values them. But right now …'

I want to assure him things will change, *must* change. The problem is, I don't feel the reassurance of those sentiments for myself.

Perhaps he sees something of my own despair, and shifts the topic.

'When can I see her?' he asks.

'I'll find out,' I promise. 'What's the best way to contact you?'

'You could always drop by the markets.'

He sketches the position of his stall in one of the market hangars on a scrap of paper and passes it to me. Then, hand on the doorknob, he struggles to say something else. I wait patiently, the door open a crack.

'I'd have her stay with me ...' He opens his other hand in a gesture of helplessness. 'But the Residents Committee has strict rules about long-stay visitors, and even here I can't guarantee her safety.'

'I understand,' I say. 'Don't beat yourself up over it. She has a good support team right where she is.'

As I leave the apartment, a door on the other side of the landing closes softly and my internal radar pings. Is it coincidence? A neighbour with nothing better to do? Or someone keeping an eye on Braheem Rani and his visitors?

14

Sometimes I push the gender envelope so Inez and I can smooch in public, and tonight — back from Braheem's and needing the company of my girlfriend — I'm ready to hit the town.

We get changed in my bedroom, horsing around with each other's underwear, then each other. It's too much for Nitro, who makes himself scarce. We collapse, laughing, on the bed, and I marvel how at ease we are together, and how quickly unafraid I've become of her seeing me with all my defences down. She leans over me suggestively and opens one hand to reveal the jet cufflinks I've been chasing.

Despite my almost complete lack of class in the clothes department, occasionally I quite like wearing a suit. It's the feeling of containment it imparts: a kind of camouflage. My ever-practical girlfriend, on the other hand, has decided to go high femme for the evening. I smile as she shimmies up and bumps her hip against me, that suggestive curve sheathed in something shiny.

I place my hand on her other hip and slide the material up to reach the slim band of her knickers. Then, backing her up against me, I slip my fingers down inside the flare of one hipbone. I get to the plump edge of her mound and she twists towards me, capturing my hand between our bodies. We deep-kiss, pressed together.

For an evening, we'll 'pass'; but that doesn't mean our antennae won't be up the whole time, gauging the reactions of the other participants in the glam parade and the varying safety of our surroundings. Maleness and femaleness are both performances that contain anxiety for me — but in different ways. Tonight, I pack my jocks and bind what little in the way of breasts I have to hide. It helps to have a strong jawline, and a stippled-in five o'clock shadow is less obvious at night, but it's my voice that's the giveaway — the timbre too light — so Inez will do most of the talking.

The gusty winds from earlier have died down, leaving a sharp clarity to the air, the temporary reprieve bringing people onto the streets in droves.

Call me a Luddite, but the city's way more atmospheric now we have traffic restrictions and power outages. Trams slip quietly along the main thoroughfares, horse-drawn buggies clip-clopping beside, the drivers doing a booming business. Zipping past them and the sedate three-wheeler taxis is a near-silent miscellanea of bikes and scooters.

It's hard to imagine wanting the city back as it once was: noisy and impatient, the smog of exhaust inescapable.

Arm in arm, we approach a group shawling up at the top of Little Beatitude Street. They take no notice of me, but Inez, *une femme idéale*, attracts both jealous and admiring glances. Another time, another costume, there'd be baleful stares and mutterings of *perverts*.

Further down Little Beatitude, we step beneath the ornamental gateway that heralds Chinatown. Here every street and alley is lit by rows of lanterns, and the spruikers call us in to eating houses as we pass, each trying to outdo the other with promises, invitations.

I love this place for its mosaic colour and rambunctious market style, everybody busy behind windows packed full of food. Buyers and sellers mingle, the runners with their carts of produce ferrying between restaurants and shops, while those in come-hither finery beckon from the warmly lit doorways of underground bars and gaming houses. In the once-bright city, these details were subsumed by an over-intensity of light. Now they are brought out, individual and distinct, like jewels.

As we make our way among the other walkers, I wonder which of my subtleties might be a tell to the observant eye. What I *hope* they see is a suited man whose particulars have been eclipsed by the gorgeous woman at his side.

We steer left into a laneway. At the end, a single red-lit lantern on a metal chain is suspended from a hook embedded high up in the brick. Madam Lush herself shepherds us beneath her establishment's carved oak lintel, down the wooden steps to fine Szechuan food and the best in bootleg wine.

Two more hours and we're strolling the city, our bellies full and guards lowered. The dark cloaks us protectively, a besotted couple taking a romantic turn. We enter a narrow walkway into a square. Too late I realise we're in Lord Place.

The Neighbourly Arms is busy, patrons spilling out into the square, the groups around the kegs raucous. We walk with tension now, gripping hands. Just past the tavern is a service alley lit by a bare bulb. Beneath it, a woman in a spangly dress is head thrown back in an ecstatic clinch. The reason is leaning against the wall, his face in shadow, his hand up her skirt.

I do a double-take.

'I think I just saw Marlene,' I whisper to Inez, and can tell by her expression that she saw her too.

Nobody we know goes by choice to the Neighbourly Arms. I drag back on her arm for another look.

'Leave it,' says Inez. 'The company she chooses isn't our concern.'

There's a heat behind her words that I don't understand, but she's right. Why should I be surprised if this is Marlene's way of getting over Gail?

Past midnight we arrive at the speakeasy and waggle fingers at the peephole, then sail in past a stolid Rosie to whom nothing is a surprise any more. Gabe, Marlene's twice-weekly replacement, takes our coats. He's polite to the point of disinterest, and I find myself missing Marlene's acerbic remarks.

Downstairs, the press of people at the bar fans out to the couches where reclining bodies sprawl amid the smoke and hubbub, while on the dance floor the fit and fearless are gyrating at the poles. On the far side of the room, every alcove has been taken. We find two stools one end of the bar. Trin, who spotted us coming in, takes our order.

Inez leans against me. I can smell the vanilla scent in her hair and the honeys of her skin. It's like swimming into softness. My finger ends tingle with the anticipation of later, laying her back and peeling off the shiny dress moulded so deliciously to her form, then parting her legs in search of other honey, diving into heat and darkness for the pearl between her lips.

The sharp, interrupting smells of cigarettes and aftershave invade. I draw back from Inez to find Crusher standing bullishly between us.

'Meg says to tell you you're running out of time,' she mutters in my ear.

Silently I curse Meg for sending her minion to muscle in on Inez's and my private space.

I try to straighten on my stool. 'Tell her I'm still thinking,' I say, and am horrified to hear my words slur.

As Crusher hefts, tanklike, back to Meg's alcove to deliver my reply, anxiety begins to circulate its warning chemicals through me. I'd promised myself I'd deal with the situation calmly, a day at a time, but tonight I'm with Inez and less than sober. Unhappy thoughts filter like bitter grounds through my foggy brain. I'm playing to keep Meg's offer on the table, but what will stalling buy me, apart from trouble?

Inez jogs my elbow. 'What was that all about?' She gives me a comical, dishevelled look.

'Meg's made me an offer I'm not supposed to refuse.'

That sobers her up instantly. 'What kind of offer?'

'To work for her. She thinks Gail's going under.'

'That's outrageous! The gall of the woman — you'd never do that. And Gail is *not* going under just because she's been targeted by a crank.'

Inwardly I squirm. Not so outrageous. News of the bogus kit — and EHg's adamant disassociation from it — has been the topic of the week in the speakeasy, but although Gail has plenty of supporters here, she's in more trouble than Inez or anybody knows. Anybody except Mojo Meg and me.

Suddenly I feel tired and a bit ill. The bubble of euphoria I've been floating in all evening has burst and I just want to leave. I ask Inez home with me, but she makes an excuse. The magic has been snuffed out for her too.

I'm placing out money on the bar for Trin when Crusher returns and slaps an envelope into my hand.

'Down payment,' she says. 'Meg thought you could use a little encouragement.'

She leaves, no chance for argument. I stare at the envelope.

This is wrong, so wrong. Meg, the consummate tactician,

has just corralled me into looking like I'm already a willing player, while I let it happen, too shocked to respond.

Inez interrupts my stupor, her voice tight. 'You're not going to take it, are you?'

'No!' I exclaim. It comes out louder than I intended, and Trin looks over to see if we're okay.

'What are you doing, Sal? Making money deals with Meg is like playing poker with the Devil.'

The worry is apparent in Inez's voice; the uncertainty in her eyes hurts to see.

We gather up our things. I motion *It's fine* to Trin, who's watching without seeming to. On our way out, I drop the envelope, unopened, on the table in Meg's private alcove. Meg makes no move to retrieve it, her eyes like chips of resin fixed on mine.

Inez pulls on my arm. 'Let's go,' she says, low and angry.

My gal leads me determinedly away, up the speakeasy stairs to collect our coats then out the peepholed door. But the damage has been done, the seeds of doubt sown. Meg knows it. We all know it.

15

My mobile buzzes under my pillow in some deep, dark hour of sleep. I'm pulled out of a bad dream, Inez inside the speakeasy shouting at me to leave. I squint at the little glowing screen, Albee's home icon flashed up, and answer to a loud crash on the other end of the line then silence. The jag of fear that shivers through me chases away all grogginess.

'Albee?' Mobile pressed to my ear, I lurch out of bed past the half-hidden bundle that's Nitro and grope for clothing, the light switch.

I ask again, but there's nothing more from the other end.

My heart rate ratchets up.

'I'll be there soon,' I promise into the phone. *Please don't let this be like before,* is what I'm thinking. There were three of them with cricket bats last time. He was in hospital with multiple fractures for several weeks.

I call triple-0 from the bathroom, giving the operator

Albee's address as I plug in for a quick subdermal of Courier's Friend. Outside, I run with the bike into the back lane. Then I'm in the toe straps and sprinting. His place will take me twenty-five minutes at full tilt along the empty streets. With emergency services stretched so thin these days, it's likely I'll get there first.

Twenty gut-twisting minutes later, I'm bumping across the footpath, the ambulance screaming up the road behind me. I wave them into the driveway. The stretcher is wheeled out, and the three of us converge at the side entrance. The security screen isn't snibbed and the glass door behind it is ajar. *Bad.*

I propel myself inside on shaky legs, the blood hammering in my ears. 'Albee?'

Neither sound nor movement in answer to my call. *Double bad.*

Light filters through from the back. I lean the bike and lift a hinged section of the counter, then race with the ambulance officers down the aisle to the workshop.

He's sprawled on the ground near his workbench, the lamp above it still on, his phone a metre from his hand. He's always said I'm '1' on his speed dial.

'Albee!'

I go to crouch beside him, but one of the officers holds me back. 'Don't touch him, mate. Let us.'

She speaks to her colleague. 'Could be another one.'

The stretcher is released to floor level. A rubber cover with lipped sides and handles goes on the trolley. Then, before my disbelieving eyes, they open a kitbag and begin to speed-change into protective clothing.

'What's your friend's name?' Ambo A asks, pulling on a bootied zip-up suit.

I tell her, watching Albee helplessly from two metres away. His face is a sheen of sweat, his mouth slack and dribbling. I look for the rise and fall of his chest. Then I hear him wheeze.

'Were you with him when he collapsed?' Ambo B this time.

'No,' I answer. 'He rang me. I got here when you did.'

Ambo B puts on a double layer of rubber gloves. 'What substances is he likely to have taken in the last twelve hours?' He adjusts his googles and mask. 'Was he suicidal?'

Suicidal? I shrug uselessly.

The forensically clad duo instruct me to stand well back as they move in on him.

Ambo A leans over. 'Albee, can you hear me?'

She's insistent, trying to draw him back to consciousness. He responds with guttural noises and muscle twitching.

The two begin a series of monotone checks and responses, working in swift coordination. One pushes something into Albee's mouth while the other lifts a watery eyelid then takes hold of a wrist. A blood-pressure cuff goes on his upper arm, a sensor clipped to the end of a finger. A mask goes over his face and his chin is tilted sharply up. Attached to the mask is a PVC bag with an inflatable reservoir and a line to a small oxygen tank hooked onto the trolley. As Ambo A begins to squeeze the bag, Ambo B presses something that looks like an adrenaline pen into one limp forearm and watches for a response on the portable monitor.

'Let's get those fluids in.'

I stare at Albee's lower half. His feet are bare and the bottom of his shirt is buttoned up wrong. I notice his jeans' fly is undone. In an impulse of decorum, I want to zip it up. As one of the paramedics shifts, I get a partial view of my friend's face. His eyes flutter briefly, and I think he's trying to speak. My joy turns to terror when out comes a horrible gurgling sound.

'Here we go,' warns Ambo A, ripping away the mask and airway protector. Rolled swiftly onto his side, Albee throws up on the floor.

Ambo B gets a plastic tub from the kitbag and shakes a white powder onto the vomit. I look at the container. Sodium bicarbonate.

He turns to me. 'A cup of warm water,' he commands.

I find a cup in the kitchenette, fill it, and return to the workshop. Ambo B is sopping up the powder-covered mess with paper towel. He takes the cup, adds a scoop of bicarb and pours the solution on the floor, sopping it up with more paper towel. Then the cup, the sodden wad and one layer of gloves go in a sharps bin.

Agonised, I hover at the edge of the workshop. It reeks of vomit and something else my panicked brain won't put a name to yet.

Ambo B has taken over squeezing the bag. Ambo A tightens a tourniquet on Albee's upper arm and taps for a vein inside his elbow. The intravenous line is attached, then something syringed in.

'Two of atropine,' says Ambo A, and a wave of terror brings spots dancing in my vision. I lean heavily against metal shelving. The thought of losing my long-time friend is unbearable.

Now they're opening Albee's shirt. I crane around them. The white scars across his chest are revealed, one below each nipple. I panic that they'll suspend their ministrations — some have before with him, realising what it is they see — but they're attaching little pads, the leads connected to a machine on the trolley.

Both pairs of eyes are on the machine as it begins to blip. It's mighty slow. Surely that's not his heartbeat?

They do a speed-search across his abdomen then his arms, moving onto his feet and calves. I panic some more when they take scissors to his jeans, cutting them from hip to trouser end. The fabric cleaves apart, revealing Albee's pale skin covered only by boxer shorts. They check the fronts of both thighs before rolling him onto one hip and lifting away the waistband to peer at a buttock cheek. It's while repeating the procedure on the other side that they pause.

'There,' says Ambo A at a purplish mark inside a sizeable swelling on Albee's right cheek. 'Delivered IM, like the others.'

'Delivered what?' I squeak.

'Intramuscularly.'

'Third one in as many days,' says Ambo B.

'Third *what*?' I plead as they readjust Albee's shorts.

Ambo A looks back at me. 'OP poisoning — organophosphate. Whatever your friend *thought* he was injecting, it was laced with a pesticide.'

I'm horrified. My eyes smart with tears.

Ambo B breaks open another ampoule and syringes it into the IV line.

'What's that?' Fear beats in my throat like a trapped bird.

'Atropine. It's an antidote.'

I try to process what I've just been told: Albee injected a pesticide into himself, and so did two others the same way before him. It seems completely impossible. In the thirteen years I've known him, he's tried a variety of anti-oestrogens then straight testosterone, and for the last few years he's bought EHg product exclusively from Gail. Any little extras, such as new recipes of Courier's Friend, he gets from me. Using another company's product is just something he'd never do.

The ambos use the rubber cover from the trolley to lift Albee, rolling him onto it, then raise the trolley to waist height and rush it between the bike-shop shelves, rails rattling and IV bag jiggling. As they're sliding him in the back of the ambulance, the muscles of his legs and arms start to spasm, working like a broken wind-up toy.

'Do something!' I shout.

They already are.

'Five of diazepam,' Ambo A, busy with the airbag, calls to her counterpart. The shot goes in, and Albee spasms some more. I can't bear to watch.

The doors slam on the lit cabin. Ambo B peels his protective clothing into a biohazards bag and climbs in the driver's seat. As the vehicle wails down the street, I dash inside and grab the keys to the panel van off the hook behind the counter. Leaving my bike, I pull closed the security screen and glass door and race through the workshop into the backyard.

The Sandman fires up immediately. Its tyres screech out of Bike Heaven's driveway. Gunning the engine, I follow in the wake of the siren and flashing lights.

It's already a busy Wednesday in the Emergency Department. Staff to and fro behind the half-glass doors, someone moans, a child cries out. I fill in an information form for Albee at the reception desk, and am grilled again on what contact I had with him before the ambulance arrived. I say none and ask why, and am informed that his skin and bodily fluids — even his breath — are contaminative to others, and that right now he's being washed down and his clothes incinerated.

Nothing I can do to protect him now, I turn wearily to the waiting area. Painted salmon pink, with seats to match, its low table is stacked with *House & Garden* magazines from the previous century. Half a dozen people sit in various attitudes of defeat: there are those waiting to be helped and those waiting for a verdict — and no way will I sit there with them.

I walk down the linoleum corridor to call Gail. Halfway through my second sentence the tears come. I slide into a crouch against the wall. Gail guides me through the details before we ring off.

Back at reception I'm informed that when they're done washing him, Albee will be moved to Intensive Care.

'Can I go there?' I ask.

The nurse makes a quick appraisal. 'Family members only,' he warns, then says softer, 'They'll be too busy to let you near for a while. I'd get a snack and a cuppa from the all-night cafeteria. It's better than the stuff they have up at the ICU.'

There's a sign pointing along the corridor to the place he means, but the Tum-Tum Tree café is not where I want to be right now. Nor is it here, staring at off-pink walls and twiddling my thumbs. I need to search Albee's place for what he took, and remove any incriminating evidence before other interested parties decide to conduct their own treasure hunt. The police I'm not worried about. It's those self-appointed guardians of the moral good at Neighbourly Watch Central.

I ring Gail again as I'm walking towards the exit. We agree for her and Anwar to meet me at Bike Heaven.

It's still dark outside. I sit in Albee's panel van and stare at the pair of fluffy dice hanging from the rear-vision mirror. As long as I've known him, he's had a love of kitsch. I lean my head on the steering wheel.

It's usual, if a bit awkward, to self-inject into a buttock, but I'm convinced Albee didn't do it by himself. There had to be someone else there who'd been let in and who left in too much of a hurry to close the front door. Albee is too careful to have forgotten. So was the jab in the bum with his permission or by force? I don't like one bit what image rises next: my friend lying on his bed, face down, pants down, someone behind him administering the dose.

Shivering, I turn the key in the ignition and the heater up full bore. The van clunks along Temperance Street and Atonement, then left onto Saviour for the straight run down into South Melbourne.

Pesticide … surely not something the inner-city emergency services would encounter often? The two previous call-outs had given the ambos the heads-up and almost certainly saved Albee's life. I don't want to think about whether or not the others had survived, but a spate of poisonings in quick succession says there's likely more of the substance being circulated in the marketplace.

I swing into Albee's street. Not a light on, nor a soul about. In this neighbourhood the doors would stay bolted at the sound of a siren, nobody caring to see what kind of emergency vehicle is arriving and who's being put in it, nobody wanting to know that much of anybody else's business.

Pulling into Bike Heaven's driveway, it suddenly comes

to me — the other sickly thing apart from vomit that I'd smelt in Albee's workshop.

It was perfume.

I bypass the front counter and ceiling-high aisles of shelving and begin my search in the workshop area, careful to avoid the place where the vomit was cleaned up.

Unlike the clutter in the aisles, Albee's work space is immaculate, each tool with its allocated place on a pegboard or in plastic slide-out trays below. The bench is a well-used surface with clamps both ends, the shelves underneath holding cleaning fluids and neatly folded cloths. Eight bikes hang from the ceiling rack at the back wall. There are more in the shed outside.

I empty the rubbish bin. If someone else brought the stuff, there might be the telltale remains of packaging, like wax off the seal of a polyshell, or an empty ampoule; if Albee did it to himself then fell ill straightaway, there's sure to be. Trouble is, I don't know how long it was between the dose and its effect, and because the stuff was injected into a muscle rather than a vein, it would have been slower onset. Slow enough, for instance, for Albee to get dressed … badly.

Nothing obvious in the workshop. I move on to his flat, starting in the bathroom where it's standing room only between the shower, washbasin and toilet. I check the cistern and the shower recess, then the set of narrow shelves behind the mirror, removing a few items I wouldn't want the snoops to see and popping them in my backpack. Done there, I enter the studio space.

Albee's living room is also where he sleeps, the bedding on the fold-out couch in disarray. A lava lamp sits beside it, the globs of goo collected at the bottom of a nasty green suspension. The dentist I went to as a kid had one of these, based on some misguided notion that we, the waiting, would find it comforting. To me it's a piece of the past never meant to endure — but try telling Albee that.

There's one clothes cupboard. I search it first, and relocate another few items from the underwear drawer to my pack. I close the cupboard and go to the bed. As I peel back the doona, a scent wafts. I lean down and take a big sniff. It's the same perfume. Whoever my friend let in his front door, he also allowed into his bedroom.

Albee! Who did you accept dirty kit from? Who, apart from Gail and me, would you trust enough to risk that? And if it wasn't trust but coercion, then who had laid him down without a fight and injected the stuff into him?

I cast about the kitchenette, one chance to find his personal stash before someone with less kind intentions does. After a fruitless search of the cupboards, I find it in the cutlery drawer. I should have realised that Albee's 'sorting like things' mentality would put the sharp objects together. I separate the velcro tabs and unroll the canvas. There are single-use syringes of T in one pocket, and antiseptic swabs in another. If he'd used anything from here in the last few hours, he had the chance to put it away.

I add the canvas roll to my bag of incriminating goodies and return to the workshop, getting down on my hands and knees for a last check of the floor — and see something nasty at the back of the workbench. It's a large gob of phlegm that Albee must have vomited up before the ambulance arrived. It occurs to me that the Ethical Hormones lab could analyse it for what he took — and that this may be my only way of finding out. Now Albee's in the hospital system there's every chance I'll be locked out of the information loop, even denied access to him.

I eyeball the stuff, cursing. If it's as toxic as they've said, I can't just scoop it up. Then I remember Albee's welding helmet and gloves in one of the aisles of shelving.

Speedily I search the kitchen cupboards for an empty jar and a spoon, then don the helmet and gloves. Down on the floor awkwardly with the spoon, I ladle the viscous gloop into the jar and screw the lid tight. Helmet still on, I deposit the gloves and dirty spoon in the kitchen tidy to seal up and dispose of later. The floor may need another bicarb treatment, but it will have to wait. I remove the helmet and go to Albee's bathroom to scrub my face and hands.

All done, I place the jar on the bench and stare out the workshop windows. Beyond the glass, the sky is lapped in cobalt. Soon dawn will be arriving in ever-paling shades of blue.

Headlights sweep the shopfront. I'm waiting in an unheard-of role reversal: the courier handing over a package to their boss for speedy delivery.

16

I step through the main entrance of the Jesu Christi Hospital with the first of the fruit-and-flowers brigade, passing by the florist's stand just inside that's touting gaudily to the forgetful. The ground floor is busy with scrubs and stethoscopes, trolleys and crepe-soled shoes, a stream of uniform wearers and clipboard holders beginning the duties of the day. The only people not bustling are those in slippers. These vague souls wander between the lifts and cafeteria, or make for the smokers' area outside, where a hunched contingent of self-harmers are getting in some unnecessary practice.

I check at the main desk for directions to the ICU, and am pointed to the lifts. Two floors up, walking along the short corridor to a pair of locked doors, I realise I smell bad and probably look worse. Stale sweat and saggy-bottomed cycling pants aren't going to help me swing the difference between seeing Albee and being sent away.

I press the intercom button and say who I'm here for.

There's a pause. 'Are you a relative?' is the query.

'Albee's my brother,' I reply. It's the truth — just not the one they mean.

The door release clicks.

The nurses station is directly ahead. A doughnut-style arrangement set centre-room, it overlooks the entire ward, which is divided into several open-fronted sections containing four beds each and a lot of gadgetry.

Two heads are bent in discussion over the paperwork. One glances up. I try to imagine what she sees: a person with cropped hair, broad shoulders and a lean frame, no hips or breasts to notice, but no telltale stubble either. Clean-shaven, boyish ... too boyish for a girl, and too girlish for a boy.

'I'm here to visit Albee Wainwright,' I tell her.

She refers to her notes. 'Are you Salisbury Forth?' She eyes me sceptically.

I refuse to be shamed. 'That's me.'

'The ED information has you down as "friend".'

That was before I realised they'd only let relatives in. I shift to deferential. 'I came in with him and the ambulance. I'm hoping to sit with him for a little while.'

'He's in isolation. I'm afraid you can't go in.'

She motions to the right-hand door of a portholed pair, both with signs on them. Obediently I read: ACUTE ORGANOPHOSPHATE EXPOSURE. ALL PERSONNEL MUST WEAR THE PERSONAL PROTECTIVE EQUIPMENT PROVIDED.

The left-hand isolation door opens and a nurse comes out just as a loud beeping starts a flurry at the station. 'Wait here,' my interrogator says brusquely, and they both rush off.

I sidle to the other isolation door, and push.

Inside is an anteroom with another portholed door. I go close and peer through. Albee's there, hooked up to a raft of equipment. I don't know if he's sleeping or unconscious. I cast about the anteroom: a desk and chair, a wet area with a shower cubicle and a sluice sink, and two industrial-size biohazards bins. The personal protective equipment is on a table beside me. I glance back through the outer window at the nurses' station. No one back yet. I saw how the ambos did it, so why can't I?

The scrub suit and gown go on first, then the shoe covers, goggles, mark and gloves, the finished effect entirely claustrophobic. I take a deep breath and ease open the connecting door.

Sounds hit me first: the rhythmic hiss and suck of the ventilator on its stand beside the bed, and the beep of the heart monitor, its readout making peaked waves on the screen above. My own heart thuds in my ears, and my throat squeezes painfully to see Albee's solid frame made frail and insubstantial amid the paraphernalia of life support. The tube coming out of his mouth to the ventilator is held in place by tape on his cheek, while an IV line from a fluids bag on a stand disappears under more tape at his collarbone. Another line connects at his wrist then loops to a second stand. More tubes trail from beneath the covers to collection bags at the bed end.

I go to the far side of the bed and place my gloved hand on his above the covers. 'Albee.' I lean over him. 'You have to pull through this, because I refuse to live a single day of my life without you. So wherever you're listening from, I want you to know I'm waiting for you, and so are all those beautiful broken bikes that will have to be fixed by someone else if you don't get a hurry on.'

I search for a sign he's heard me, but all I see above the hospital gown are familiar features slackened into an unresponsive mask of grey.

The door swings open and a nurse comes in, kitted up.

'Actually, you were supposed to *wait*.' Her voice is muffled, but not enough to hide the anger. Hands on my shoulders, she turns me around to inspect me. 'Your friend's in isolation for a *reason*. If you've done your PPE wrong, we'll have to hose you down — unless you want to end up as a patient too.'

When she's satisfied I've not put myself at risk, she busies herself with the electronic pump on the IV line, then checks the screens and various fluid bags before turning again to me.

'You can have ten minutes in here with him. Then we talk out there.' She points to the anteroom.

I nod gratefully. 'Thanks,' I mumble into my mask, but she's already swishing out the door.

Ten minutes goes fast. At the rap on the inner porthole, I squeeze Albee's hand gently and tell him I'll be back very soon.

Her protective layers shed, the irate RN bristles. 'You shouldn't have gone in there by yourself like that.'

'I'm sorry — it's just I …' My voice cracks. That Albee not die is all I can think.

She softens minutely. 'Time to get out of that gear.'

She instructs me in the removal and dumping of the disposables into one biohazards bin and reusables into the other, then takes me to the sink to oversee my hand-washing. When she addresses me again, her tone is more conciliatory.

'By the way you got kitted up, it looks like you've already had a lesson in the safety procedures.'

Silently I thank the ambos for their unwitting instruction.

She looks intently at me. 'There appear to be no family members listed for your friend.'

'I'm the long-term stand-in,' I say.

She nods. She seems to get it.

I'm heartened enough to try her with a question. 'Can you tell me what's happening?'

'We need to help him breathe, so we're keeping him tubed and ventilated for now. His blood pressure was very low, so we're bringing it back up with drugs and fluids. I'm afraid we won't know for a few days how much damage has been done elsewhere.'

I try to take it in. It's like digesting a brick.

'You called the ambulance?' she asks.

I nod.

'If we got to him early enough, there may not be irreparable damage. Either way, he's in a lot of trouble right now.'

'But there's a chance he'll be okay?'

'A chance. I won't lie to you: his heart and brain function are the main concerns. It all depends on how long it was between the overdose and the antidote, and what else he had in his system to complicate things.'

'He didn't do it deliberately,' I say croakily, and she gives me a sympathetic look. I know she doesn't believe me. Why else would someone inject an organophosphate into themselves?

I'm choking up again, but there's something else I need to ask her. Albee is at the mercy of hospital protocols now, and I need to find ways to protect him. As ill as he is, he could be in danger of being outed as a gender transgressor to the NF watchdogs. All it would take is a quick word in the ear of a local card-carrier for Neighbourly Watch, and he'd be put on the pervert register for future attention.

I feel the stress rise as I try to frame my question. 'Albee has had some operations …'

Her response is measured. 'We have no interest in his other condition.'

Normally I'd take exception to that word, but right now I'm just enormously grateful she's onside. Some of my tension eases off. Albee's personal nurse, at least, isn't going to report him.

'We're not all slavish followers of NF precepts,' she says grimly. 'Some of us still think our job here is to help sick people, no matter who they are.'

I have to ask. 'Have the police been in?'

'Not here — check down at ED. But I can tell you they won't be interested in taking it any further.' She gets the look of someone who's had to explain hard stuff to upset relatives many times. 'They'll call it in as an unspecified OD; they don't care about the circumstances or the type of drug. Then they'll sit on it for another week to see if there are any new incidents, specifically ones involving high-profile persons. If there aren't, they'll decide it's not enough fatalities to warrant the manpower required for a public safety alert and a proper investigation. With so many dodgy backyard sellers, the field of potential suspects is enormous, and the city cops are overstretched and under-resourced. If anything, they'll hand it over to Neighbourly Watch to follow up. After all,' she adds wryly, 'they're the only ones around here with seemingly endless resources.'

This comes to me as no surprise. On the surface, the community's attitude is a moralising one: users of kit deserve whatever misfortunes befall them, and who cares about a few dead blasphemers and deviates? But the demand for the products of hormone manufacturers like EHg, NatureCure and BioSyn, and the roaring trade we all know the CEO piss farms do, paints the real picture. The community, far from being an abstainer, is a voracious consumer of banned kit. It's just that it's also in complete and utter denial.

'Has anyone else been in to see him?' I make it sound casual, but she knows where I'm going with this.

'One Neighbourly Watch rep, just before you.'

I have to work to hide my dismay. How the hell did

they get to know so quickly? Gail's information network may transcend the usual bounds of time and space, but Neighbourly Watch Central comes in a close second. Lucky for us it's that way around.

She frowns. 'He sauntered in, flashing his badge, then proceeded to make a nuisance of himself, as they usually do. Pretty soon he realised he wasn't going to be asking the patient any questions and left. There's been no one else — no family members enquiring as yet.'

There wouldn't be. Albee's family are all Word of God Brethren, and they pushed him out of home when he was twelve. Which brings me to my next request.

'His biological family won't be visiting,' I say. 'But he has a family of friends who'll come and sit with him if they're allowed. I can give you some names.'

'You're asking me to put them down as relatives?'

'Yes.' I hold my breath and wait.

She sighs, tired already at the beginning of her shift. 'Alright.'

'You're terrific,' I say. And mean it.

She screws her mouth into a rueful smile. 'Glad to hear it. Now if only the doctors would tell me that occasionally.'

She waits by the outer door. 'Time to go.'

I take one last look at Albee through the porthole, sending a silent plea to the patron saint of gender transgressives. It's the closest thing to a prayer that I can manage.

Outside, opposite the hospital's main entrance, the borrowed panel van is a blaring advertisement for seventies kitsch. I cross the street and do a quick check of my bike in the back, then I call Ellie, an old friend from the youth refuge. These days she's the facilitator of a Melbourne gender support group, and I can trust her to put the word out to the others on the family list straightaway so Albee won't be left alone.

I ring off then stare for a bit at my phone. When Inez and I parted company outside the speakeasy, she was still angry with me, but I need to let her know about this. I text a brief message and end it with an 'x'.

Almost immediately a message comes in, but it's not from her. I read the display: *Yr prsnt dlvrd 2 bthdy prty*.

Thanks to Gail, my little jar of evidence has made it safely to the hidden facility of the Ethical Hormones group.

The rest of Wednesday is a blur. Gail has another courier do my deliveries while I go back to the hospital, tag-teaming with Ellie. 'Any change?' I ask, and she shakes her head.

Every patient on a ventilator in the ICU is 'specialled' — allocated their own nurse. I ask the one on duty for an update, but she's less forthcoming than the last, saying only that Albee's stable.

Ellie sticks around awhile, and together we watch the blips on the ECG monitor, willing his traumatised heart to pump and his mind to resurface undamaged. When she gestures she has to go, we hug like astronauts in our protection suits; one life in the balance, ours circling above in a holding pattern.

Late evening and lying exhaustedly on my couch, I glance along the hallway and see a white envelope pushed under the front door. Instantly I think of Inez. I retrieve the envelope — a sealed blank — and bring it back to the couch. The sheet of paper inside is crudely hand-printed: *EVIL IS UPON YOU. CHANGE YOUR WICKED WAYS AND SAVE YOURSELF.*

I fling the paper and dive off the couch to make sure the doors are locked, front and back, then peek furtively through the blinds of my bedroom window to the darkened street. This is more than a warning lobbed in public at a suspected transgressive. Now they know where I live.

Back on the couch, I cuddle Nitro to me like a furry hot-water bottle as my mind swings chaotically from one bad scenario to another: Roshani, Albee, the EHg and Gail — and now some nutter connected to the prayer groups fixed on me. I think of the failed delivery to Cutters Lane, no reports yet of other couriers being attacked by prayer groups. *What if they've been following me?* I could have been putting everyone I know at risk.

Gail rings in the middle of my panic.

'The results from your sample came through while you were at the hospital,' she tells me. 'They found traces of an agricultural insecticide along with low levels of testosterone and a questionable growth hormone. There's no indication of a sedative.' She pauses. 'Albee would have been aware when he got the jab. It must have hurt like hell.'

I grip the phone. Someone did this to my friend and then abandoned him.

I hear her acknowledge a muffled voice.

'I'm at the warehouse with Anwar,' she expains. 'He's been speaking to the technicians in the lab. They suggest conducting a more detailed assay of the sample, in case any impurities deposited during the distillation process help to pinpoint the farm's location.'

'They can do that?'

'Not at their facility, but they know a private forensic soil-science lab that can. They'll feed the results into the National Soil Conservation database to see if any of the elements find a geographical match. It won't help Albee's current situation, but it might bring us one step closer to the source.'

I ask about the surveillance at Ferguson's.

'Nothing yet,' she answers.

I tell her about my two warning notes, adding, 'I didn't realise they were aimed at me personally until tonight.'

She's silent a moment. 'Save yourself from what, exactly? If they know you're a transgressive, they believe you're already lost. I'll organise a team to watch your flat. And *you* need to watch your back.'

I rub tired eyes, every fibre in me stressed. 'It'd be better for you if I were working for Meg right now,' I say quietly.

'We'll cross that bridge if we have to,' is her noncommittal reply.

We ring off. I pad barefoot into my pocket-sized kitchen

and lean my hands on the sink, staring out at the shadowed pebble path winding through the dunes. Right now Albee needs me; but so help me, I will search for the people who did this to him, and when I find them I will hand them to Gail and her fixers on a platter.

17

I haven't been able to reach Inez all morning. Normally we'd have texted each other a couple of times by now. I've sent her two more messages since the one about Albee, but there's been no response. It's making me antsy.

Home from my vigil at the hospital, I walk distractedly around the flat opening and closing things, not sure why I opened them in the first place. Several times I try to make a cup of tea, boiling the water then forgetting to fill the pot. Even the cat catches my air of anxiety, scratching at the back door to go out, before changing his mind.

Close to 11 am I remember Nitro's twelve-thirty vet appointment, and hurriedly organise a van with Gail. On my way out I meet the house-watching team she promised. It relieves my worry about Nitro being left alone, but still I ride a paranoiac route to Cute'n'Cuddly. When I get there, I'm told to take my time with the van and a couple of days off.

Back home, I load Nitro into his cat carrier and strap him in the front seat beside me, then we're on our way to Max's.

I chat to him, an uncomplaining passenger, as I drive — but it's more for my reassurance than his. He's done this trip many times and doesn't mind his little portable home, lined ever so comfortably with a kitty futon. Of course, there's a risk in taking Nitro anywhere, and I always drive the route across the river afraid of being stopped by traffic cops or an emissions patrol for some petty misdemeanour. Today it's worse than usual, every person happening to glance my way a potential threat.

Max's place is two blocks behind the select boutique shopfronts and cafés that make up Toorak village. I swing off Toorak Road into his street and glance up at an impressive canopy of dappled limbs, the plane trees reaching from both sides to the middle. Below their mid-green benevolence the verges are so lush that I suspect an illegal supping of the city mains.

As with every other property in the suburb, the Toorak Vet Surgery has a grand entranceway and electric gates. I press on the intercom and, after an initial reticence, they rattle open, the result of too many visitors and no time for home maintenance.

A wide, sweeping drive leads to a verandahed Federation cottage with wooden fretwork and gable ends. There's parking for half a dozen cars out front — no inner-city bolthole run on a shoestring, this. The practice takes up the front section of the house; the rest of it — and there's plenty more — is where Max lives with Penny, his partner of twenty-five years. She's a qualified vet nurse and his full-time assistant now their kids have flown the coop and have lives of their own. Max could take on other workers, but he and Penny prefer it this way. Like those doctors still with licences to practice (in greatly reduced numbers since the 'blitzkrieg' on reproductive technology) his services are in demand, but his books are closed.

I survey the surgery's neatly stacked shelves as Max palpates my cat's ample belly on the treatment table.

'Got a bit of a tum there, matey.'

Nitro weighs in at half a kilo more than last time. Max looks at me disapprovingly over his half-glasses.

'I'd stop with the treats if I were you. From now on I think we'll go for the low-cal kitty bites.'

I gesture remorse while Nitro lies on the hard metal bench and purrs, unperturbed. My cat is an alien.

We've been making these visits since he was a six-week-old fluffball glowing in the palm of my hand. Back then, eight years ago, his kind were no longer flavour of the month, but he was still a *legal* alien. Max, at great risk to himself, kept us and others like us on as clients after the Unnatural Practices Act was forced through parliament by Nation First and the pet exterminators were given their orders to go forth and round up all abominations of nature not handed in by their tardy owners across the amnesty period. According to Nation First, these weren't God's creatures but monsters made by science, and they were to be got rid of. But what loving pet owner would willingly give their phosphorescent bird or bunny to the Animal Patrol, knowing what was going to happen to it?

Animal lovers everywhere responded by building more secure boundaries and secret enclosures. Now low-wattage creatures of all kinds lurk behind the barred façades of the inner city's apartments and terraces and creep inside the protective fences of suburban gardens. The authorities, however, aren't stupid. They suspect the community of subterfuge, which is why the pet exterminators still patrol the streets in their vans, trying to catch us out.

Max squeezes up a furry roll and sticks in the vaccination needle, then inspects eyes, ears, teeth. All this Nitro submits to with good grace. I wish I could say the same for my own medical appointments.

All done, Max finds a treat from the shelf behind him and palms it over to the cat. 'Just one,' he warns us both. 'Special for today. I shouldn't need to see him again for six months. You okay for other supplies?'

'Yes, thanks.'

I buy everything I need here: food and worm tablets, supplements and accessories, even bedding. All check-ups and vaccinations are taken care of without a single thing being written down, no paper trail or computer files for the tax auditors or animal inspectors to find. According to the meticulously kept records of the Toorak Vet Surgery, I am not a client and Nitro doesn't exist.

Max walks me to the front door, scrutinising me before opening it. 'How are you bearing up?'

I've given him the annotated version of Albee's accident. 'I'm okay.'

He nods. 'Albee's as strong as an ox. He'll pull through.'

Our next port of call is five minutes up the road, and Nitro's favourite place after Max's. It's where my cat gets to prowl a real garden with something other than desert tussocks to piss on.

I ease the van to a stop in front of Checkpoint Charlie. Today's SOS guard stares impassively through the reinforced glass. Another day, no precious cargo, I'll ask how they keep from getting cabin fever in their little booth.

When Gail isn't home, the request re-routes to her mobile. I lean out to punch in the code and look in the lens. The permission lights green and I hear the lock mechanism disengage. Then the van is gliding around tree-lined curves, heading for the turn into Salmon Close.

The second keypad attended to, we roll through slowly opening gates onto gravel. I press the manual release on the other side. The gates swing together, meeting with a decisive clang, and my relaxation response comes, Pavlovian.

The house ahead is all shutters closed. I stop beneath the oaks that straddle the driveway, their branches intermingling. Gail calls one 'Grace' and the other 'Majesty'. Acorns crunch underfoot as I heft the carrier beneath

Grace and set it down, Nitro shifting restlessly inside, pushing against the little plastic door for me to unlatch it.

The moment of seeing my cat step delicately out onto cool green grass is always a joy. He sniffs, saucer-eyed, ears twitching, before dropping cheek first and rolling ecstatically onto his back. I clip the extend-a-leash to his collar while he's pedalling air, eyes gone to slits, in cat pleasureland.

He begins to stalk the terrain, slinking through the undergrowth as if he's a jungle cat, not an electric purple exotic bred for city life. Our slow perambulation takes us to where a bank of rhododendrons forms a protective horseshoe about a herb garden, a sundial on a pedestal in the middle. The herb varieties are planted in a wheel shape, separated by brick inlay spokes. Nitro creeps onto the camomile and bats with slothful imprecision at a cabbage moth, while I sit on a bench positioned to take advantage of the view through the horseshoe down to the bottom of the garden, where hydrangeas hang their heavy heads in damp, peaty shade and spiky thickets of japonica harbour a multitude of wrens. I smile at their busy chatter, the return of the birds to suburbia a special joy. For a while it seemed like they never would.

We move on through a grove of stripling birches, their light-refracting leaves ashimmer, then along the shelter of retaining walls where the camellias are budding up for autumn and the dogwoods turning shades of magenta. Back at the oaks, our circuit made, Nitro sharpens his claws on hoary bark.

This outing is always a pleasure, but today it's marred by worry. It's not just Albee's situation. The anonymous warnings rankle, and the attack on Roshani still haunts me. I don't want to think about Meg's job offer complicating everything, but it's impossible to keep her sharp-eyed unpleasantness out of my mind.

I remember Inez angry in the speakeasy, and can't believe I let the whole charade happen. That Gail didn't scotch the idea of me working for her rival is a measure of how bad things have got; meantime, instead of telling Meg I'm not interested and putting an end to it, I have to keep her hanging on my answer — something Mojo Meg does for no one.

I make a call to the ICU and am told 'no change'. Nothing else to do, I settle myself at the base of Majesty while Nitro sniffs a dandelion at full stretch of the lead. Clicking the release on the recoil mechanism, I let it reel him in, then lean down and nuzzle into fur that's caught with bits of twig and leaf. He begins to knead himself a place beside me, purring rhythmically. Silently, I apologise to him in advance: while I'm working for Meg, both of us will be barred from the sensate pleasures of Gail's private grounds.

I lean my back to the bark and gaze up. In my perfect world, I'd have a place like this. And I wouldn't have to sneak in and out of it, terrified of the long arm and enquiring eyes of Neighbourly Watch. There'd be no more scary prayer groups monopolising street corners and writing threatening messages, and no government-employed pet exterminators gunning for my cat.

Cool grass tickles my bare feet as scents rise from the loamy earth. Exhaustion drags on my limbs. I close my eyes … then jolt upright. Even here, I can't allow sleep. Displaced from his cosy nest, my cat stretches, bum up, tail wafting. Reluctantly, I stand too.

My afternoon gets progressively pulled more out of shape, like a woollen jumper in the spin dry. The flat, normally a retreat from the world, feels cluttered and oppressive. Not rostered to be with Albee again for another few hours, I decide on a sitz bath — filling it unthinkable these days — and turn on the hot tap. Nothing comes out. I swear profusely. Somehow I've used up the day's metered allocation, and it's only 4 pm.

When my mobile finally beeps, I'm sure it's Inez; but it's Gail to say two members of the Red Quarter militia have caught a street hawker at the Shangri-La and can I go over. Glad for the distraction, I hop on the bike and pedal more ferociously than necessary through the traffic, getting sworn at by pedal taxis and trams alike.

As I ride, I wonder how a little blip like this in my relationship can throw me so badly. There could be any number of reasons why Inez hasn't replied: misplaced her phone, called out on an emergency job …

It was the look she gave me in the speakeasy after Crusher left the envelope. One she's never directed my way before. A look of *doubt*, rising disappointment riddled through it.

18

The day waning but dusk not arrived, Madams Row is unlit as yet, its buildings imbued with an air of closed expectancy. I lock the bike below a geranium box then rap on the Shangri-La's crimson door, and am surprised when Savannah herself opens it. In a high-collared cheongsam the colours of a coral reef, she's breath-stoppingly attractive. She welcomes me in with a slightly distracted air, her mind on something else.

That something is in her kitchen.

The street hawker is lurching about, mumbling and gesticulating peculiarly. He has that pelvis-forward-shoulders-back walk I associate with madness, as if his internal gyro has been knocked out of whack. What he was trying to offload is sitting innocuously on the kitchen table.

He's watched by two people: one at the door and one leaning against the sink. Both are dressed in black, and could be scenery movers for a theatre company but for the subtle energy compressed in the workings of their bodies.

The guard positioned by the door glances at us both as we walk in, but addresses Savannah. 'We can't get any sense out of him. He's not just off his face, he's off his rocker. It'll take a month in detox to bring him down — if ever.'

'Where did you pick him up?' I ask her.

'Outside La Petite Mort, shouting at the top of his lungs. Not hard to miss, and even easier to catch.'

'Great sales technique.'

'More like giving it away,' she says. 'But most people here have heard the news and would be too wary to buy. We think he was paid in pills first then set loose with his wares.'

It makes no sense. 'Why would they do that?'

'You tell us.'

The guy is tall as well as skinny. His arms dangle weirdly and his joints seem too loosely strung, as if on loan from someone else's body.

His mumbling gets louder. Biting dogs and ferocious angels have the monopoly of his mind — and someone with bleeding fingers. His jerky movements still momentarily. I check his hands. No blood.

A chime dings softly in the kitchen. Savannah excuses herself and steps out.

I sit at the table and reach for the polyshell. The wax medallion pressed into the midriff seam is unmistakeably EHg's. Closer inspection reveals it to be a patch job, same as the last.

The guy steers suddenly to the sink, shaking his hands over it vigorously, as if something's clinging to them. I'm

189

reminded of Lady Macbeth. If this is a guilty conscience, was it something he saw or something he did?

I look questioningly at the guard closest.

'No friggin idea,' she answers.

She leans across the metal draining board, stopping his hands with the strength of hers, and tries to persuade him to the table. His arms go, but his body refuses to leave the sink. He shrieks as she twists an arm behind him.

Sat forcibly, he looks around, wild-eyed.

'Feel free to ask,' she says to me.

I proffer a hand. 'Salisbury Forth.'

The whites of his eyes are glazed, red as maraschino cherries, his pupils tiny black pits. His gaze wanders off me to the door.

His guard leans over and gives him a little shake. 'Pay attention, mister.'

I hold up the egg. 'Can you tell me who gave this to you?' I ask, and he recoils from the question as if it scalds him.

'Bleeding fingers,' he mutters, rocking in his chair. Madness defeats the best interrogation techniques.

A woman's anguished wail rises suddenly from another part of the bordello, stopping us all momentarily. Something — someone — has broken through the perfectly veneered world that is the Shangri-La.

A door bangs. I force my attention back to the street seller and start again.

'I'll pay you for more,' I say invitingly, but head tilted to his shoulder, he looks at me as if I'm the loony.

When Savannah steps back into the room, her expression tells us nothing — her manner as seamless as ever. She, on the other hand, can see by our faces that the situation hasn't changed.

'I'll make the call to the psych unit,' she says to the guards. 'As for this …' She picks up the polyshell. 'I'll take it to Gail myself.'

She draws me with her out along the corridor. I start to say something, but am signalled to silence by a brief finger to the lips. We're passing the clients' parlour.

We enter the salon our first meeting was in. Savannah motions me to a chaise longue, then crosses to the cabinet of curiosities I'd tried not to stare at last time. Her being right by it, I do now.

She lifts the latch and opens a latticed door to adjust something fallen off its stand. My imagination is already firing up, picturing how the various devices might strap to a body — or inside it. She catches me looking and a smile crinkles the corners of her mouth. Not for the first time I think that here is a woman who loves her work.

'A world of untapped potential,' she murmurs, and I get the feeling it's not the objects in the cabinet she's referring to.

I blush.

She closes the lattice and comes over to sit by me. 'I'm worried for Gail's safety,' she confides.

Hastily I regather my wits. 'I agree this isn't about selling; it's to show us the stuff is out there doing damage. But that doesn't mean the threat is aimed at Gail personally — more likely at EHg, and her by association.'

Savannah shakes her head slowly. A bastion has been breached in the heart of transgressive territory. 'That may be so,' she says softly, 'but I need you to find out who these people are.'

She takes my hand in both of hers in a disconcertingly intimate gesture. I feel a strange mix of emotions as I look into hazel eyes flecked with gold, the fragments of colour being caught by the light.

As alluring and formidable as she is, I feel ill-equipped to do what's being asked. There's a certain focused simplicity to being a bike courier — not to mention a rather reassuring anonymity. You make the drop swiftly, often under cover of night, and leave. Right now I feel like an L-plater shoved onto a racetrack mid-event and told to drive for my life. Except it isn't my life. It's Gail's.

'I want that too …' I start to detail my unsuitability, but Savannah interrupts.

'I know you'll do whatever it takes.'

The crimson door closes. I click on my bike lights and cycle distractedly down the Row. Two blocks along, I pass a prayer-shawled figure crouched, weeping, in a doorway. I stop and look back, wondering if there's anything I can do; but they startle like a rabbit when I enquire, and are gone into the dark of a side alley before I can even turn my bike.

19

Inside Tallis's light-filled office tiredness weights me to the chair, the strain of events beginning to show. My host observes me with a keen eye and waves away my apologies about not getting back here sooner.

'Braheem seemed genuinely upset by what happened,' I tell her. 'I believe him when he says he's spoken to no one about his sister being a surrogate.'

The memory of the door closing across the landing niggles, but not enough to mention. Instead I say, 'He'd really like to see her.'

Tallis hands me a glass of water from a filter jug. 'That won't be a problem. The crusaders for the moral good keep a sharp eye on maternity ward admissions and discharges — it's why we have a birthing centre in the Red Quarter and don't use the hospital system unless absolutely necessary. Having lost the baby, Roshani's no longer a target.' She pours herself a glass. 'She could spend some time with

Braheem at the markets this morning. We'll supply an escort, just in case.'

She means someone from a Red Quarter protection team. I think of the CCTV at the Tea House. Better for Roshani to visit her brother out in the public eye than at that place with its invisible observers and creepy politics.

Tallis looks enquiringly at me. 'Would you like to go too?'

'Sure.'

I'm not due at the hospital until twelve thirty, and the market's on my way. A darker thought worms in, unwanted: *it might be me who needs the protection.*

Tallis, not privy to my morbid thoughts, looks pleased. 'It'll do Roshani a lot of good.'

Roshani, Geeta. Two names for two places. At Braheem's I'd realised the letters of their family name, Rani, were contained inside her alias.

'What happens for her from here?' I ask.

'She'll have ongoing counselling and access to all the medicos she needs. When she's ready, she'll be helped to relocate outside the Red Quarter and find other work. Given what she's been through, her surrogacy days are likely over.'

This is my moment to bail out gracefully, but it seems so unsatisfactory to leave it there. *Someone* sicked the prayer group onto the poor woman.

'Do you still think the leak might have come from inside the organisation?'

'I don't know.'

She lowers her voice as if the walls have begun to listen

in. 'Those privy to her surrogacy agreement — the Red Quarter madam who negotiated it, and her medical and social supports — are all people I trust implicitly. Roshani is writing us a list of everyone she's had dealings with since entering the program, and we'll go through it name by name. The other surrogates have been told of the attack and questioned about her, no animosity there that we can detect.' She sighs. 'As far as their own safety goes, we don't require them to stay exclusively in the Red Quarter before they're showing. After that, any trips outside need our approval. But we're not here to be the police; ultimately, all we can do is caution them to be extra vigilant when outside the precinct.'

I put down my drink and the light through the window catches in the glass, striking me as quite beautiful. It's best not to look at what's been sieved out by the filter. In the last few years, serious cracks have begun to show in the city's infrastructure, prayer meetings no solution to aging utilities.

I get to the piece of news I've not wanted to say, telling Tallis I'll be uncontactable for a while. She gives me a candidly appraising look, but doesn't push for an explanation.

'Well then …' She levers herself up out of her easychair. 'Shall we go ask Roshani if she'd like to visit her brother?'

Before we leave the room, she turns to me. 'On behalf of the folk here, I want to say thanks again for everything you've done. If there are any changes to the situation, we'll let Gail know.'

'I'd appreciate that,' I say, and exit her calm, sunny office with regret. Tallis Dankner is someone I'd be glad to have for a friend and confidante — especially now, as I prepare to walk alone into the tiger's lair.

Roshani leads the way through the market hangars past the lusty spruikers of the fruit and veg section then along the haberdashery and clothing rows, seemingly oblivious to the Red Quarter chaperone discreetly following. It gives me the chance to marvel at the improvement in her, a transformation from the stricken person I saw lying in a hospital bed.

Braheem's Lucky Charm jewellery collection is tucked between a stand of scarves and a stand of leather goods. The reunion is gratifying to witness. As brother and sister hug delightedly, I find myself thinking it might be the last heart-warming thing I'll be seeing for a while.

'Sam!' Braheem clasps my hand.

It takes me a moment to connect to the name I'd used in his visitors book.

'Salisbury, actually. I just didn't want to tell the Tea House.'

He nods, unsurprised, then calls across to his scarf-selling neighbour. 'Rashid! Can you watch the goods for half an hour?'

Rashid, a portly man with a keffiyeh flung about his shoulders, good-naturedly assures Braheem that he'll direct all potential customers to his own stall instead.

I glance back along the aisle and see our chaperone inspecting a candle stand.

We go to a café on the street opposite the market entrance. Friday trading in full swing, it's crowded, but convivial. Braheem commandeers a table by the window then goes to place our orders at the counter. The mood is so happy and relaxed, I hate to spoil it, but I can't help one question while his sister and I are face to face.

'Geeta — is it okay to call you that now?' I wait for her assent before continuing. 'I'd like to ask you something I asked Braheem.'

She stares a moment at her nails, then nods.

'I'm trying to work out how someone might have got wind of your "condition". Was there anyone outside — at the Tea House, for instance — who took a particular interest?'

Her shoulders droop a little, but she recovers quickly. 'Since the — since Sunday I've been over and over it. But I never confided in anyone except Braheem.'

I see the raw hurt and am sorry to have raised it. 'I'm not questioning your integrity or Braheem's in any way,' I say gently.

She replies a little defensively. 'We're good at keeping secrets.'

Braheem had said much the same thing at the Tea House. I wonder where this is going.

She looks across the table at me, a challenge in her eyes. 'Has he told you why our family emigrated to Australia?'

I shake my head.

'Our parents came from the same district in Uttar Pradesh. Both families were scheduled caste, or *Dalit*. In India that means "untouchable". For the kids of those families, life is hard and school is not a given. My father was one of the few to break the bonds of caste and get an education.'

Braheem arrives with our coffees. I look up quickly. How will he feel about her telling me this?

She smiles thanks at him and keeps talking.

'When the affirmative action laws forced public universities to give some slots to so-called "backward class" applicants, he went to Delhi University to study medicine. There were massive protests at the time, and he had to claw his way past the kind of discrimination that would have been glad to see him fail. His eventual success meant our childhood in Delhi was privileged, because of his position at the Gene Research Institute. But we were still, and always would be, Dalit.'

Braheem is silent, eyes on his sister.

'My parents were afraid Braheem and I would always struggle because of the attitude to caste, so when Australia was looking for the kinds of skills our father had, we packed up and came here. Our parents wanted us to grow up in a place where Dalit had no meaning, but you soon come to realise that every culture has its own version of untouchable.'

She looks away, suddenly embarrassed, and belatedly I realise she's referring to people like me. Braheem shifts uncomfortably in his seat.

I think back to my teens and early adulthood, and all the confusion I felt over who I was. Those who present as androgynously as I do are a walking, talking question mark for the community to feel perturbed about. Some even seem to think we've been designed deliberately to mock them.

Briefly I flash to Inez. I'm untouchable to her too now. I let the pain trickle through me as I sip my coffee.

'Your parents had no regrets about settling here?' I ask.

Braheem shakes his head. 'They still missed home, which is why they took a trip back there with Geeta when we were in our teens. Our father died a few years ago of cancer, and our mother returned to India permanently last year.'

Both parents gone, at least they still have each other. I can't help a moment of envy over their close sibling relationship. Then the resemblance strikes me.

'You two look remarkably alike ...'

'We're twins, by IVF,' Geeta replies. 'Braheem is my older brother, but it's only by a couple of minutes.'

'Ah,' I say, one more piece of the Rani family puzzle slotting into place.

The coffee break over, I scribble my mobile number on a serviette. 'In case you think of anything, or just want an ear to bend,' I tell Geeta as she gets up.

On an afterthought, I turn to Braheem. 'Who lives in the apartment directly opposite you?'

He looks surprised. 'Marcus and Laura Nancarrow. Why?'

'Just curious. Are the Nancarrows on the Residents Committee?'

'Marcus is.'

'And who deals with the CCTV footage?'

'The committee shares the responsibility. The footage is downloaded to an old computer in the basement.'

'Who looks at it?'

He frowns. 'I don't honestly know. I don't think anybody cares that much any more.'

I don't want to alarm him, but maybe, just maybe, the Nancarrows do.

I'm en route to the hospital when I get a call from Gail.

'Bad news,' she says. 'Early this morning I took Savannah's polyshells to Ethical Hormones to get the contents tested. The one she handed me several days ago is the usual execrable hormone-farm mix, but the one she delivered last night is a different story. The ampoules all contain the same combination that poisoned Albee: growth hormone laced with an OP, along with a raft of incidentals like floor scrapings and insect parts.' She lets that sink in, then says bitterly, 'Even without insect killer this stuff is toxic waste — not fit to be buried, let alone put in a body.'

I feel ill. This means the EHg logo isn't just being used to sell bogus kit, but bogus kit spiked with an organophosphate. Gail's situation has just spiralled from a business-ruining scam to a life-endangering vendetta.

20

Inez and I are arguing across a candlelit table at the edge of the Glory Hole's dance floor. I've told her I'm going to work for Meg. She hasn't taken it well.

Elsewhere in the room it's still Happy Hour, the bar area already five deep, and the tables and alcoves filled with people arrived from work and ready to play. Miserably I press an index finger to a glob of leaked wax as some nameless house mix begins to drum out an insistent beat. This afternoon's conversation with Gail ended with the news that the surveillance at Ferguson's had netted nothing, the space unvisited by all but a family of brazen, scampering rats.

Now I lean towards Inez, desperate for her to understand. 'I know how it looks, but I'm asking you to believe me when I say it's out of necessity, and I just can't explain yet.'

She replies, just as intense, 'What's to explain? You've accepted Meg's money offer. But the person *I* know wouldn't work for that piranha under *any* circumstances. So who exactly are you?'

I feel the squeezing pain of having to withhold from the one I most want to confide in — and watch as a new thought dawns on her.

'Gail put you up to it, didn't she.'

My perspicacious girlfriend. *Now* she's angry.

'This is some double-play she's cooked up, dangling you like bait to the wolf pack. She's exploiting your loyalty! Have you ever thought you might be just a little *too* loyal?'

I don't bother to say how I haven't.

'Sal, your hero is not all sweetness and light. Sure, she champions ethically made hormones and pays for the APV's outings, but don't forget it *suits* her for us to rustle the competition's horses and put them out of business. She may have cleaner politics and better people skills, but underneath she's as ruthless as Meg. You don't have to go along with it. Say no to both of them before it's too late.'

I'm reminded weirdly of the anonymous warnings. I never knew Inez thought any of these things.

It's true Gail has my unswerving allegiance, but I owe her a debt I can never repay. She gave me a life, and I'm living it. Inez, though, feels locked out — injured that, after everything we've shared in our time together as co-vigilantes and lovers, I don't trust her enough to say what's really going on. But while this flushed and angry woman confronting me is smarter than I'll ever be and can hold her own in all kinds of situations, she'd have no hope against Meg's sly tactics and the heavy hands of Crusher and Snarl. I shudder inwardly. *I* have no hope against Crusher and Snarl.

'I suppose you're going to disappear, no explanation, from the APV too?' My girlfriend fixes me with a withering eye.

I nod. I won't risk Meg getting her hooks in there.

Inez pushes back in her chair. 'I realise you've got a lot on your mind, especially now with Albee, but I gave you more credit than that. I thought you lived by a set of principles and weren't just a gun for hire.'

I feel her every accusation go in like a blade, and can't say a word in my defence. She gives me one last searching look in the hope I might tell her something to make it all better.

I don't.

I watch as she gathers up her things, leaving for the APV meeting we should both be at. My last chance to plead for trust and forbearance has just slipped away, and I know in my already aching heart she won't be seeking me out again. Gutted, I stare at my untouched drink. The exhilaration of new love, just two short weeks young, has been crushed under a heavy boot. Meg's boot.

I glance across the dance floor to the row of cushioned alcoves. The curtains to Meg's private space are drawn back. She's been watching us argue from a distance all the while. I feel my jaw clench.

Before Inez's arrival, I'd stood at Meg's 'office' table and announced I was available for work. She'd looked at me through slightly narrowed eyes and asked, 'What brings the change of heart?' 'Bills to pay,' I'd muttered. Snarl had smirked — a contortion of her features I'd not thought possible. Meg's hard gaze had stayed on me, but she'd nodded slowly.

The only thing to be gained from this sorry episode is that Meg already knows what Inez thinks of her, and seeing us at loggerheads will shore up her belief I've deserted Gail.

Crusher saunters up, her black tee-shirt stretched to its limits by barrel ribs and worked biceps. She claps me on the shoulder. This, I'm guessing, is a demonstration of her nicer, friendlier side. I feel the eyes of the room watching.

'Girly trouble?'

'Something like that.'

'Never mind — plenty of others around with all their curves in the right places and their plump bits begging for a poke and a jiggle.'

I can't believe I'm hearing such misogynist crap.

Crusher leans close. A terrible habit made even more excruciating by smoker's breath. 'Meg's ready to give you your first job,' she says. 'Welcome to the club.'

I watch her shovel her bulk back between the couches, people looking up then away. She has nowhere to go but her boss's alcove. Working for Meg has effectively separated her from any community she might have found here. Right now she doesn't seem to care, but I wonder about later. Fate is good at flipping the tables.

I look down. Placed on mine is an envelope. Inside it are my pick-up and delivery instructions for the next day, along with the money that Crusher had failed to give me the first time round. I skol my drink and pocket the envelope, my only desire now to escape the claustrophobic air of the speakeasy.

It's pretty sad. I'm drinking alone in a dingy sports bar in St Kilda, downing vodka slammers and wishing I could turn back the last several days and do them all again. I squint at my watch. Paul will be taking over from Ellie at Albee's bedside now.

There's no use dwelling on my shattered love life, or the dismal lack of result at Ferguson's — except, being in my cups, I do: I give regret full rein. If I'd just said a flat no to Meg the first time, the question of working for her might never have come up; I'd still have a girlfriend, and every day would be the shiny and exciting thing it was before. I'd been a long time in the relationship wilderness before Inez's warm presence wrought its magic on my life. Now she believes me made of flimsy moral fibre, and I'm afraid that even when she finds out the truth, it will be too late to restore the trust between us.

Crusher and Snarl leap unpleasantly to mind. How long before I turn into a cliché too? Couriering for BioPharm, with its reputation for being not quite cruelty free, will shoot to hell any credibility I have within the APV; just as the news of my association with Mojo Meg is going to oust me from my social circle as fast as if I were strapped in an ejector seat. I remind myself the change of boss is temporary, but secretly I'm afraid that once Meg has her constrictor grip on me, she won't let go.

I place my hand over the refilled shot glass, bang it on the counter and take a fiery swig. The other punters — all three of them — are hunched over their drinks, not interested in their neighbours or the giant TV screen above us blaring an overwrought commentary on some blood sport with a ball. What a merry lot we make for the bartender, who's busily sending phone texts and smirking at the replies. A love interest, I'm guessing. Lucky him. I raise my glass again for the last of it to dribble down my throat and cauterise my tonsils.

I'm an easy drunk. Normally, I'd be afraid of losing the faculty to choose between flight and fight; but tonight I want it this way. Let the alcohol leak its slow fog through me, acting on the plugs and passages of my heart, numbing them against the disappointment of forfeited love.

I lay some notes on the counter and steer myself through the door. Somehow I manage to cross the street without being run over before stumbling along the darkened walkway that leads to the sea. What was a sunny day has turned black and blustery and cold. Above me the clouds are being shredded like confetti in night's stratosphere. Once, they might eventually have made rain, but these days they just mysteriously dissolve into the empty reservoir of the sky.

Ahead, the fun park's smiley entrance menaces. I shudder, and move on to where St Kilda pier pokes a ghostly finger from the shore. Walking its weathered boards, I have to put one hand on the railing to steady myself. Past the bleak stretch of grey shoal beach to my right, I can just make out the beacons of the Tasmanian ferry terminal. There hasn't been a ship for a fortnight — the ferry company's licence revoked for shoddy maintenance and leaks in hulls. People will be rowing themselves there soon.

I stop at the end of the walkway beside the permanently closed café building, and consider scaling the chain-link to get to the observation tower further along the breakwater. From there I could throw myself into the sea. It's an inviting thought in a cold, miserable kind of way. The ocean-dwelling predators, at least, would find nothing to distinguish transgressive from normal flesh, loyal friend from traitor. For them I'd simply be a meal. Guess that's why all the fairy penguins have gone.

The alcohol works its acids up my gullet. I grip the rail and hang my head, then give in to the inevitable and heave onto the rocks below. Wiping my mouth with my hand, I sag onto the ground, as full of self-loathing as I've ever felt. And think of my family.

The last time I saw my mother was eight years ago, shortly after she and my father got dunked in the municipal swimming pool, baptised in the spirit of Jesus.

She told me she always knew I would be going to hell.

They say blood is thicker than water, but the question that followed me through childhood — *girl or boy?* — thinned my own family's loyalty and washed away their love. People stopped asking the question in my adolescence; instead, it became a silent accusation in their eyes and their awkwardness. My parents realised that calling me a girl and giving me girly things wouldn't make me *be* a girl. And so they sat back and watched me career towards uncertain adulthood, knowing I would never miraculously turn into a 'normal' daughter — at least not without institutionalisation and electrodes.

At sixteen I left school and home and found my way to a squat in St Kilda. I visited my family every once in a while. They tolerated me, but I could see they wished me gone. Five years later, with their panicked conversion to evangelism through Saviour Nation, they made it clear they no longer wanted anything to do with me. It pained them, they said, but it was better this way. Better for us all. The fact that I'd never even *tried* to behave as a girl had increasingly strained their sense of rightness and credibility with others, and now it strained their standing in the church community. All this had taken its toll on them. Why else would my father have ulcers and my mother hypertension?

I didn't fight it; but to be excommunicated like that, at twenty-one, is to be made skinless to the world.

I think of Helen. It must have been hard on her to have a failed role model as an older sibling, and more times than I care to remember, the accusations would come at me like javelins: *Why do you have to be so different? Why can't you act normal?* All that hurt and anger had been laid like a blanket over our history, suffocating the good and leaving only the bitter taste of blame. But a shared childhood grows deep bonds, and in some indissoluble way, she's the one who knows me best.

I finger my phone. Being late on a Friday evening, Michael might answer. He's like a Doberman protecting her from the likes of me. How ironic I'm the one who could help them achieve their long-sought miracle by fixing them up with the right kit from Gail. In their eyes, though, that would make me not only a gender transgressor and social outcast, but a drug peddler for Beelzebub too.

I tap in the number for Helen's mobile. It clicks into a recorded answer, then her voice cuts in.

'Hello? Sal?'

My number must still be in her phone.

Suddenly Michael is there. I hang on, stoppered by a paralysing anxiety.

'*You* don't call my wife. *Ever.*'

The line goes dead.

I slump, desolate. How will the rift between us ever heal? Last time I visited, Helen said if I came to her home again, she'd get the local chapter of Neighbourly Watch to see me off. Something in me broke then — something I'd clung to, deep down, despite all experience to the contrary. It was the belief my family would ultimately cleave to its own and accept me: that they would love me, regardless.

Inez once told me her folks wouldn't care who I was or how I fitted into her life, as long as we made each other happy. On the strength of that, I began secretly to hope I might become part of *her* family — a late add-on to the Moran mob — because in my reality, it's not blood that's thicker than water, but the potentising qualities of acceptance and respect.

'Take me home,' I mumble.

The taxi driver turns and looks at me through his bulletproof bubble. 'And where would that be, mate?' He's a grizzled fiftyish and has seen too many of the world's woes.

I slur out the address.

He takes one last regretful look at what he's let in his nice clean SEC cab, then swings the vehicle into the traffic lane, saying, 'Don't puke on the upholstery.'

I'm too spent to reassure him. Closing my eyes, I lean back into the smell of leather and disinfectant.

Home is where the cat is: Nitro, who loves me regardless of my shortcomings, and who welcomes me plaintively at the door, pressing for my attention, even if it's just because he knows who fills up the bunny bowl.

I'm ashamed to say it, but out on the pier it wasn't the pricking of my conscience over Gail and the EHg crisis or even Albee's dire situation that had drawn me back from the brink. It was the thought of Nitro waiting for his dinner.

21

I ring Max in the small hours, too self-pitying to apologise for waking him.

'Is it Albee?' he asks.

'No.'

He waits for the reason I called.

'I have to take a leave of absence from the APV,' I tell him. 'And I probably won't be contacting friends for a while.'

'You alright?' The concern is apparent in his voice.

'Yeah,' I say, heavy and unconvincing. 'Just gotta do some stuff.'

'The sort of stuff that needs a minder for Nitro?'

'No — but thanks for asking.'

'We'll keep the porch light on.'

'I'm counting on it,' I reply, and feel the resurgent flare of an old warmth.

Max is referring to a ritual established in the early days when I first got to know him and Penny. Back then, seventeen years old and unable to find my place in the world, I was drifting between jobs, having left school early

211

with no graduating credits. Gender-wise, I was swinging between extremes — and hating myself. Nothing worked. Nothing felt right. It was a canker in my spirit, a spreading necrosis eating me up. Then along mooched Ninja, the black tortoiseshell moggie, a scratched and scruffy wanderer who crept through my open window one terrible hot summer and attached himself to me like a familiar. It turned my days around. I finally had someone — if a little worse for wear — to come home to, someone to cuddle.

Max had a practice in St Kilda near where I lived. I met him then Penny because of Ninja's penchant for street fights and regular need for stitches. I even ended up working for a while as Max's part-time assistant to pay for the surgery bills. He said I should think about vet school, but I could never have afforded the bridging course and upfront fees.

Gradually, with Ninja and my job as daily anchors, the swinging pendulum that was my gender identity stilled around the midway point, and I began to make peace with the gender transgressive I was and would always be. Then, in the summer before the pandemic took hold, Ninja was bitten by a brown snake. Max saved my cat that day, but not three weeks later when fate put him and his envenomed reflexes in the path of a concrete truck. We had a ceremony, Max, Penny and I, burying Ninja in their leafy back garden under the plum tree.

My battle-scarred street cat was at rest, but I was a mess again. Max and Penny rescued my sorry arse from a few bad situations on St Kilda pier, reminding me I had an important place in their lives. That reminder was a precious gift: a no-strings acceptance, and open invitation to doss down in their spare front room anytime — hence the reference to the porch light. These days it may be more a metaphor, but it's as comforting as ever.

'Stay safe,' Max says, and we ring off.

I go to bed, but I don't sleep. I watch Nitro stretched out above the covers beside me glowing like a fuzzy nightlight.

In four short hours, I will get up and go to work for Mojo Meg. I will become a courier of BioPharm's not-so-ethical products and, to all those I know and those I love, a turncoat, having bitten the hand that's fed me these last seven years.

Prestige Couriers Inc is in Banana Alley, a service road running along the north bank of the Yarra at the bottom of the CBD. The building is a set of barrel vaults sitting between the water and the railway viaduct. With a sauna and solarium one end and a gym the other, it's mighty public, but there's plenty of eye candy to distract the curious from the unassuming roller door that was once the rear of a nightclub and is now the workers' entrance to a busy distribution hub. Day and night a bevy of cyclists spin in and out of here like helmet-clad worker bees, the legit business hiding a much more profitable sideline. Meg is a brazen operator.

Her premises take up the middle four vaults, each one extending from Banana Alley to Pilgrim Street and connected to its neighbours by archways excavated through metre-thick walls. The entire block of tunnels used to be where fruiterers stored their goods before market — hence the name, which has stuck despite the place going through several personality changes since. It's only a matter of time before the zealots on Melbourne City Council's renaming committee get to it.

My Saturday deliveries made, I wheel in, exhausted and cranky. But it's not from the exercise or the close-of-trade traffic. It's no fun being harangued by dissatisfied customers, especially the rich and snooty kind. Not trusted with the more exclusive clients, I've been put on beginner's duty, delivering goody bags of pituitary tonics and do-it-yourself collagen injections, herbal pheromone mixes and libido boosters to the beauty salons along Chapel Street, Melbourne's high-fashion row, and along the way doing more than my fair share of kowtowing to their vanity and niggling grievances. These are the people for whom 'tightening their belt' means a course of liposuction. Give me the Red Quarter customers any day. BioPharm does a roaring trade south of the Yarra, and Meg, as sole distributor, has the market sewn up.

I lock my bike in the rack between a fixed-wheeler and an all-terrain hybrid and join the queue of couriers dropping off their panniers along with any undeliverables. In the next-door vault, I open one in a bank of lockers and remove my street clothes — slouch jeans, hoody and lightweight hikers — then shower in a draughty cubicle, the brick curve above me coldly lit by light-saver neons. Seems Meg has decided the only heating her workers need is the internally

214

generated kind. Leaving, I pass several others rummaging in their lockers or silently checking their bikes, everyone intent on getting away from the place as quickly as possible.

At the beginning of my shift I'd been informed by Snarl that 5 pm is drinks at the pub in Scots Alley, just up the street. I would have begged off, but it's been organised to welcome me into the fold — Crusher slapping me playfully around the chops and adding, 'Don't make us come find you.' (I heard afterwards from another courier that her real name is Sandy, while Snarl's is Merlyn. I couldn't hide my incredulity at the latter. 'Don't say her name like that,' he'd replied, looking around nervously. 'She's sensitive.')

My bike left in the rack, I set off, crossing beneath the broad arches of the viaduct to Scots Alley, a history-imbued passage linking Pilgrim Street to Pilgrim Lane. Once, its row of warehouses sat harbourside, and it was a busy trading area for goods carried by the steamers, including hessian sacking, French champagne and gold. I look for the entrance to the Rob Roy pub. An unmarked door in a scummy recess, it takes careful notice not to miss.

Inside, the pub is the adamantly unrenovated kind: years of drinkers spilling their food and drink on the carpet and wearing deep concavities in the ancient upholstery, and *proud* of it. The bartender looks as worn as the décor, gravity doing its heavy work on him.

I find Crusher and Snarl — Sandy and Merlyn — tipping back beers in a wood-panelled booth. I look for the others I thought would be here too. No joy.

They welcome me in their individual ways: Sandy with a robust backslap, and Merlyn with a thin smile dragged from the gloomy depths.

I slide in, the smell of the booth making my nostrils twitch. I'm afraid that if I sneeze, it'll raise the dust of some old soak who carked it in my seat. Sandy goes off to get the next round while Merlyn and I stare at each other across the way. I want to ask about the other workers, but don't dare.

Sandy is back mercifully fast, setting down two schooners of dark ale and the lemonade I requested. Not that I'd tell them, but I'm still recovering from the poor-me session in St Kilda.

'To the newbie.' Sandy raises her glass.

'Aw, shucks,' I say as they swig. Could be that Meg's minders are just desperate for other company. It must get lonely — boring, even — the two of them against the world.

Another round is called for far too soon. My turn, I go to the bar and try to meet the eye of the bartender. He moves away to serve someone else. I lean in, wondering what will help my chances, and see that below the counter he's wearing a kilt. I'm no tartan expert, but this one I happen to know because of my father's father. A die-hard Scot from Dundee, he'd weathered the parochial Aussie suspicion of blokes in skirts to don his tartan every day. This one — his regimental — he'd worn on special occasions, including at his funeral.

'Did you serve with the Black Watch?' I ask in my best nice voice, and the barman turns to me, surprised.

'That's right,' he replies in an unmissable Scots brogue, which makes me nostalgic for my grandad. 'Forty years wi' the regiment: Ireland, Iraq, Afghanistan … More flippin' theatres than the West End.'

'Here's a long way from there,' I say.

'Married an Australian, didn't I. We ran a youth hostel in Warburton till the fires took it. She hied off wi' an English backpacker half her age and I ended up in this place.' He wipes the bar with an ancient tea towel then cocks his head at our booth. 'Same again?'

'Thanks.' I feel like a boy scout who's just earned his first merit badge.

'Salisbury Forth,' I say, reaching across a hand.

He takes it in his big, surprisingly soft one. 'Cam MacLeod.'

Another round on, Sandy and Merlyn have loosened up and so I get bold.

'Meg thinks there's someone working for Gail who wants to take her down,' I say, trying to keep it casual.

'A greasy pole-climber,' Sandy replies.

'Any suggestions who?'

'Well, it can't be *you*, that's for sure.' Sandy laughs loudly at her own joke.

Merlyn surprises me by coming out of her mollusc-like shell. 'I'd be taking a good hard squiz at her 2IC,' she says darkly.

Fancy Merlyn using military lingo. Gail's second-in-command is Anwar. I stare at my lemonade. There's no way on Pan's sweet earth it's him.

'Got proof of that?' I ask.

Sandy taps her nose. 'Not for us to say, is it.'

These two know nothing. How could I have thought they would? I feel a sinking despondency as I glance along the patrons lining the bar. This subsection of the city's underworld is different to that of the Glory Hole. Here the atmosphere is brooding, angrier. Some would likely belong with the speakeasy crowd if they weren't too repressed to know it. Unfortunately, it's these all transgressives have learnt to watch for, being the most likely to lash out at a suspected 'perv'. It makes me a teeny bit glad I'm with Sandy and Merlyn, who are matching each other schooner for schooner and show no need for a toilet break. They must both have industrial-strength bladders.

My stomach gassy and acidic from lack of food, I give up on lemonade and go to the bar to check the blackboard menu. All the meals are dead animals with breadcrumbs or brown sauce, so I opt for peanuts and crisps. As I'm heading back to the booth, Meg arrives through the door. No one but me seems surprised. I realise the other two knew she was coming.

Cam calls me back to get the generously poured whisky sitting on the bar. 'For the boss,' he says.

His boss too? Makes sense she owns the place.

'Sandy and Merlyn helping you settle in?' she asks as I pass across her drink and lay the nut and crisp packets on the table.

'Yes, thanks.'

I don't feel talkative. I've been pushed one too many

times off my balance beam today. At least I don't have to wait long for her to get down to business.

'EHg won't survive this smear campaign, run as it is from the inside,' she says in a flat, uncompromising tone.

My heart thuds unpleasantly. *The worm in the apple* … She's saying someone close to Gail is capable of that?

'It'll collapse, and there'll be a smack-down brawl for Gail's territory. You'll be glad to be out of it.'

I say nothing.

She takes a delicate sip from her glass. 'Anyone made C&C a buy-out offer yet?' she asks casually.

It's impossible to tell whether she knows already and wants confirmation or is on a fishing trip. The joke's on me joining her 'gang' to glean information, because I'm sitting opposite a master.

'Not my business,' I reply gruffly.

'Don't seem to know much about anything, do you?' Meg sips again. 'I like that about you, Salisbury. You're charmingly incurious.'

Before I have time to react, she floors me with another announcement.

'Tomorrow I'm starting you on some knock & drops.'

The Sabbath has no meaning to Meg any more than Gail — but trusting me with her prize clients so soon? While I'm digesting that news, she lays down her trump card.

'Prestige Couriers is in the happy position of being able to take on C&C's distribution area and service its client list,' she says. 'And so my question to you is, would you rather Gail's reputation be destroyed and her territory fought over by the pack, or a genuine competitor step in early in a friendly, bloodless takeover?'

Bloodless ... heartless ... Beyond the protective umbrella of C&C, hormone distribution is a murky business open to bullying tactics and blackmail. Welcome to Meg's world.

'You're her star performer,' she presses. 'You've worked for her for several years — am I right? Even if you've spent all that time with your ears politely closed, you'd have a mental list of her buyers, past and present. I'd wager you could mark on a map every address you've delivered to.'

Her predator's eye is on me. I'm too afraid to look up, lest she see the truth of a kinaesthetically wired brain written on my face.

She presses harder. 'Under the auspices of BioPharm and Prestige Couriers you could continue on as you have — for top dollar *and* with top protection.'

She tilts her head at Sandy and Merlyn. Sandy blinks owlishly and I almost laugh.

So this is my true value to Meg. I'm to hand over the company secrets — Gail's buyers list — to give her the advantage in the grab for territory; and in return her minders buy me drinks instead of breaking my arms.

I've been naive. Now I feel vulnerable. What if it's been her all along, steering the ship into the iceberg?

I picture her, flanked by Snarl and Crusher, explaining to

Gail's regulars the sudden change of supplier; the coldly persuasive nucleus of a company whose many tentacles are about to be inserted like cancer into the bones of the Red Quarter.

Meg brushes an errant speck of dust off her tailored lapel, and gets up. Her bodyguards follow suit.

'Think about it,' she says again, and then I'm alone in the lumpy leather-and-horsehair booth, staring morosely at empty glasses on sodden cardboard coasters.

When I'm really anxious, or really angry, I get on my bike. Tonight I'm both, riding through the streets of Fitzroy and Abbotsford to my favourite circuit at Yarra Bend Park.

I've let off steam this way since I was six years old and given my first two-wheeler: a Dragstar with shiny pink tassels sticking out the ends of the handlebars. I took to the tassels immediately with scissors, much to my parents' dismay, that being another of their attempts to colonise me as a girl. I can remember feeling, even back then, if I didn't do something with my pent-up energy, I would explode from it. So I'd hop on my bicycle and ride as hard as my young body could manage. The revelation was discovering my strength, my capacity to go fast. I'd power up the hills then freewheel down, every corpuscle chorusing YEEESSSS! That bike — which I eventually stacked in a ditch at the bottom of a very big hill — was my joy, and my lifeline. But I made sure the next one wasn't pink.

I exit the street and judder across the warped boards of the footbridge over the river, then am leaning through the curves of the Yarra Park track, the lamplit edges of the parkland swishing by like a fast-forward movie.

I've never been someone who gets calm by being still. Riding is my meditation. Eventually, the motion unsticks my thoughts and they begin to flow like wind through a leaky building.

Meg's earlier observation of me as 'charmingly incurious' flurries through. For me, couriering is about getting the deliveries to their destinations at speed and unnoticed. That's where the pleasure has always lain. In all the years I've worked for Gail I've never wanted to know who the addressees are or what the packages contain. Why would I?

After three-quarters of an hour, my hands and cheeks are prickly with cold while the rest of me sweats under the layers; but the ride has done its calming work. I swig from the bike's water bottle, and head for the hospital.

Food moved to the top of my needs list, I swing by the Tum-Tum Tree café for a bowl of congealed vegies and pasta. It's passable fare, but in truth I have no interest in it other than as fuel for my body, the mush bypassing my tastebuds en route to my stomach.

The lift is stifling and I strip off a few more layers. As I'm let through to the ICU, those on duty behind the desk glance up briefly. I make for the right-hand isolation door.

The sign is gone.

Wondering, I enter the anteroom. No biohazards bins, no personal protective equipment. I look through the porthole: an empty bed frame.

Panic hits. Terrified, I turn to exit and bump into the nurse coming in.

'Sorry,' she says, seeing my agonised face. 'We thought you knew. He's out of iso now.'

Albee pronounced non-contaminative at last, his room has been cleaned and all the bedding and disposables, even the mattress, sent to the incinerator.

As I follow the nurse around the central station to the other side of the ward, I wonder about the patient in the other isolation room, and how many others there've been. If this were the rash of poisonings we'd feared, Albee's room would already have a new occupant. EHg's scouts must be doing a good job of snatching the dirty kit from the streets as it lands.

I'm led to a section containing six beds, Ellie greeting me at the first. I look down at Albee's still form. 'He's made good progress, right?'

'You bet,' she replies. 'They're going to start lightening up on the sedatives to see if he's ready to breathe on his own. If he shows the right signs, they'll take the tube out.'

I reach for the outline of an arm under the covers as together we watch our friend, neither of us verbalising the lurking fear: *what if he comes to consciousness and isn't the same old Albee?*

My wristwatch says 10 pm. I'm sitting in a vinyl armchair procured by Sarah, the nurse I angered on my first visit, and holding Albee's hand as I talk low-tone to him, when I feel the muscles flicker in his fingers. It's a tiny twitch, his fingers closing slightly on mine, and could be some autonomic response — but I'm not so sure. Was it something I said? I've been telling him about Inez, and just described her storming out of the speakeasy.

I wait for another message. That there's nothing more doesn't dampen my hopes. He's shucked the OP residues from his body, and now he's as good as squeezed my hand. Well, nearly.

Slouched sideways in the chair, one leg over the armrest, I doze, entering a disturbed half-dream. Images play on the screen of my sleep: Helen looking out at me through the barred windows of her house; the street seller shaking bloody hands over the Shangri-La's sink; Geeta being pelted with rocks by an angry prayer group. I come back to awareness with a start, Mojo Meg's last words, *Think about it*, ringing ominously in my head.

Paul arrives from his chef's shift to take up vigil. I lean over Albee and kiss him softly on the cheek.

I've decided I need to let Gail know Meg is convinced it's sabotage from the inside, and that I'm being pressured for the details of her buyers list. It means breaking the pact of no contact, but I have to go see her tonight.

22

At Checkpoint Charlie something is badly wrong: my ID won't verify, but the SOS guard waves me distractedly through anyway. I ride into Gail's cul-de-sac and pass police cars leaving. Her gates are wide open.

Dread settles on me like a lead weight. I lean the bike inside the hedge and walk slowly along the driveway between terracotta urns, up the steps to the unlatched entrance.

'And you are?'

Coated and casual, the speaker blocks the threshold. Something about him is vaguely familiar.

'Sal Forth.' I reach out my right hand.

'Sal …' He looks me up and down. 'That short for Salvatore or Sally?'

'Salisbury, actually. After the cathedral.'

He blinks once, thrown briefly. A hand emerges like an eel from his shirtsleeve. Shaking it is like squeezing a bladder of air.

'Doug Smeg, Neighbourly Watch. The good detectives were kind enough to give me a tingle and bring me in as community observer. You know how the Local Incident Committee likes to have its *t*'s dotted and *i*'s crossed.'

He waits for me to appreciate his wit. I don't.

I peer past him through Gail's glass-enclosed portico and open front door into the living area. These days Neighbourly Watch gives everyone permission to stick their noses in other people's business.

'I live nearby,' I say, and wave my hand non-directionally, although I'm sure this won't wash with Doug, who probably has the NW dossiers on everyone and their aunts and uncles for blocks around. 'Nothing serious, I hope?'

'Overdose.'

His words register like a slap.

'Seems the kit was laced with something else. The ambos could do nothing for her. Damn shame — fine-looking woman. Morgue's admiring her now.' His nuggety eyes are fixed on mine.

No! Pain slams into me like a wrecking ball. My eyes burn, the shock stoppered in my chest. *I will not cry out.* Not with this smug bastard watching.

I set my foot on the next step to get past, but he moves swiftly to prevent me.

'LIC investigation scene. Sorry,' he says, slick and mean.

Still blocking my way, he reaches past a potted cycad to slide open a drawer in the roll-top bureau beside it, and calmly picks through the contents.

This can't be happening.

Everything in me wants to pummel him aside to find out for myself that it isn't true, but I see the regulation-issue taser at his belt and know he has the power to make an arrest for any violation he cares to think up.

'They confiscated a dispenser and some contraband, but not enough to constitute dealing, as such ...'

He lifts out a blister strip of Courier's Friend — its telltale electric blue a brief flash before it disappears into his pocket — then assumes a disinterested air, as if his mind has already turned to other things.

I hold down the stab of rage. No way would Gail keep kit or equipment at her house. Someone must have planted it.

I force my expression blank. I want to rip his throat out.

'Where did they take her?'

'You'll have to ask the constabulary that, I'm afraid.' His lips stretch into a smile. The cops are gone. 'How coincidental,' he says mildly, 'you turning up like this in the unfriendly hours. I'm assuming we're both on the same page, *Ms...ter* Forth?'

I look at the menace in his flat, pasty face and know exactly which page. The one that, if all Doug Smeg's clothes were to be removed, would reveal the injection marks of a long-time steroids user.

Call me Ms or Mister, I don't care, but keep your evil hands off Gail's things.

'I have no idea what page you're on, Doug,' I say, low and even, 'but I doubt it'll ever be the same one as me.'

Then I take my leave down Gail's neat drive, the blood drumming a fearsome tattoo in my head, his eyes like leeches on my back.

The speakeasy is aflutter with the news of Gail found dead in her home from a dose of tainted hormones. How I made it here from Toorak, I don't remember, but after ringing Anwar, I'd stumbled in and collapsed on Rosie's broad shoulder.

A full shot glass appears at my hand. It isn't the first. I surface from my stupor to concerned faces looming in and out of view, the speculation rife around me. But it wasn't me who told the news. It arrived before me. Doug Smeg, or someone in the constabulary, has a high-speed connection to the speakeasy grapevine.

'… anaphylactic shock,' a voice says loudly. 'Something toxic in the kit. So much for trusting Ethical Hormones.'

'Fancy Gail of all people getting her own medicine wrong,' someone else chimes in.

'Getting greedy, more like — or desperate,' another replies. 'I always thought she looked too good to be true.'

'Yeah, right,' I say to my empty glass, and the bar goes quiet around me.

The room is suddenly oppressive, the smell of alcohol and kit cloying. I start for the door, but a hand places itself on my arm. Merlyn steers me firmly over to Mojo Meg's alcove, its tasselled curtains secured to give a bird's-eye view of the bar. I wait unsteadily at the table as Meg drums baubled fingers lightly on its surface, Merlyn and Sandy standing point duty.

'My busy little courier.' The fingers drum.

'Busy no more,' I say, unable to mask the bitterness. 'I quit.'

'I'll ignore that because you're upset. Sad news about Gail, but we all step over that mark sooner or later.'

'This was premature.' Grief and drink have made me unwary.

The fingers still. Mojo Meg's eyes glitter in the lamplight. 'I'll give you that. It's not like Gail to capitulate.'

I'm on the edge of an avalanche of sobs, but Meg is the last person I want to break down in front of.

'You went there?' she probes.

'Yes.'

'And found her?'

'No.'

'So who did?'

I blink soddenly. Doug Smeg said the police had called him. But who called them?

'I don't know.'

Meg is having her own thoughts, some of which might be about why I went there in the first place.

'Who told you she was dead?'

'The Neighbourly Watch guy who was rifling through her things.'

She says nothing to that.

'Take the day and sleep off the booze,' she orders. 'Be in my office Monday, 9 am.'

I linger, bleary-eyed, until I realise I've been dismissed. Lurching up the speakeasy stairs to the door, my second attempt to leave is stopped by Marlene. Knocked out of her usual superiority, she sniffs, eyes red-rimmed, and reminds me in a throaty lisp to collect my cycling gear.

Rosie puts an arm around my shoulders, turning me away from the storeroom where my bike is stashed. 'You're not leaving here on that,' she rumbles in my ear. 'I've called you a taxi. Want someone to see you home?'

I shake my head.

'Chin up, mate,' she comforts. Then the door locks behind me and the spyhole closes over.

The taxi is already at the top of Wickerslack Alley. I make for it, the gossip at the bar replaying in my head.

'Yeah, right,' I say again, to the stinking bins and stacks of cardboard boxes. I know better — two things better: Gail didn't do kit, and didn't need to, being one of the rare few who'd retained their full complement of hormones in the wake of the pandemic. My business-savvy employer was a walking, talking fertility factory, a modern-day wonder, so no way had she overdosed.

I'm on my couch, crying into Nitro's purple fur. Gail was my boss, but she was also the rock of dependability around which my fickle, unfocused life revolved. And she was family to me.

Reaching in my jacket for another tissue, I pull out a slip of paper. It's a number with a scribbled message: *We need to talk. Marlene.*

Marlene never wants to talk to me. So why start now?

I flick the paper to the floor. She can go talk to the wall. Two weeks ago I was cracking jokes with Albee in his workshop and happily couriering for Gail. Now Albee is in a coma and Gail is dead.

The wail rises in my solar plexus, pressing up my windpipe into my throat. Nitro riding my lap, I launch back in the couch and let loose. Nitro leaps. I wail harder. It becomes a guttural scream, raw and primeval; I swing round on my knees and begin to pound at the back cushion.

When my arms have become too weak to punch another time, I slump into hiccupy sobs. Nitro returns to the couch and begins to knead himself a place beside me. I stroke him, feeling his warmth; the vital spark coursing through him the same one that runs through me and connects us all, including Albee in his deep sleep. But not Gail. Not Gail ever again.

23

Anwar said he'll ring me when he finds out where Gail's body has been taken; meantime, I have to go be with Albee.

My bike's still at the speakeasy, but the panel van is parked outside. I climb into it, grief-stricken and drunk, then sneak along every side street between home and hospital in an effort to avoid the notice of the roving Temperance Units and emissions patrols.

Driving, I think of Marlene's note. There's nothing I want less than a mutual sob session, but maybe she has something useful to say. She's got cosy at various times with a number of Gail's competitors, and occasionally I wondered if my boss was using her as a source. Information, even from Marlene, would be welcome right now, because while I believe there'll be no lack of takers for Gail's territory, I can't bring myself to believe anybody would be so desperate as to kill her for it.

I find a parking spot around the corner from the hospital entrance, and text off a message. If Marlene wants to talk, let her.

Overhead, a single old-style neon shines down, punctuating the dark of the deserted street. Drained, I stare across the parade to the buildings of the university precinct. Behind them the sky is beginning to lilac up. How many dawns have I seen lately? Too many. I blow my nose, zip up my jacket and step out of the van.

Five hours later, the Glory Hole's statuesque cloakroom attendant is waiting for me in the Good Bean and attracting the interest of the regulars.

Frank clasps my shoulder with a thick hand, the droop of his eyes telling me the news of Gail has reached his establishment. He shoots a glance down the row of tables.

'One of yours?'

'You could say that.'

Marlene has pretensions to a Lamborghini lifestyle and never visits what she calls the bohemian section of town, but has made an exception for me. As for getting past Frank, she's in luck. He has his own set of identifiers that decide entry to, or rapid exit from, the Good Bean. Top contenders for the latter are Nation First politicians and exponents of B2N; next, known snitches for Neighbourly Watch. Clearly he's decided Marlene fits none of these.

Her eyes are rimmed Hepburn-like with liner, her cheekbones subtly rouged. A dove-grey jersey dress with fur trim sheaths long, graceful limbs above stiletto ankle boots. She looks suitably downcast, but this is a woman who, even in sorrow, knows how to dress for effect.

I say hello and sit, feeling woolly-headed from grief and lack of sleep, unable to dredge up any small talk. She saves me the trouble by launching straight in.

'We've not been close,' she begins, 'but we both had a very special connection to Gail, so I'm hoping we can help each other.'

'Sure.' It comes out a bit lame, but this is more than Marlene has ever said to me in one go.

'I heard about Albee. How is he?'

'Still in a coma.'

She tuts sympathy and sips her latte. 'Of course you know Gail and I were lovers?'

I nod, not sure Gail would have used that word in relation to her.

'She was my first,' she adds from under her lashes.

I assume she means lesbian bedmate, but she could mean vegetarian cooking teacher for all I know. I wait for what might be next.

She reaches for a hanky, then dabs expertly at her made-up eyes and says, 'I've asked myself a million times: why did she do it?'

Marlene knows as well as I do that Gail is too smart for this to be an accident, but, unlike me, she's assuming Gail did it deliberately to herself. For a moment I'm lost for an answer. I finger my mobile in my pocket and wonder why Anwar hasn't got back to me.

'I don't know,' I say wearily.

A coffee appears at my elbow, the lush aroma reaching my nostrils. Distractedly I stir in the *crema* with my teaspoon while Marlene fiddles with her hanky, building up to something.

'I heard you were at her house afterwards. I don't suppose you saw anything there addressed to me?' she asks.

'Actually, I didn't get past the front door, thanks to an overly diligent member of Neighbourly Watch.'

Her eyes narrow ever so slightly, and a tiny warning light blinks on in my hindbrain.

She treats me to an especially shiny look. 'I fell head over heels for her,' she confesses. 'I'd be devastated if she left me nothing, not even a note. We were … soul mates.'

I feel an involuntary recoil on those last two words and shift in my chair to cover. Now she's getting really spooky.

'Like I said, Marlene, I didn't even get in the door.'

She sags in exaggerated disappointment, then presses in close. 'I'm going to let you in on a little secret.'

Please don't.

Too late.

'We were planning to have a baby together.'

My mouth opens in an 'O' and stays there.

'I think you know already Gail was a fertile,' she says *sotto voce*. 'What you might not know is that she'd been selling her eggs through a Red Quarter broker: the madam of the Shangri-La.'

Savannah. Marlene knows a hell of a lot for someone who I thought was just a casual fuck.

'Anyway, she promised me one of her egg sets, and I've been having the fertility supplements and uterine rejuvenation shots to be ready for the embryo transfer.'

Gail's egg implanted in Marlene's rejuvenated womb? I don't want to ask about the dollop of donor sperm.

'Unfortunately, her silly broker refused to take me on as a recipient, and so Gail was going to sign a special permission for a set to be released directly to me for my procedure. I know she wouldn't have forgotten.'

'Silly' is the last word I'd use to describe Savannah, and as far as I remember from Tallis, the donor–broker relationship is a secret kept between those two. I suppress the spurt of anger, and shrug.

'If I come across anything with your name on it, I'll be sure to hand it over.'

Marlene's shiny look tarnishes. 'I'd like to believe you wouldn't withhold from me, Sally — but I don't.'

My shoulders tighten. My *friends* know never to call me that.

Her tone drops further into hurt. 'If you can't bring yourself to give your blessing to Gail's and my fertility arrangement, perhaps you could find it in your heart to do one other little thing, for her sake?'

I curse silently. 'What do you want, Marlene?'

'I posted her some very soppy love letters, which I'd be mortified if anybody else read. You were closest to her, so you might know where to look for them.'

I'm surprised she doesn't think of Anwar as Gail's closest friend, but let it slide. I suppose she still believes my boss was bedding me.

'Maybe she entrusted you with some of her personal effects?' she presses. 'They say suicides often do that before the … event. It'd be protecting Gail's privacy if I had them — and saves you from getting into any trouble later.'

Trouble with whom? Now she's pushing all my buttons.

'I've got nothing for you,' I say. 'Sorry.'

Marlene draws herself up haughtily. 'Have it your way and play the dumb courier,' she hisses. 'Just don't be surprised when there are repercussions.'

She swivels expertly out of her chair and swishes down the narrow aisle beside the counter. Frank lifts his pear-shaped posterior off a barstool and goes behind the register, but she sashays right past. The front glass rattles and then she's gone, an angry swirl of movement out the door.

Left with her bill, I sit awhile trying to get my head around the notion of Marlene and Gail having a baby. Eventually, I give up. It's as counter-intuitive as a Cute'n'Cuddly dung beetle and my imagination just won't go there.

Marlene can look for her own letters. She doesn't need my help. Besides, I can't see Gail keeping them. Seems to me, the desperation to conceive has consumed a number of Marlene's other capacities, including niceness. I'm wondering what 'repercussions' might be headed my way when Frank comes over, bar cloth slung over one shoulder.

'Your boss left something with me earlier in the week,' he says quietly. 'Said it was to go to you if anything happened to her.'

He gives my table a perfunctory wipe, then removes a manila envelope from the big front pocket in his apron. My name, Gail's handwriting. It clinks as he hands it over.

I cast a guilty look towards the door. Something for me and not Marlene. I half-expect a jersey-clad cyclone to come swirling back to denounce me for being an arrant liar.

'Another coffee?' Frank asks.

My stomach is saying no, too much caffeine already poured into a foodless cavity.

'Might as well.'

I poke diffidently at the envelope then cast my gaze across the Good Bean customers, their backs hunched and heads together over the tables — all, it seems, with secrets to share. I'm not sure I want to open mine.

I tear the end of the rectangle then tip it, and a set of keys lands on the table. A little shake and a second envelope slides out, embossed with the plush letterhead of Curlewis & Yang, Barristers & Solicitors. In the envelope is a certified copy of Gail's Last Will and Testament. The first page reveals Frank to be executor of the will. I glance down to where it says 'Residuary Estate', and there my eyes stop. My name is written in as sole beneficiary. Gail's protected Toorak citadel is her last gift to me.

Tears prick, the pages blur. I lower my head to my arms on the café table and weep soundlessly.

24

Anwar's seated behind the desk in Gail's secret office at Cute'n'Cuddly — and he looks like crap.

'Hey,' I say wearily. He'd rung just as I got home from the Good Bean and was sinking into a pit of exhaustion on the couch.

'Rough night,' he replies in his understated way.

There's a chair placed my side of the desk, but I don't want to sit in it. I close the door and choose my usual position against a filing cabinet.

He leans forward with a concise intensity.

'She's disappeared.'

'Pardon?'

'There's no record of her arrival at either of the city morgues, and nothing in the Ambulance Service's log about a pick-up in Salmon Close. In addition, the police say they never attended a call-out to that address.'

I can't process what he means. 'Someone else took her body?'

'If there was a body. I think she's been abducted.'

My mind races back twelve hours. I didn't see the ambulance, just the police cars. Or was it that I saw the blue flashing lights zoom past and *assumed* that's what they were? Then there was Doug Smeg from the Local Incident Committee blocking my way as he'd delivered the news.

Anwar interrupts my runaway thoughts. 'The SOS guard said the ambulance and police cars arrived at the northern neighbourhood entrance at 11.45 pm, and left the same way several minutes later.'

'If she didn't call them, how did they get into her place?'

'Good question.' Elbows on the desk, he steeples his fingers. 'Her gates were jammed open. The security system had been disabled and the surveillance hard drive taken. I found her mobile in pieces on the back patio.'

I remember Doug's searching hands. 'The LIC rep was looking for a drugs cache,' I say.

'Describe him to me.'

'Big mean guy called Doug Smeg. More 'roids in his system than is good for anyone.'

Anwar looks interested. 'Sounds like the go-between who arrived here Monday with an offer on Cute'n'Cuddly. He was representing a syndicate that preferred to remain anonymous — as did he; but we have him on camera.'

He opens Gail's I Spy screen set in the desk, and brushes it with a finger. Then he swivels the image my way and I'm looking at Doug Smeg sitting in Gail's front office.

'Yep.'

He flips the cover down. 'The deal was simple: cash upfront for a company in financial freefall. But their man was too self-interested to be just an intermediary. He informed us Neighbourly Watch had Gail and every person working for her targeted for "special attention", and, as a bonus if she agreed to the sale, he could make her problem go away. She didn't appreciate being treated to the same tactics the NW racketeers use on the hormone farms, and he left unhappy. I'd say that's when they decided to up the ante.'

My heart leaps in my ribcage at the thought of Gail still alive, then just as quickly bogs in a quagmire of terrible possibilities.

'They could have killed her by now.' I hate to think it, let alone voice it.

Anwar frowns down at his fingers. 'Mr Smeg must have got quite a shock when you showed up. But whether his news was the plan all along or a spur-of-the-moment decision, it made for an effective blindside and sent you away. You didn't call the police because you thought they'd been. No reason to mobilise a search, we begin to grieve — that is, until we can't locate her body.'

I leave my leaning post and plonk myself in the spare chair. 'This morning I got a package from Frank at the Good Bean,' I say quietly.

He nods. 'I know.'

'So Gail must have thought there was a chance of something like this happening?'

'She felt it necessary to cover every base. Frank was just acting according to her instructions. Her contact in NW will find out about our LIC representative, and how far up the food chain he really is.'

'What about our discovery at Ferguson's?'

'A dead end. We pulled out the surveillance equipment yesterday.'

'And the informant who told Gail about Barrow Road?'

'Even I don't know who that was. But it might be worth asking around the street racers again to check if they've seen or heard anything new.' He opens his mobile and copies a number onto a slip of paper then passes it across. 'Titania gave me her details.'

I suppress an arch comment about his superior people skills.

'She'll know how to find Skinny,' he adds. 'He and Lola would be the ones to get the word out to the rest, I imagine.'

I kick my heel slowly against the chair leg. 'I was meeting Marlene Bott at the Good Bean.'

'Oh?'

'She wants her love letters back.' Even now, discussing my boss's private life feels wrong.

Anwar is matter-of-fact. 'Gail mentioned she was getting some grief from an over-amorous party.'

Marlene had certainly showed her over-amorous side, but seemed more upset over the loss of what had supposedly been promised her than of her 'soul mate'. That's the fertility crisis for you. Her revelations about Gail selling her healthy eggs through a broker were no great surprise — viable ova fetch big money — but that my employer gave a toss who they ended up in is anathema to everything I know of her.

'Did Gail ever mention anything to you about wanting a baby?' I blurt, and Anwar looks genuinely shocked.

I take that as a no.

Feeling shaky and nauseous from no sleep, I go home for a kip. Late afternoon, I call Titania. Briefly I explain, and she gives me Lola's number.

Lola registers the urgency. 'Hold on a sec,' she says.

She's back fast. 'He says meet him under the Angels Gate Bridge in an hour.'

I thank her and ring off. Street racers being middle of the night types, I thought I'd have trouble winkling them out before dark.

By the time I get to Fishermans Bend, dusk has settled in all its nooks and crannies and Barrow Road is gloomy and forlorn, too many empty-socketed eyes facing across the river to the twinkling lights of humanity. Skinny parks his burbling monster — a different one to the other night, and a smidge more compliant with the emission laws, but still scaring the birds from their roosts in the concrete arches above.

Arm in arm with Lola, he strolls appreciatively around Albee's panel van, calling it 'my ride' despite assurances I'm just minding it for a friend.

'What's the stress?' he asks.

I tell him the situation with Gail, and describe Doug Smeg. He listens without seeming to, his eyes roving the unlit site, the street behind. Finally they come back to me.

'She special to you?' he asks of Gail.

'Very,' I say, and my chest hurts with an unsayable fear. I scribble down my mobile number and hand it to him. 'This is me, twenty-four hours.'

He passes it to Lola for safekeeping, and she pops it in her studded shoulder bag. If anything turns up, we can both trust her to remind him to call me.

'No promises,' he says.

That's good enough for me.

My mobile beeps in my pocket. I excuse myself. It's Ellie telling me to get myself to the hospital.

Albee has woken up.

Ellie beams at me from the far side of Albee's bed. Sarah is nearby, flicking through clipboard notes. All hospital decorum flung off, I rush over.

'Lazybones,' I say into his ear, and feel him chuckle.

I straighten towards Sarah. 'When? How?'

'We extubated him this morning. Usually there's some disorientation at first, but he came to very calmly.' She looks down at him. 'Wish they were all like you.' She moves his call button closer to his hand, then turns to us. 'His heart rate is staying nice and steady, so do me a favour and don't excite him.'

The three of us are left to our reunion. I can't stop smiling at my friend in the bed. His face has thinned to wan, but he's the same old Albee.

'We missed you,' I say. I take his hand in mine, holding it as if it might break. He seems so fragile beneath the crisp hospital linen.

Ellie pulls up the armchair. 'Don't you dare do anything like that again,' she tells him sternly.

Albee looks befuddled. 'What did I do?' he croaks, then winces, his windpipe still sore from the tube.

I glance at Ell then back to him, and go for the unadorned truth. 'You used some bad kit,' I say softly. 'Not just your average bad — stuff laced with pesticide.'

He takes in my words then closes his eyes. 'I don't remember ... it's all a blank.'

'Don't even try yet,' I say as he reopens his eyes and stares up at the hospital ceiling. 'When it comes back, we'll be here. You won't have to remember alone.'

His fingers squeeze mine weakly. Give him back his workshop with his beloved bicycles and the old assured grip will return in no time.

Sarah swishes back, and Ellie and I are shooed away. I go without trepidation, knowing his nursing team very well now and no longer terrified on his behalf every time his clothes have to be removed.

Ell and I head down to the hospital foyer, where I give her the news that Anwar thinks Gail is still alive.

'That's wonderful!' she replies, then her enthusiasm falters.

I draw her over to a seat by the florist's. 'Out with it.'

Her eyes are anxious, their blue-green framed perfectly by shoulder-length auburn hair. She's always had a genuinely unaffected beauty.

'Sarah says Neighbourly Watch has been keeping tabs on Albee, wanting to be notified when he wakes up.'

And now he has. My stomach takes an elevator drop. I don't want them asking Albee any questions.

'Ell, I think there's more to this than Albee making a mistake with his bedmates or his T. I'm trying to find out what happened, but until then we can't let them at him.'

Her look in reply is one of such immediate understanding, all the years of persecution still resident, that I want to loop a charm of protection around her for what she's suffered — and may yet — in the name of truth to self.

We hug goodbye, and she makes for the lifts while I quicken my step for the door, passing the usual huddle of smokers puffing their sick lives sicker. Funny how, with so many things declared immoral, this vice slipped through the policy net. But then, Nation First has never been averse to corporate sponsorship.

I walk along the road towards the van, thinking about Neighbourly Watch. There wasn't much they could do while Albee was in a coma, except get his address. So now there are two things I need to do before I go back home.

The security door to Bike Heaven is hanging open and Albee's flat has been completely trashed. I pick my way through the mess. They'd ignored the shopfront and workshop and come straight in here. It's a thorough job: every cabinet and drawer in every room emptied, the contents strewn. Was this the person who injected Albee covering their tracks, or Neighbourly Watch after evidence? It's lucky I took the kit that first night. Whoever did this would have found nothing.

Leaving, I tape over the shattered pane in the glass door and try to close the security screen — but it won't snib, the jamb chiselled away. All I can do for now is tape it closed too.

My second job is in Toorak.

Thanks to a contingency override set up by Gail, Anwar's and my ID codes verify automatically now at Checkpoint Charlie. The barrier begins to whine open, the guard not lifting his gaze from his TV screen. I wonder what his counterpart thought last night when the 'emergency' vehicles barrelled in and out. Not much, I guess. The world could explode both sides of the perimeter and these guys would still be sitting impassively in their sentry box minding the gate.

I clunk into gear and drive on. Albee's van, with its fluffy dice and shag pile carpet, is beginning to feel just a bit too comfortable. If I'm not careful, it's going to make me soft.

I re-enter my code on the number pad outside Number 5, and Gail's gates swing apart. The van bumps across the boundary towards the darkened house, the security lights triggering as I pull up.

The door to the portico is locked: Anwar said he'd secured the house. I get out the set of keys bequeathed to me. On the key ring is an engraved tag with the words CARPE NOCTEM. Gail's little joke, and the code for her alarm.

The beeping starts once I'm through the portico and inside the front door. I punch in the number equivalent of each letter and press 'Enter'. The beeping stops. Yay, me.

The sensor on the foyer lamp registers my presence and light pools out. The living area is peculiarly undisturbed, given what must have happened here last night. At the far end is a set of French doors opening to the back patio. I look out at shadows, thinking about Gail's broken phone and Marlene's love letters. I need to see for myself that the letters aren't somewhere in the house. As for the donor permission, this is where Marlene's story really jars. Or is it just that I don't want it to be true?

Gail being a minimalist, the ground floor is easy. I search to the back of every neatly organised drawer and cupboard, and then go upstairs. The cedar-framed window on the landing looks down onto a stand of almost leafless birches, winter come upon them in the few days since Nitro and I were strolling the garden.

I rifle through the desk in the study, knowing she'd never leave the important stuff easy to find — but then I'm assuming Marlene's letters weren't. After a quick check of the spare rooms, I enter the main bedroom, though I'm not comfortable doing it. Presuming Gail is still alive, her private space is exactly that.

Back down in the living room, I sit on the couch feeling thwarted, nothing to prove or disprove Marlene's assertions.

Mumbling expletives, I haul myself to my feet and go reset the alarm. In the portico I pause beside the roll-top bureau, reminded of Doug's fingers crawling like a fleshy pink tarantula through its contents. I slide back the lid. There's a pair of gardening gloves and secateurs, a stack of nursery labels, some pens and string ... Did I honestly believe I would find something those searching hands hadn't?

Marlene and her stupid letters.

Defeated, I squat on the outside steps, remembering Gail's will tucked in Frank's big apron. Nitro would have no qualms assuming ownership of the property, but to me this will always be my employer's house and I an interloper to privilege.

I stare at the line of terracotta urns. What had I imagined after Marlene flounced out of the Good Bean? Each missive arriving in Gail's letterbox; her walking back to the house knowing who it was from and chucking it.

I step onto gravel. Leaning over the urn closest, I shine the torch down inside — and let out a triumphant yip. Several envelopes are at the bottom. Not tied nicely together or wrapped for protection against the elements, but dumped in there like rubbish.

I use a stick from the garden to retrieve them: nine in all, addressed to Gail in a flowery script. Only one has been opened. Maybe it gave tone enough of the rest. There's a hint of scent. I bring it to my nose and time stops its beat. It's *that* scent, the one that wafted up from Albee's sheets the night he was rushed to hospital.

I'm up to the fourth letter, Nitro sitting like a pudding on the others laid out on my living room floor. Anger at Marlene vibrates in me like a wire. If she was at Albee's that night, she could have given him the OP-laced kit.

The night marches on. My body enters a twilight zone of exhaustion, rest something only other people get to do. Marlene, meanwhile, has gone from florid rehashings of her and Gail's sex together to incensed at having been ousted from her beloved's bed and removed from C&C's buyers list. This is not the cosy picture described to me in the Good Bean. It seems Gail didn't bother to reply, which really ramped her up.

Nitro comes over to butt my shin. I stroke his plush fur and pick up letter number six. Prurient fascination aside, I'm heartily sick of Marlene's manipulative tones, her confessions of undying love alternating with remonstrations over 'injustices suffered'. I skim-read six, seven and eight and open number nine.

It's in the last paragraph that she lets it slip. Nitro's purr machine pauses momentarily at my horrified '*Oh no*'.

Little wonder Marlene wants her letters back.

I ring Anwar, and after a short discussion we ring off. Next I text Marlene that I've found her correspondence and to meet me at the Shangri-La at 9 am. Then I crawl into bed with the cat, and sleep.

25

I don't know if Albee's ready for this, but I'm counting on the sense of smell being one of memory's most powerful triggers. With all nine of Marlene's letters secreted in my daypack, I'm walking in the entrance of the Jesu Christi Hospital under the cotton-ball pinks of yet another dawn to ask him, just out of a coma, to take a sniff.

Moved out of the ICU to a medical ward, he's in a room of four beds, his by the window. I enter quietly, but he's not asleep. He's propped up on pillows, his body free at last of tubes and machinery, Paul beside him in the vinyl armchair carted from the ICU.

Paul goes off to find coffee. I swish across the privacy curtains and pull up the chair, searching my friend's face for evidence he's strong enough.

'Albee, I want you to close your eyes and sniff something, then tell me what it reminds you of.'

He looks at me, amused, until he sees my seriousness. 'Not a pair of your smelly old cycling socks then.'

I laugh. 'Think yourself lucky.'

His eyelids flutter down trustingly. I draw one of Marlene's envelopes from my bag and waft it near to his nose as he breathes in, out, and in again.

Nothing.

I make a wad of five envelopes, the scent stronger. 'Try again,' I suggest, and he takes another sniff.

I'm thinking my idea is a stupid one when his brow furrows. 'Oh,' he says, and his eyes fly open. 'That's Marlene's scent.'

Bingo.

'I remember she was … We were fucking.'

'Albee!' I can't help myself. 'With *her*?'

Even someone freshly woken from a coma can look embarrassed. 'She's very attractive.'

'How could you have let her give you a jab?'

'Did I?' he asks, and my heart sinks.

'Please, Albee, is there anything you can recall beyond the fucking bit?'

He frowns, eyes unfocused to the past, the memory cogs trying to turn.

'She'd brought some T as a present,' he says. 'Told me it came special delivery from Gail. Normally I wouldn't, but I was due for a shot anyway, and the polyshell had EHg's logo on it. Not to mention I was already pretty far gone from what we were doing. She can turn the sex energy on like a solar flare.'

Marlene has never turned the flare my way — a small mercy for which I'm grateful — but there's no doubt it's a powerful talent, because she'd managed to bed not just one but two of my dear friends. I stuff the envelopes in my bag, anger rising. Even if she didn't know the kit she'd injected into Albee was dirty, she pretended ignorance to me about it in the Good Bean, which makes her a liar, and a coward for deserting him.

Albee seems suddenly drained. I lay my hand on his. 'I'm sorry to spring that on you.'

'Don't be,' he says. 'Ellie's told me what's been going on while I've been napping.'

I glance away, no words to describe the last few days. Looking back, I murmur, 'If anybody wants to know, you can't remember a thing, right?'

He nods. 'Find Gail,' he says.

Paul arrives through the curtains with coffee and raisin toast from the Tum-Tum Tree café. We sip and munch awhile, Albee gone very quiet beside us. I have a fair idea what he's thinking about.

'A busy Monday planned?' I ask him.

'No rest for the wicked. They want to get me up for a walk after the white-coat brigade's done its rounds. Meanwhile, Paul's going to contaminate my mind with subversive literature.'

When not chefing for a restaurant in the city, Paul writes potboilers for a flourishing underground press. He holds up a dog-eared paperback, the title *Knock & Drop* splashed blood-red across the front.

'Catchy.' I down the last of my coffee then check my watch. I have to leave.

As I bend to kiss Albee, he whispers, 'How's it going with Inez?'

I straighten. 'It's not.'

He regards me with serious eyes. 'You know what they say about people in comas being aware of everything going on around them? It's true. As one-sided as it must have seemed, I remember the conversation we had just before I woke up.'

It was the night I poured my heart out to him; the night I felt a flicker of movement in his hand. I get a flush of embarrassment.

'She hasn't answered her phone or replied to any of my messages since the argument.'

Albee looks at me sympathetically. 'Don't give up trying.'

At the end of the corridor, I see Sarah at the nurses station talking to the nurse unit manager. She falls into step with me as I head for the lifts.

'Just getting an update on the troublemaker,' she tells me. I hear affection in her voice. 'Seems he's going leaps and bounds.'

'You'll be keeping an eye on him then?' I ask hopefully.

'As long as the hospital board doesn't decide to rip up my contract. They're purging the current nursing list of suspected subversives, so we're having a staff crisis.'

'Will you be okay?'

'Yeah. I'm good at hiding my light under a bushel.'

We get to the lifts. I press the 'down' arrow, then turn to her. 'Now he's awake, I'm hoping to ask you another favour.'

She waits, understandably not jumping in to say anything yet.

'Ellie told me about the visits from Neighbourly Watch.'

She grimaces. 'As if we have the time ·or energy to kowtow to their demands. Some Nation First politician called up too, concerned about the poisonings. Luckily I could reassure him Albee was recovering, because the first two didn't. What's the favour?'

'Tell anyone who asks that he has amnesia and may never remember what happened to him.'

'No probs,' she says. She knows exactly who 'anyone' refers to.

The lift bell dings, the door opens. Inside, I watch the numbers light in descent.

Sarah gets out at Level 2. I suppose she thought it was going to be worse — like asking her to fake an entire family for the ICU visitors list. For that, and all the other things since, I can't thank her enough.

I'm walking to the tram stop on Temperance when I get a call from Geeta.

'Hope this isn't a bad time?'

'Not at all.'

'You asked me who I confided in,' she begins, and I slow my step. 'Nobody outside, like I said, but there was someone

256

from SADA. She vets applicants for the Ovum Recipient Program, so I didn't put her on the list I made for Tallis. We met for coffee a few times, then I stopped going.'

'Why do you want to tell me about her?'

'I feel guilty saying it, but she was a bit strange.'

'Tallis should hear this.'

'Could you do it?' She sounds so vulnerable.

'She'll need the details from you,' I warn.

'I know.'

I ring the SANE office while waiting at the tram stop, but get the answering machine, so leave a message for Tallis saying Roshani has some new information. I don't add that her fears of an internal leak may yet be realised.

The tram rolls up. I slip the phone into my jacket and board. Next stop Marlene at the Shangri-La. It's going to be an effort to stay cool and calm at this meeting, because inside I'm seething. Marlene's been stringing me along. Not only does the perfume on her letters now connect her to Albee and his brush with death, but in letter number nine she threatened that if she didn't get her donor permission, she'd wreak havoc on Gail's 'too perfect reputation' along with her 'bitch-faced broker's house of business'.

26

The Red Quarter is decidedly less atmospheric beneath the cover of an overcast sky. With the welcome lights at every entrance extinguished and the windows shuttered behind their metal bars, the buildings on Madams Row look worn out. Even the trees seem tired in their shawls of autumn leaves, ready to get on with winter hibernation. I try not to remember where else I'm supposed to be right now, heading to the Shangri-La for a showdown instead of my scheduled work appointment with Mojo Meg.

As I walk briskly along the Row, I see Marlene approaching from the other direction, her high heels tip-tapping and diamanté shoulder bag swinging on its strap. She gives a little wave, and we meet at the bordello's entrance.

'Oh, Sal,' she gushes, as I allow her first into the tiled portico. 'Thank goodness. I was so worried my silly love letters would fall into unscrupulous hands.'

No danger of that — now.

'I trust you didn't betray a besotted lover's confidences by reading them?' She laughs prettily but looks at me hard. 'And you found the donor permission to show Gail's broker? That's why we're here?'

'I thought you could sort it out with Savannah straightaway,' I reply. 'I'll vouch for your character.'

She's annoyed at that, but hides it in another gush of false gratitude. I lift the knocker and rap on the red door.

Savannah answers, a stilettoed figure in dominatrix black, and Marlene launches into a rehearsed spiel, vying with her host for most solicitous. I could tell her not to bother. Savannah's charm is built into her every atom, while Marlene's is a veneer as easily dissolvable as battery acid with bicarb.

I'm aware of two people arrived silently behind me: the Red Quarter protection team promised by Anwar. Marlene catches sight of them and swings around. Trapped all sides, it's dawning on her she's been set up.

She fixes on me. '*You*,' she says through her teeth.

The two usher her inside. 'No need to paw me,' she says to them, heavily aggrieved. 'I'm just a kitten among you predators.'

Yeah, a werekitten.

Down the corridor we go, Savannah leading, then into the kitchen, Anwar already sitting at the table. He greets Marlene courteously, but she decides to ignore him. Seems we have the haughty Marlene back.

The protection duo move together, seating her in one swift action before positioning themselves by the exits.

I'm impressed.

Savannah sits opposite Marlene, crossing her long black-clad legs. 'Let's discuss your letters first,' she says, and Marlene tightens her lips.

Haughty *and* unresponsive.

I take the envelopes out of my pack and lay them on the table, then go lean against the sink to watch the thing play out.

Marlene bristles with umbrage. 'I don't know why Salisbury tricked me here like this, but I've done nothing to deserve such harsh treatment,' she announces to the room.

Ever the innocent, ever the victim. The calm demeanour I'd promised myself completely cracks.

'You injected Albee with dirty kit,' I say hotly.

This is not where Marlene — or any of us — thought we were going to start.

She turns to me, horrified. 'I thought it was EHg's stuff.'

'But you didn't get it from Gail, did you.'

Marlene knows her letters have told all that, and more.

'I would have if I could!' she exclaims. 'But being made *persona non grata* and taken off her buyers list meant getting any of her precious product was like sucking blood out of a stone. That's what happens when you're no longer the famous Gail Alvarez's preferred lover. She was very cruel, you know, very heartless with my affections.'

So much for not speaking ill of the dead.

'Where did you get it then?' I ask.

'Someone came to the speakeasy offering T at a bargain price.'

My look of disgust elicits a retort.

'I'm not made of money,' she sniffs. 'I can barely afford the hormones for my own requirements. If a box of polyshells dropped off the back of a C&C delivery van, so what? I was angry with Gail, so I bought one. I thought it would make a nice present for Albee.'

'How kind of you. But you must have smelt the stuff was dirty before you gave him the jab.'

She looks suitably chastened. 'I may have got a whiff, but we were too far gone in our little seduction game to stop. We were in the throes of passion. He was begging for —'

I stop her there. 'I get the picture.'

Savannah intercedes, velvety smooth. 'Who did you go to for your own supply when Gail refused you?'

'Mojo Meg,' Marlene answers defensively.

'But BioPharm's goods are just as expensive as EHg's,' Savannah responds. 'How could you afford it?'

'She's been kind enough to give me a discount in return for a bit of industry gossip. Nothing important.'

I'll bet. 'So you sold Meg information in return for your hormone fixes,' I say angrily.

Marlene rounds on me. 'Do you think on the Glory Hole's wages I can afford to buy premium blend? Maintaining a fertility regime is very expensive, and using

EHg's products put me into debt. I asked Gail for a minuscule discount to help me cope, and she ditched me.'

I'm completely unconvinced. 'Maybe Gail ditched you because she didn't want to play yummy mummies with you. If you really want to get pregnant, why not make another arrangement with a different broker?'

'I've spent a fortune preparing my womb for this. I don't want just any old person's egg attached to it. Of course, I don't expect someone like *you* to understand about quality chromosomes.' She casts me a dismissive glance. 'Why would I settle for a bitzer when there's pedigree?'

I feel everyone in the room wince at that one. And she's yet to mention the quality of the other part of the baby equation: the sperm donor.

Anwar speaks, voice quiet. 'Marlene, you're here because we believe Gail didn't OD and isn't dead.'

I wait for her to exhibit shock.

Momentarily at a loss, she looks at us brightly. 'Well, that's wonderful news, isn't it?'

I'm outraged. 'Is that all you have to say?'

Savannah's expression is registering that she's had enough. As she unfolds her legs, the buckles on her leather corselet glint. One hand resting on the table, she leans over Marlene.

'You play the defenceless female because that's how you control the game; but you're going to tell us the truth now.'

'Get off me, you cow,' Marlene spits.

Savannah smiles, unfazed. 'I'm not the one you should be worried about. See those two strong silent types?' She motions to the protection duo. 'They're very good at control. And unless you tell us what you know, so we can find Gail and fix the mess someone's put her in, they'll be controlling your personal space twenty-four hours a day.'

Marlene huffs contemptuously, but she's gone pale beneath the pancake.

'They're excellent at what they do,' Savannah assures. 'While you're here they'll search and strip you of hormone patches and subdermal implants, then they'll escort you back to your house and go through your possessions. They'll remove every gram of kit, including all those pills and powders you've stashed for a rainy day. Next will be the beauty preparations that have obviously become necessary to your daily life. By the time they're finished, you won't even have a toothbrush. Nor will you be allowed to go out for replacements. You'll have to face the world without props or potions of any kind, as dowdy as a Hausfrau.'

Savannah's words are wielded like a whip. I remember the beautifully plaited set I'd seen in the parlour cabinet. No props needed here. Marlene is forced back in her chair as Savannah leans closer, her dominatrix alter emerging like a black moth from its chrysalis. Slowly she inspects Marlene's body.

'You've spent a fortune on surgery and hormones — I can see that. *Unfortunately*, once the supplements and special treatments are stopped, the effects will leach out of you like water through sand. That latest vaginal rejuvenation won't last; those breast implants we can have syringed out. Soon you'll be scrounging for old troche packs, fingering up the crumbs like a coke addict; but nothing will slow the withering on the vine.'

Marlene is looking decidedly sick, her bravado punctured. The Shangri-La's chess-playing madam — a practised observer of the human psyche — knows how deeply she's committed to the trappings of femininity.

Savannah presses harder on Marlene's weak spot.

'Oestrogen-deprived, your cunt will dry and your womb will shrink — such effort for nothing, so much money wasted. You'll be a washed-up vamp with all the sex appeal of road kill.'

Suddenly her tone changes. 'But that's just half the story,' she says silkily. 'Because shortly we're going to start injecting you with T. If you're *lucky*, we might even find a way to make it interesting, like you did for Albee.'

Marlene stares up at her, appalled. 'You wouldn't,' she squeaks.

Savannah smiles. 'Try me.'

Marlene's composure completely shatters. Collapsing onto the Shangri-La's kitchen table, a low wail comes out of her, winding into a caterwaul of anguish.

'Monsters! You don't know what it's been like, watching Gail take herself every month to Cutters Lane. Number 137 gets all her ova! How dare she sell to people she doesn't even know and not spare me a single egg. Is that fair? Is that caring?' Her voice scritches up the decibels. 'Since that stupid vaccine, I've been stuck like a genie half out of the bottle — and unlike *you*,' she stares straight at me, 'I don't enjoy it here. I deserve a full complement of my rightful hormones.'

I look at her face contorted by anguish and can't feel offended. After it got out about the additive in the vaccine, the reports were everywhere of premature ovarian failures and plummeting sperm counts. Then came mass panic, everyone trying to conceive or store their fertile eggs and seed before reproductive shutdown.

'We trusted them,' Marlene sobs. 'No side effects, they said. But what they did was criminal: they stole our parenthoods. I always assumed one day I'd have a baby. Then I couldn't even *buy* one from my fertile lover. What was wrong with bringing her down a peg or two to make her grateful that I would *want* to have her child?'

'What did you do?' I demand.

She stops sobbing. '*I* didn't do anything.'

'Tell that to Albee.'

She regards me from beneath her lashes. I realise how much she hates me.

Savannah signals and the protection duo move in. Marlene squeals, and Savannah holds up a staying hand.

'Let's try that again,' she says. 'Who's making Gail "grateful" right now?'

Marlene turns nervously from one unfriendly face to the next. 'If I tell you, will you keep those two robots away from me?'

The protection duo don't even blink.

Anwar responds. 'All we want, Marlene, is to get Gail back unharmed. Beyond that, we have no interest in you.'

She brushes ineffectually at a strand of hair that's escaped its stylish coiffure while he sits calmly opposite, the picture of mild containment, as if he's come visiting for a nice cup of tea.

He smiles encouragingly at her. 'Help us now, and that will be the end of it. Otherwise, I'm afraid …' He glances at Savannah then the protection duo, his meaning clear.

Her shoulders slump. 'His name's Doug Smeg — he's a Neighbourly Watch official,' she says almost inaudibly. 'He was very supportive after Gail dumped me.'

Anwar freezes at the name, but Marlene doesn't notice. She continues, eyes downcast.

'The batch of fake EHg kit was his idea. I just helped with the drop-offs in the city. He said if we gave Gail a bit of a shake-up it would make her more amenable to my situation.'

'And bring down everything she's built across the last ten years,' I cut in.

Marlene ignores me. 'All he wanted in return was the opportunity to be my sperm donor. He's very keen to continue the Smeg line.' A flicker of her old self reappears. 'Not that I'd ever burden a child with *that* dreadful surname.'

I want to gag in the sink. And someone should tell her that her own last name, Bott, isn't much of an improvement.

'Who supplied the kit?' Savannah asks.

Marlene chews on one plump, carmined lip. 'He said he had a mate working at a hormone farm who could provide the goods. I didn't ask how, or which one, and he wouldn't have told me anyway.' She looks up. 'But I swear on my grandmother's shroud the stuff wasn't meant to *poison* anyone. I went to him after the accident with Albee and he got all creepy — said he'd "sort" it. I could tell it wasn't in his plan. Something went wrong at the supplier's end. I told him I wanted out of the arrangement, but he convinced me that if I held my nerve a bit longer, he could persuade Gail to sign the donor permission. He just needed the chance to put his "unrefusable offer" to her without her minders around.'

I exchange looks with Anwar. She believed Doug would do all this just to be a daddy?

'You didn't think he might have been after something else from Gail?' I ask.

'Does it *matter*? He was my last resort.' She eyes the letters on the table, then me. 'Actually, I was expecting her to sic her bloodhounds on me over the last one of those; but she didn't …'

She hasn't worked it out yet that Gail never read it — just me. I don't enlighten her.

'So I agreed to get him through her gates,' she says.

I suppress an impulse to walk over and slap her. 'Gail wouldn't have let you or him on her property.'

Marlene gives me another dirty look. 'Says you. I rang her from the neighbourhood gate and said I could put things right between us by giving her some information I'd heard about the sellers of the fake stuff, if she'd just let me in. I'd already sob-storied the SOS guard into promising not to tell anyone I'd been there begging for forgiveness from my ex. He was an even easier mark than you, Sally — you're *such* a romantic. After that, all I had to do was smile at the camera and press my pinky to the pad.' She pauses. 'I was walking through her front gates when the ambulance and police cars sped in. He never told me that's what he was going to do.'

'Where did they take her?' Anwar asks for all of us.

'I *don't know*. I never even got to the house. Doug told me to go, and leave the rest to him. There was still a chance of getting the permission signed, so I did like he said and went to my shift at the Glory Hole. Then he rang to say Gail had been temporarily relocated, and to tell everyone there I'd heard she'd overdosed.'

So it's all been one big act. She got the kit from Doug, lied to Albee then me about what she injected him with, then mourned Gail's 'suicide' in the Good Bean. How can we trust a single word she says?

'Why the note in my jacket?' I glare at her.

'I panicked over someone finding my letters at Gail's and blaming me for what Doug might do to her.' She straightens in her chair. 'In case you haven't got it yet, he's not a man to be messed with. And you shouldn't be sitting here accusing me. You should be protecting me.'

On impulse, I reach for her diamanté bag and yank it off her shoulder. The contents upended on the table, I light on a small scent bottle. Pulling off the cap, I take a sniff. That perfume again.

'Not your usual,' I say drily.

The sly Marlene resurfaces. 'That one's for special occasions.'

'Like poison-pen letters and seductions involving organophosphate?'

She's unabashed.

'Why Albee?' I ask, voice tight. She has the capacity to crawl under my skin like a tick.

'It was fun. He was willing.'

'You nearly killed him!'

I can't believe that a couple of minutes ago I was almost feeling sorry for her about the infertility business.

'It wasn't my fault Doug's supplier spiked the kit,' she retorts. 'Albee was payback: you stole Gail from me, so I seduced your special friend.'

A look of triumph steals across her features. Savannah squashes it in one deft move.

'Since Salisbury didn't in fact "steal" Gail from you, we could balance up the issue of payback by starting you on your first shot of T straightaway,' she suggests, and Marlene recoils from her as if she already has the needle in her hand.

It's such a neat ploy, I almost laugh. Testosterone is the very antithesis of femininity to someone like Marlene.

Savannah capitalises on the shock. 'Doug never intended to negotiate the donor permission on your behalf. You must know that by now. He used you to get to Gail then ditched you,' she says flatly. 'You've no protection from him, or us. The only way out of this without *punishment* is to persuade him to hand her over.'

Marlene looks at her as if she's mad. 'Like he'll do it just because I ask.'

Anwar casually delivers his bombshell. 'It might help you to know we've located the hormone farm where Doug got his supply.'

I blink at him in surprise. Does he mean the results have come back from the soil-science lab?

'How could you?' Marlene asks, suspicious.

'What you distributed as EHg product had so many contaminants, a forensic analysis could pinpoint its place of origin,' he answers.

She's silent, digesting the news.

'You said yourself the poisoning wasn't in Doug's plan,' he reminds her. 'What will happen when that farm is outed anonymously by us as the source? Hormone farms may be endemic, but they're still illegal and their operators are punishable by law. The police will be required to investigate, no matter how influential the shareholders are. The shareholders, meanwhile, will come after the perpetrators. When they track down Doug — as they surely will — he'll throw *you* in their way to save himself.'

It's a scenario not hard to imagine, but leads me to another question Marlene can't answer. Why would Doug's supplier want to put an OP in the kit and bring their grand scheme crashing down?

'We're offering you the services of Gail's relocation network in return for your cooperation,' Anwar urges. 'Or do you want to live the rest of your life afraid, always looking over your shoulder?'

Marlene's gaze stays on the table, but I can see her wavering. How ironic if she ends up a client of Harry Tong, being the last to deserve his meticulous attention.

She looks up at Anwar. 'I won't be relocated to some outback shithole. My terms are a guaranteed supply of my hormones: regular deliveries, gratis.'

'That can be arranged,' he replies. 'If you help us now.'

She smirks at the protection duo, thinking she's turned the tables on them and Savannah. 'Then I'll do whatever you want.'

'Deal,' says Anwar. 'If there's anything else you've neglected to tell us, this is your chance.' He waits expectantly.

She brings two scarlet-tipped talons to her forehead in mock salute, and instantly I flash to the street seller in the Shangri-La's kitchen. The realisation drops. *She* was his nightmare, the one with 'bleeding' fingers. She gave him the kit to sell in the Red Quarter, but he remembered only her luridly painted nails.

'Nothing more to report, sir, Guide's honour,' our new recruit tells Anwar, and in my guts I know — we all know — she's lying.

27

A light wind has picked up and is hurrying the leaves from the trees along Madams Row. A cyclist scoots past: such a smooth, economical way to travel. Compared to that, walking is tedious. Next stop for me is the speakeasy and my bike locked in its storeroom. Even a day without it is too long.

'We don't think Doug's in it for the next generation of Smegs, do we?' I say to Anwar.

'That's assuming he can sire another generation,' he answers. 'The fear of ending up the last one in the family tree would be a powerful motivator for some. But no, I think Marlene wants a baby, and Doug is after an empire.'

The Doug Smeg Distribution empire. We know he got the idea from Marlene and the kit from a farm worker, but whose interests apart from his own was he representing when he came to Gail with the offer on C&C?

I shoot Anwar a quick look. 'And the proof we have identifying the hormone farm?'

'None. The tests came back inconclusive. It just had to sound plausible for Marlene, to keep her from doing any more damage.'

'So what now?'

'A proposition that Doug will go for — or information from someone that circumvents the need.'

Marlene's cooperation may be secured, but we still don't have the leverage we need to persuade Doug to give up Gail. Pity Miss Snooty isn't valuable enough to him to offer a prisoner exchange.

'What if Gail's been forced to sign over C&C already?' I ask.

'She'll hold out,' he replies quietly.

We part company just beyond the street's bollarded exit. It's a carryover from the pandemic days when the whole area was cordoned off as a plague zone. These days the barriers are left there to keep things out, not in, it suiting the Red Quarter's current residents to control the type of traffic moving through the enclave.

Anwar makes north for a pedal-taxi stop on Temperance, an empire to keep from the brink. I continue east, and ten minutes later am heading down Wickerslack Alley.

If Madams Row seemed worn out, then this laneway is exhausted. The brick is dingy, its graffiti old and uninspired, and every alcove exudes an unpleasant backstreet mix of body fluids. I pass someone sleeping under cardboard, a pair of bright yellow runners sticking out. A lucky find in a city bin? More likely a gift from the Salvos.

I round the corner to the hidden stretch of alleyway and the entrance to the Glory Hole. It's unlatched and unattended. I'm a bit surprised. Their security measures aren't usually so slack, the city rife with roving gangs looking for ways to express their surfeit of anger and disappointment.

There's no one in the coat-check nook. I take a quick look down the steps past the dance floor to Meg's alcove. The curtains are drawn back and it's empty. Lucky me.

Rosie is over at the bar, no sign of Trin. I stand at the entrance to the storeroom behind Rosie's usual doorkeeper's position — where my bike was and isn't now.

Rosie glances my way. I gesture to her and she hops off her stool. 'Sal!'

As she comes hurrying up, I look at her, heart in mouth.

'Where is it?'

'Sal —' she starts, then her eyes flick over my shoulder as both my arms are seized in an unfriendly grip.

'You took your time,' Merlyn says in my ear.

'Where's my bike, Rosie?' I ask.

'In our truck, like where you'll be next,' Sandy says as they haul me out the speakeasy door, my feet pedalling air.

'Help would be good,' I call to the Glory Hole's pierced and tattooed doorkeeper, who seems rooted to the spot.

'Don't go blaming her,' Sandy admonishes. 'We told her if she tried to help, we'd come back and break her Harley.'

The ride is super cosy, squeezed between my taciturn abductors in the cab of their sleek black cruiser. I manage to crane around and look through the window behind to check they weren't telling fibs. Three stars for honesty. My bike is there.

We don't ride far, gliding down Pilgrim Lane then into Scots Alley, pulling up outside the unmarked entrance of the Rob Roy. I'm surprised it's not the barrel vaults of Prestige Couriers. Then I remember who owns the pub.

We enter to stale air and dim lighting, no help to be had through windows thick with grime. There's a scatter of punters slumped in various stages of alcoholic decline. If I spent my daylight hours in this place, I'd end up that way too.

Cam polishes glasses behind the bar. If he sees the three of us enter, he doesn't acknowledge it. The Rob Roy is strictly a mind-your-own-business place. I wonder how many deals made under duress he's turned a blind eye to.

Prestige Couriers' head girl sits in the same booth as last time, dressed in a navy blue blazer and matching skirt and doing business with two trucker types. We wait while Meg wraps up and they shake hands. As the two heft by me to the door, I spy an Australia Post insignia on their shirts.

Meg motions to us. Merlyn slides first into the bench seat opposite her, then Sandy inserts me before seating her own bulk.

'A rose between two thorns,' I say chattily.

No one smiles.

'Not at work this morning, Salisbury,' Meg says. 'Problem with the alarm clock? Or a sudden change of heart?'

'My heart was never in it,' I answer. 'And now my probationary period has expired, I've decided not to take the job.'

'You forget: you're mine already.' Her voice is hard as flint. 'I bought you. You work for Prestige Couriers and BioPharm now.'

'I'm nobody's,' I say angrily. 'I *chose* to work for you, even though you made it rather hard to refuse. And you can have the advance you foisted on me back in full — the money's still in the envelope.'

I no longer care about Crusher and Snarl making origami of my limbs, or Meg, piranha-like, devouring what's left of my tattered reputation. She's been swapping kit for information with Marlene, happy to sit back and watch Gail go down.

Meg looks like thunder. I'm saved by her mobile buzzing on the tabletop. She answers it, her expression going from angry to incredulous. After a few curt words, the phone disappears into her navy blazer.

She regards me for an overly long moment. 'Anwar Mustafa has just told me some extremely interesting news, which I believe you're aware of already.'

It's just a tiny bit satisfying to see that the Mistress of the Compendium doesn't know everything, after all.

'*If* he can get your other party to bring his prize to the table, I've agreed to the Glory Hole being the location of proceedings. Of course, Mr Mustafa will owe me. Nothing for nothing. I'm sure he's eminently capable of handling the situation without a fuss, but I have it in mind to keep you with me as surety against losses.'

No way! My body's electrics begin to fire off distress signals like scattershot, every fibre in me clamouring for escape, but with Meg's heavyweights placed each side, there's nowhere to go — except under the table.

My captors grab at me, but get a handful of my jacket instead, which I manage to Houdini out of. Then I'm crawling cockroach-like from the booth and bolting for the exit.

Outside, I dash to the rear of the truck and wrench on the doorhandle. It opens. I thrill with relief. My abductors were so preoccupied with me that they forgot to lock their vehicle. I drag out my bike, praying it hasn't been damaged, and look to the Rob Roy's entrance. Why aren't they snapping at my heels? It's too good to be true. Meg must have told them not to bother.

I start running triathlon style, sticking one foot in the toe strap nearest and swinging the other leg over the frame. My hands glove to the fit of the handlebars and I assume racing position, swishing down the alley then left onto Pilgrim Street. Dodging pedal cars and slow-lane cyclists, I speed east, the wind a cleansing cool on my face, thoughts rushing through me like water in a sluice gate.

Meg and Marlene's *quid pro quo* — hormones for information — has to be how Meg got wind of the insider sabotaging Gail's business. She saw Marlene's obsession had taken a nasty turn, and suspected her of deeper involvement, then used that to try to sway me into throwing my lot in with Prestige Couriers and spilling the beans on C&C's buyers list.

Barrelling left into a laneway, I begin to dogleg north.

So why now offer up the Glory Hole as the venue for our hoped-for exchange with Doug? Maybe because she likes to know everything about everyone, and this way she's assured a box seat.

I ride into my street — and a brawl outside my house. The team of two organised by Gail to watch the property are hustling someone in a prayer shawl to their vehicle. A hysterical someone.

'Sal!' she cries when she sees me.

I tell them it's my sister and they stop, nonplussed.

One holds up a rock. 'She was about to lob this through your front window, this on it.' In his other hand is a piece of paper. I don't need to read what's printed there.

'*You* did that?' I say to Helen. 'And the other ones?'

She looks at me beseechingly. 'I need to talk to you — in private.'

With reticence the pair release Helen, and tell me they'll be outside if I need them.

Key turned in the lock, I push on my front door. This will be the first time my sister has stepped into my home. Nitro cruises up, his tail wafting like a lure, but she hardly notices. I don't bother to introduce them.

I confront her in the living room.

'So you put that note under my door the other day. What about before that? Did the prayer group just happen on me at the Good Bean, or have you had them follow me around?'

'You're not hard to predict,' she replies. 'You've been going to that café every Saturday for years. You even tried to take me there once.'

I think back to my failed delivery in Cutters Lane. 'And the attack in the Red Quarter?'

'The Red Quarter?' She frowns. 'I don't know anything about that.'

I feel like my head is going to explode. 'Just tell me. Why the rocks and cryptic messages?'

'I couldn't think of any other way to scare you,' she replies simply. 'I thought if you knew the prayer groups were targeting you, you'd stop couriering and lie low for a while.'

'*Why?*'

She doesn't answer, just stares, unseeing, at the cat. Then she says, 'If Michael finds out I've come here, he'll kill me.'

Her face crumples. I lead her to my couch while Nitro heads for the safety of the bedroom, a doona to commandeer.

She bends forward and grips her knees. 'I lost my baby, Sal,' she blurts.

'You were pregnant?' I ask, incredulous, and she shakes her head. I'm afraid she's going to clam up again.

I sit by her. 'Helen, if ever there was a time to talk to me, now is it.'

She gathers herself to speak, not looking at me.

'After the vaccination drive, when we were both still fertile, Michael and I made deposits in the Family Health cryo-banks. Preserving sperm or ova was frowned on by Saviour Nation's worship leaders, but it wasn't forbidden.' She fingers the rough fibres of the prayer shawl fallen from her shoulders. 'I would never have considered going against the NF edicts once it was denounced as an unnatural practice, but Michael discovered how attractive politicians who have children are to the voting public. It was his suggestion we enter a surrogacy arrangement and I fake my pregnancy. I'm ashamed to say I leapt at it. I've wanted this for so long …'

The tears begin to flow. I find a box of tissues and place it by her, then go lean on the wall beside my bookshelf. I've never seen her like this.

'We were about to announce our miracle, and how I'd be going somewhere quiet for my confinement — pregnancies are so risky these days — when the surrogate miscarried and I lost my little girl.' She breaks into another round of sobs. 'Now Michael thinks he'll lose his seat to his running mate who's a fertile with three kids.'

'When was this?' I ask.

'A week ago.'

A week ago I was hauling Geeta off the pavement.

I stare at her.

'Was it you crying on Madams Row last Thursday?'

She nods. 'I'd just been given the news by the broker.' She pulls a tissue from the box and blows her nose. 'For you of all people to come past on your bike …'

The eerie wailing in the Shangri-La comes back to me. 'Your broker is Savannah Rose,' I say quietly.

She gives me a quick, surprised look then nods. We're both silent.

'So why try to stop me from couriering?' I ask again.

'To get you away from Gail Alvarez before it was too late.'

I jolt. I've never hidden the fact I bike courier, but how does she know I work for Gail?

'Too late for what?'

'You think I'm closeted from the real world, as if being a politician's wife is all tea and scones,' she accuses. 'But you don't know anything about my life, or what Michael's been involved in outside the church and Nation First. *His* baby is a syndicate called Gateway Enterprises. He calls it his retirement fund.'

I search my memory banks for where I've heard the name before.

'They specialise in company buy-outs: driving the target company down, then stepping in while it's in freefall and offering the owners a quick exit, cash upfront. Then they repackage it and sell it at a profit. Cute'n'Cuddly was their latest target, but something went wrong. Then Michael had a big argument early yesterday with his go-to guy, a disgusting man called Doug Smeg.'

I come off the wall so hard I shake the bookshelf.

'You've met him then,' Helen says drily. 'He did something — I don't know what — that puts everything at risk. Whatever bad things you think about Michael, Doug's the one you should watch out for.'

'How do you know all this?'

'The phone calls and meetings were held in Michael's den at home. I'm not a snoop, but I heard things — like, for instance, that *you* work for Gail Alvarez's distribution business. You have to understand, Michael will do whatever it takes to protect himself and his position in the party, and he's going to use its full force to go after Doug. It'll end up a massive exposé to make Nation First look good and Michael squeaky clean. Doug and Gail will be set up as collaborating in some greedy scam linked to the products of a hormone farm.' She pauses. 'Whatever else you do apart from deliver soft toys, I don't care, but I don't want you rounded up like a criminal with the rest. Our family has been through enough.'

I chill. 'So this is really about saving family face?'

She looks at me. 'Sometimes I've wished you weren't family — it's been so hard, living with the shame. But this is different. I won't let that psycho hurt you.'

I'm guessing she means Doug.

'Michael is very fastidious.' Helen starts shredding her soggy tissue. 'He records all his phone conversations in case he needs to use them against someone. They go on a jump drive in a locked drawer of his desk. When things went wrong and the buy-out of Cute'n'Cuddly stalled, he was going to pull the plug, but Doug wasn't happy about that at all. Whatever he did next, Michael went ballistic about it over the phone.'

My thoughts race. Could 'things going wrong' have been the poisoned kit, but Doug wouldn't give up his dream of the Smeg Empire?

'I think I know the reason why Michael went ballistic,' I say to her. 'Saturday night, Doug abducted Gail.'

Her lips press together. 'That would do it.' She contemplates me a moment, then produces a key from her pocket. 'This is to a numbered box at the GPO on Beatitude Street. In it are the phone files that link Michael — and Doug — to Gateway and its activities. I told him Doug came to our house this morning and took the jump drive.'

My breath catches. 'You'd organise something like that?'

She gets a strange expression. 'I did it all by myself.'

She's right: I don't know my sister any more.

'Michael's trying to work out how to get the files back from his ex-collaborator, who doesn't have them.'

'So it'll be your word against Doug's?'

'Yes.' She hauls off the couch and hands me the key. 'Sal, I need this — and you do too, now. If Michael's vendetta against Doug goes ahead, it'll destroy Gail's company, and I'll be seen by SADA's brokers as too high a risk to enter another surrogacy arrangement. But while Michael thinks Doug has the evidence to damn him, he won't go public. Our family will be protected, and the fertility centres won't refuse me another chance.'

She gets a pen from my bookshelf and writes a number on the back of my hand. 'Nobody deserves to be at the mercy of Doug Smeg. Use the information on the jump drive to negotiate for your boss.'

I gape at her as she turns for the door.

'I have to get back,' she says.

I'm not sure that's such a good idea. 'Why not stay somewhere —'

'I'll be alright.' Her smile is bitter. 'Michael doesn't think I'm capable of independent thought, let alone subterfuge.'

The surveillance two are still outside the gate as promised. Their job here over, I ask if they'll drop Helen at a train station, and then watch as their vehicle turns off down the street, my surprising sister sitting in the back.

I go inside and retrieve my APV jacket from the back of the wardrobe. When Helen mentioned Michael's syndicate, I suddenly thought of the documents I'd taken from the office shredder at Greengate Farm. With everything that happened afterwards, I'd forgotten all about them.

I unfold the wad. The name Gateway Enterprises is familiar because it's written in bold at the top of the front sheet. Beneath is a memo of agreement between Gateway and Greengate to 'open up new avenues of distribution' for the farm's produce. Safe to assume they're not talking about milk.

I ring Anwar and tell him I know how we can persuade Doug to the speakeasy with Gail.

28

Darkness from a rolling power outage follows me through the city like a wave. I wheel my bike past Rosie's Harley — still intact — out in Wickerslack Alley and, in a display of trust I only partly feel, allow her to stash it again in the Glory Hole's storeroom for safekeeping. Anwar arrives, and he and I go to set things up with Trin.

Monday night is a muted affair, patrons talking softly in huddles, music low. The evening inches towards the appointed hour. After I'd collected the jump drive from the Beatitude Street GPO, Marlene, watched by the Red Quarter protection duo, had rung Doug with a message from Anwar suggesting a swap: Gail for Michael's incriminating phone files. Now, Anwar is out on Pilgrim Lane in the van and Rosie's in her usual position at the door, and I can't help scanning every walk-in for Inez; but no one's seen her here the last three days.

The protection duo turn up next with Marlene for her shift, and Gabe is sent happily home. Savannah's threatened austerity measures shelved for now, Marlene is dressed to the nines, more paste and sparkle than a Miss Universe entrant. Back in her cloakroom domain, she sounds like her old self, a string of cutting remarks aimed squarely at her minders seated each side of her.

Downstairs, the speakeasy's two resident tough guys are arms folded and stance wide outside the closed curtain of their boss's alcove, signalling she's in. Clearly Meg has decided to wait it out with us — after all, she has a proprietor's interest and a ringside seat. Her minders ignore me. It doesn't exactly break my heart, although I'd like to ask them for my jacket back sometime.

Eleven o'clock gone and twelve approaching, there's still no sign of Doug. The stress is cycling through me. What if he doesn't show?

My mobile beeps once. The signal from Anwar.

A commotion starts at the door. Our guest is here, but with the wrong company. Rosie shouts a warning down the stairs as Doug enters brandishing his Neighbourly Watch badge, five puff-jacketed Neighbourhood Values brigaders in tow.

Mr Smeg has pulled a swifty. What a surprise.

I cross the dance floor, intercepting him at the bottom of the stairs. He plants his bulk in front of me, his NW-issue taser holstered, his belt slung low like a cowboy's.

'Well, Salisbury, we meet in the unfriendly hours again.'

I feel like I've been thrust into the OK Corral. 'Where's Gail?' I demand.

He slaps a hand to his forehead. 'I knew I'd forgotten something. Show me what you have that's worth my visit, and I'll go see if I can find her.'

'I don't remember the posse being part of the deal.'

'Don't worry about them. They're here for a fun night out. Oblige me with the incriminating evidence and my people will stop bothering yours.'

The Neighbourhood Values Brigades are famous for their bothering. 'Are they in on your scheme?' I ask him.

'That lot?' He harrumphs derisively. 'Led by the nose on the sniff of coinage.'

Marlene's nook is being searched: I can hear her indignant squawks. The protection duo must be gritting their teeth, trying to look ineffectual.

'This is harassment of law-abiding citizens,' I say.

He glances casually around. '"Law-abiding" is a bit of a stretch, don't you think?'

I follow his gaze. Under Nation First's expanded anti-transgression laws, all of us here are offenders. Those from the couches and the bar area have been herded onto the dance floor, while Trin, an expression of distaste on his face, is both hands on the counter, being stood over. I admire his forbearance. If he wanted to, he'd have the guy on the floor screaming for mercy.

Two brigaders are whipping back the curtains to the alcoves, their search nearly at where Sandy and Merlyn stolidly maintain position. Last minute, Meg's minders step aside and the brocade is flung open — to an empty booth.

Meg knows better than anybody the escape routes built into the speakeasy's architecture. The wheelchair cubicle in the allsex toilets has an exit onto Sailors Walk, a passageway that doglegs to the river. With just enough space to walk — or wheel — between buildings, it's a quick getaway that I've used myself on occasion.

Doug returns his gaze to me, feigning disappointment. 'I'm beginning to suspect you've nothing to parley with.'

My peripheral vision registers Sandy and Merlyn moving closer.

I look at him and shrug, my hands open in mock regret. 'Not without Gail.'

'Like that, is it?' He tsks and taps his wristwatch. 'Oh, dear: just gone midnight. My people won't be happy, what with the place being open after curfew.' A half-dressed couple are ousted from an alcove. 'Not to mention lasciviousness in a public place, contravening Nation First's code of moral conduct.'

Those on the dance floor are being patted down for contraband, but unless anyone's ignored Trin's advice circulated earlier about suspending all transactions for tonight, Doug's lackeys will find zip.

'Your turn next,' Doug informs me.

I don't want any of those clumsy hands on me: who knows where they've been. Besides, I have the jump drive tucked under my chest wrap. I shift my weight to ease the tension building in my body, and measure the distance to the door while Doug surveys the room, pleased with what he sees.

'This venue isn't currently an NW-listed hotspot,' he says, 'but I could fix that. On the other hand, we could conveniently forget the address if you'll 'fess up that you're fibbing.' He gives me a pitying, supercilious look. 'I saw your mate in his van. Does he think I'll be so convenient as to lead him to his boss? You can tell him from me he'll be out of a job soon.'

'Not if Michael Bannister, can help it,' I reply. 'I heard the recording of what he said when you told him you'd taken Gail. Speaking of "your funeral", what was with the death-by-OD scenario at her house?'

'A moment of inspiration falling from above,' he replies mildly.

'You bastard.' I want to slug him one for telling cruel untruths. Instead I say, 'What *fell* was Marlene.'

He frowns at that. 'Miss Tell-it-all. She has a thing for people in positions of power — but I'm sure you know that. The night I first spied her at the Neighbourly Arms, it was packed with NW and Nation First heavyweights. She could have hooked onto any of them with that arsenal of charms, but I got in first and so it was me she poured out her troubles to.'

All roads lead to Marlene. How easy her betrayal of Gail was.

'She must have been desperate choosing you.'

That cuts. He smiles. 'I pumped her for information — forgive the crude pun — and she told me what Ms Alvarez puts inside her fluffy animals. She told me about *you* as well. Mainly how she doesn't like you. I convinced her I could be a helping hand, and she bought it.'

'Not just your hand helping,' I retort.

'If you have the goods, and the equipment to deliver them … Imagine: Douglas Smeg Junior!'

'Why can't I picture you as the fatherly type?'

He leans in confidingly. 'Because I'm not. But the head of a hormone distribution company, now that really rings my bell. There could even be a place for you in the new arrangement if you play your cards right.'

I can't hide my disgust. 'So Plan A was to wreck EHg's credibility then buy C&C at a knockdown price so you could start it up again as Doug Smeg Enterprises. Did it include poisoning the clientele?'

He looks momentarily dangerous. 'That cock-up was none of my doing. My flaky accomplice threatened to spit the dummy over it, and consequently Plan A was ditched for Plan B.'

The brigaders are nearly on me. I pull the jump drive from my wrap and wave it at Doug.

He makes a grab for it, but he's slow and heavy and I'm not. I sidestep and catch Trin's eye.

Trin executes a lightning twist and hammers down once on his guard. The guy drops, screaming, and the room erupts, the compliant crowd now an angry mob. It helps that a number of them are Red Quarter protection team plants, supplied compliments of Savannah. Doug's lackeys suddenly find themselves surrounded by those they've just rudely searched.

Sandy and Merlyn swing into action. Their display of menace temporarily distracts Doug — and for good reason: it's aimed at him. He tries to draw his taser, but Sandy has him wrapped in her big meaty arms. I power up the stairs as Merlyn stands eyeball to eyeball with him, casually unbuckling his gun belt.

Doug twists in Sandy's embrace, seeking me out, then redoubles his efforts when he spies the incriminating evidence about to leave the building.

My mobile vibrates in my pocket. Not Anwar. I press it to my ear. It's Skinny.

'Got something you might wanna know, Andy Pandy. Macca's squeeze told Lola she saw an ambulance parked in a factory yard a couple of nights ago.'

I stop. 'What factory?'

'End of Pleasance. Place with a brick chimney. I took a squiz up there half an hour ago on my way to the meet, and saw someone leaving in a brown eco-lite — one of those enviro-friendly shitheaps some people call a ride. Could be your guy.'

I say a speedy thanks and ring off. A brown eco-lite drove into C&C last Monday when I was with Gail on her warehouse roof. Monday was also the day Anwar said Doug turned up with the buy-out offer.

I press Anwar's number. 'I think he's got Gail at Ferguson's.'

'See you there,' says Anwar.

Rosie is raining blows on the NVB hack pulled from Marlene's coat-check nook. I wonder if he thinks the after-hours entertainment is worth the promised pocket money now. I dodge them, making for the storeroom and my bike, shouting at Marlene's minders to leave her — after all, she chose hormones over protection.

'Sal, wait!' Marlene calls, and I pause.

'You'll need this,' she says in a breathy rush. She produces a key from her cleavage, that pillowy wonder barely contained in its shiny scoop top. 'It's the office spare.'

For a beat I don't know what she means, then it dawns on me. The new lock on the paint factory's upstairs room. So this is what she was holding back from us at the Shangri-La. She's known all along where Doug's been hiding Gail.

Deceitful bitch.

As I try to take the key from her, she snatches back her hand. 'I come with it,' she says determinedly.

I have no time to deliberate. 'Grab her and go!' I cry to her keepers. 'She can show you where.'

I'm already sprinting past them with the bike. Anwar and the protection team will be slowed by traffic cameras and construction sites. Not me. My way is much faster: no cameras, no detours, no road rules.

I glance back down the stairs to Doug at the epicentre of a mêlée, and suppress the impulse to laugh. He'd planned on a bit of NVB monstering to take what he came for, but now he's been detained by two experts in the threat department. Meg must have told Sandy and Merlyn to get in his way if things got messy. It's the first time I've ever had reason to thank the Glory Hole's unsympathetic proprietor for her help.

29

I am a machine, legs and lungs pumping, body tucked flat and low, eyes on the route ahead. Speeding along the city streets, a shadow with lights and reflectors flashing, a savage joy ripples through me. Adrenaline courses, quicksilver, in muscles and ligaments, joints and skin, and I feel nothing of the cold, the dark, the jolting surfaces. Tuned to the immediate, a kinetic fusion of parts, I am complete: this moment surely what I was made for.

I hunker down for the descent across Saviour and the pathway under the rail viaduct. Then I'm out and hugging the curves of the cycle track through the Docklands. The city is deserted, thanks to Sunday curfew. It gives me the perfect run. I whirr by fenced excavations, KEEP OUT signs wired to the chain-link. I'm no bigger than an insect to those concrete sentinels blotting out the western sky, each empty shell in its neglected place a testament to the human will and the desire to create — and the power of misfortune to take away.

I ease onto the pedestrian bridge and across the Yarra, its ink of cold rising from below. Barely a light shows on the other side, that black-swathed tract of industrial land become a foreign shore.

I move through the gears and grind on. The first peak of adrenaline fades; the second kicks in.

I'm on Barrow Road. The next turn is Pleasance. To my left, lights follow the arc of the freeway one kilometre away, its massive concrete girders rising slowly to the Angels Gate Bridge. I veer and Ferguson's brick chimney is dead ahead, a lodestone drawing me in.

A final burst of speed and the factory looms large, windows glinting beneath the black serrated roofline. As I angle steeply into the driveway and bump across the boundary, the rear tyre explodes and the wheel slides from under me. One foot wrenches painfully out of a toe strap, and then I'm down and skidding with the bike. The boundary fence stops my momentum, but not before I've shredded clothing and lost skin.

No time to assess the damage, I lift the bike and lay it behind the gate stuck partway across the entrance. The front light releases easily from its handlebar clamp. I drop the helmet and begin to sprint.

Anwar's van is parked out the back beside a stack of rusty drums. I flash some light on the factory window, no need this time to climb through: the door next to it yawns ajar, the lock hanging off splintered wood. Anwar's handiwork — I hope.

I'm about to cross the threshold when a vehicle noses around the corner. Not an eco-lite. The protection duo step out with Marlene and join me.

I make a quick check of the storeroom before stealing along the corridor, the others close behind. We enter the factory space and fan out, torches veiled, moonlight filtering through the roofline panes. I glance back to the square of glass that's the office window, then scan the mezzanine level with its row of squat emulsion tanks and feed lines dangling like entrails to the mixing bowls below.

No sign of movement. I take the key from Marlene's unresisting hand.

I'm halfway up the metal stairs when the door swings open and Anwar steps onto the landing wielding a crowbar.

My heart leaps into my throat. 'Anwar, it's me.'

He lowers the weapon.

Gail appears, and relief floods through me. I launch myself clumsily up the remainder of the stairs.

Anwar reaches up to a lantern hanging from a sprinkler pipe and the gantry is revealed in an uncompromising light. Gail runs a hand across her jaw. I see the marks on her cheeks from where she's been gagged.

'How excellent to see you, Salisbury,' she says. Then, 'You're bleeding.'

'Fell off my bike,' I say ruefully, and she raises an eyebrow.

I grin like a fool — until I remember who's about to arrive. 'Doug and the others will be here any minute.'

Neither of them seems overly perturbed. 'I've been making arrangements for that,' Anwar replies. Confused, I glance down to Marlene. Her chaperones have mysteriously disappeared.

A figure steps into the factory space, torch beam flashing. The beam fixes on her.

'That's my favourite frock, Marlene — bit nippy for it tonight, though.'

Marlene and her frock together with Doug tweaks a memory in me of the service alley beside the Neighbourly Arms, Marlene captured in my mind's eye, *in flagrante*. I realise Doug was the other in the clinch. Little wonder he looked familiar that night at Gail's.

As I descend the steps, three NVB lackeys emerge from the corridor. The other two are probably guarding the entrance. Coming straight from the speakeasy relieved of their tasers and nightsticks means they've calculated good odds for themselves. Maybe they didn't pay enough attention to Marlene's departure with her two buddies.

Doug's gaze goes from me to the gantry, Gail there next to Anwar still holding the crowbar. He speaks almost lazily. 'Here's a turn-up for the boys back at HQ: three curfew-breakers loitering suspiciously on private property, one with a weapon.'

Plan B a failure, he's reverted to his official role.

Marlene makes her move. 'Doug, I'm so glad you've arrived. I hope you don't think it was me who brought these people here. They found out all by themselves.'

I want to smack her for oh so many reasons. The innocent act may be her last desperate throw of the dice, but surely she doesn't think he'll buy it?

The answer is in a curt 'Shut it, Marlene.'

Mr Perspicacious.

Doug turns to the nearest of his lackeys. 'Get the others.' To the other two he says, 'Search that one.'

That one would be me.

Right on cue, the protection duo return hauling a slumped figure each. They prop the bodies against a wall then go stand in the exit.

'I was going to warn you about them before you so rudely interrupted me,' Marlene snipes.

Doug's three shift uneasily and look to their ringleader. He probably told them this would be a simple job, easy money. But with the humiliation at the speakeasy and now the change of odds, their thoughts are clear as neon: easy money is slipping from their grasp.

As Anwar and Gail gingerly make their way to the factory floor, I walk up to Doug. It's all I can do not to take a swing at him.

'We'll pass on the offer of a trip to Neighbourly Watch Central,' I tell him. 'Here's your insurance policy.' I shove the jump drive into his hand. *For Gail, and my sister.*

He pockets it, surprised.

'Michael believes you stole it from his house. My advice is, run with that. We all want a happy ending, so if you and your goons leave, we'll consider our grievances null and void.'

The protection two move obligingly from the exit, but Doug shows no sign of leaving.

He sneers at me. 'Tough talk, coming from a skinny-arsed genderbender. I wonder does that swagger of yours match up to reality?'

I stare at him. I didn't know I swaggered.

I'm worried he's about to pull another swifty when I hear it — and so does everyone else. A rumbling in the distance, like a battalion of tanks.

The rumbling turns throaty. The tanks have V8 engines and exhaust modifications. The sound rolls along the street and enters Ferguson's lot, burbling up the service road then around the back, the side, the front, until the entire building is reverberating. As the smell of petrol seeps in, I want to rush excitedly to a window and hoorah like a kid: Skinny has brought the street armada to Ferguson's.

The circle complete, engines idle soupily. Then the horns start up a tooting, shrieking cacophony. Engines rev again and blatt more fumes, then cut out. It's eerie, the sudden silence, as if all the air has been sucked from the building. Transfixed, we wait.

Skinny saunters in.

His racing leathers are a patina of famous brand names and fancy stitchwork; his metal-toed boots clip loudly on the concrete. Instinctively he seems to know who the protection duo are, and gives them a deferential racer's salute. They return his gesture with nods.

'Andy Pandy.' He grins roguishly at me and winks at Gail, then claps Anwar on the back like an old friend. Swivelling to Marlene, he treats her to a fast once-over. 'Who's the show pony?' he asks, and she huffs offendedly.

'The one with the key,' I reply. 'Not that we needed it.'

Skinny fixes finally on Doug. 'And here's Mr Important.' He struts over, facing off with his opposition even though he reaches only to the other's shoulder. 'My cavalry is bigger than yours,' he says.

Doug is circumspect enough not to reply. His offsiders have edged away from him. They take a few more steps backwards then seize their chance, retreating down the corridor. No one moves to stop them.

Outside, a cheer goes up and the horns ring out their strident tones again. The three are running the gauntlet of the street racers. If they get through the circle, it'll be a long walk back to the city.

A different sort of din starts out front, accompanied by more shouts. There's the clang of metal on metal, and smashing glass.

Skinny cocks his head at Doug. 'Mate — you're gonna need a new ride after tonight.'

He turns to us. 'When your business is done here, come tell me.' Then, boots and buckles jingling, he exits the building.

Gail limps off the bottom rung of the stairs.

'I'm sure Doug won't mind me saying we've had some rather intense discussions here,' she says. 'But while the conversation was scintillating, I'm afraid the accommodation was below par.' She looks at our sparkly turncoat. 'We spoke at length about you, Marlene, and I've had time to consider your needs. Doug brought me some documents to sign —'

Marlene is already dashing up the stairs, which puts paid to any theory I might have about high heels inhibiting their wearer's capacity for speed. I hear the office filing cabinet drawer being slid open.

Gail continues. 'A legally binding agreement …'

Marlene returns to the landing, brandishing a sheaf of papers.

Gail lifts her gaze. 'For a transfer of ownership.'

Marlene stills, not sure what's coming.

'What did he tell you?' Gail asks her from below. 'That they were my embryo-transfer documents and as the recipient you needed to sign too? Did he make you do it *blindfolded*? Because what you signed — as a witness — was the handover of Cute'n'Cuddly Pty Ltd to Doug Smeg Enterprises.'

Marlene shrieks her disappointment and flings the papers over the railing. Several sheets flutter down. I pluck one from the air and shine my bike light on it. A page of legalese in tiny print. It could be anything.

'Well then,' Marlene says sharply from above. 'I have some show and tell of my own.' Haloed in the gantry lantern's glare, she leans over the railing like an opera diva ready to spout an aria. Trust her to go for the theatrical reveal.

'It's about my sperm donor.'

I glance at Doug.

'We met here every Sunday and did it like hobos in that disgusting room. I jerked him off into a jar. It turned him on like crazy. Ask him. He especially liked it when I wore a prayer shawl.'

I think back to my first visit here. That explains the sequin in the sackcloth.

'The candles and the porn were for ambience?' I enquire.

'Doug's idea of foreplay.' She snorts. 'But he didn't care about the décor so long as he got his equipment serviced.' She turns to Doug. 'You thought you were going to be a daddy, didn't you?'

'The little fellas are excellent swimmers,' he says, and Marlene begins to laugh hysterically. She's been treading such a tightrope of manipulation and deceit, I wonder if something's finally snapped.

'I lied, Dougy,' she coos. 'Someone else was going to do those particular honours, because you're firing blanks. I saw the results onscreen at the fertility clinic and none of them were even wriggling. You've got two saggy scrotal sacs of duds!'

'You lying cunt.' Doug goes for the stairs.

He reaches her in a series of heavy-footed lunges, but she lifts one spike-heeled foot with the agility of a kickboxer and shoves it straight in his chest.

I revise my opinion of stilettos. Speed *and* accuracy.

Surprised by her unexpected force, Doug is sent down a couple of steps. He grabs the railing and the entire construction judders. He launches for her again. This time the railing snaps off in his hand like a piece of peanut brittle and he tips forward, nose to metal.

As he struggles upright, there's an almighty crack. The structure beneath him sags, unhitched from the gantry, a metre gap opening to where Marlene is on the landing. He scrabbles for a hold as the stairs tilt and strain and the anchor bolts are wrenched from their base plates. Then the entire structure buckles like meccano and crashes to the ground, Doug with it.

We rush to where he's contorting, eyes wide, on the concrete, his body tangled in rusty iron. The piece of stairway poking from his chest doesn't look good.

'Oh my God, oh my God!' Marlene shrieks from above as Doug vomits a gout of blood, and a pool of black begins to seep across the pale cement.

Anwar and the protection duo crouch both sides of him, trying to staunch the flow, but it's coming out of so many places. The next spurt gets them all.

Doug's body tenses to hiccup another viscous mass, then goes slack in a long gurgling exhalation, like a drain emptying.

One of the protection duo has her fingers pressed to his carotid. Appalled, we wait. She looks up at us, shaking her head.

'Inshallah.' Anwar passes a hand across Doug's eyes and closes the lids.

In the shocked silence, the sounds of the outside begin to filter back. Marlene totters around the gantry and clunks noisily down the far steps, oblivious to their missing bits. She crosses the factory floor, stopping a safe distance from where Doug's body has been skewered by wreckage.

'Oh my God,' she moans, hand over mouth.

'Salisbury,' Gail says quietly. 'Would you fetch the blanket from the office?'

30

Ferguson's big front doors have been dragged open, Anwar using the crowbar to break the rusty locks. Revealed outside is an impressive line-up of fetishistically accessorised custom rebuilds parked nose to tail.

The circle opens for the protection duo's nondescript van to reverse up to the entrance, then Doug's wrapped body is carried out and slid in the back while Marlene leans against a wall, sobbing inconsolably. Anyone would think she'd just lost her one true love. There's no sign now of where Doug met his demise, the clean-up executed with such clinical efficiency that I suspect the Red Quarter two have done this before.

We exit the factory blood-spattered and filthy, but it doesn't seem to bother Skinny. Growing up a gender transgressive in Melbourne's gangland 'burbs would have been a Lord of the Flies experience.

'Pleasure doing business,' he says to Gail and Anwar, shaking their hands.

He comes over to me and murmurs, 'Hot stuff, your boss. You should bring her to the Bend for a race meet. I'll show her some classier ways to get a thrill. As for you, Andy Pandy ...' He eyes me in a fresh appraisal. 'Got your place in Black Beauty reserved.'

He's an incorrigible flirt and a rock-solid ally. Small wonder Lola loves him to bits.

'See you there,' I reply, and this time I mean it.

I thread my way between two handsome fenders and cross the factory car park to collect my bike. Closer, I see the gate has fallen on it. Closer still, I see the gate is *flattened* on it. When the cavalcade bulldozed their way in, they must have run over both. I stare in dismay at the mangled blue frame and wheel rims with their spokes popped out; once such a thing of beauty and grace, a thing of joy. Nearby, my helmet is just shattered pieces of shell and strap.

I prop up the gate, then drag the bike out and carry it back across the car park, bits dropping all the way.

A racer approaches me from the pack: Skinny's rival from the night Anwar and I handed over the racing fats.

'That yours?' she says, consternated.

I nod.

'I'm real sorry. The Purple Princess went over so easy — I never saw nothin but the gate.'

I look to her truck, the parade leader. My bike was crushed by a bruise-coloured six-wheeler twin cab.

'That's okay,' I say, watching Gail help Anwar close the factory doors. 'It's just a thing. Replaceable.'

I lay the bike in the back of Anwar's van. There'll be time later to grieve.

The racer crowd have moved en masse to the middle of the car park where Doug's eco-lite has been stripped of all its bits, the sad brown metal shell now getting enthusiastically doused with something flammable.

The first puffs of black smoke go up and the racers cheer.

'We should leave before the bonfire celebration,' Gail suggests.

Dressed in a borrowed tee and trackpants while my clothes are being washed and dried, I'm sitting with Anwar in Gail's living room, ensconced in the cushiony depths of her comfy white couch. The light of early morning filters benignly through her French doors. I could almost believe the last several hours have been a trick of my imagination — except my raw skin smarts under the surgical dressings on one palm and hip, and my urbane boss is bruised and limping.

Barefoot in loose linen pants and shirt, she pours tea the colour of a Scottish burn into three pristine china cups. The sugar goes in, granules slid off a silver teaspoon. I don't know how she manages it, but everything with her is so effortlessly aesthetic.

She hands Anwar his, the chafe marks on her wrists showing against the pale fabric.

'Something's been bothering me,' I say.

She glances up, teacup poised. 'And what's that?'

'Do I swagger?'

She sets the cup on its saucer. 'Yes, you do. It's peculiarly endearing.' Her gaze is gently mocking.

Well, that's sorted then.

'I'm sorry it took so long to find you,' I tell her.

I don't want to imagine what it must have been like, forty-eight hours in Ferguson's office, Doug as keeper.

'I had the utmost faith in you and Anwar to come through,' she replies, lowering carefully into an armchair.

'Thanks to Skinny, and no thanks to Marlene.' *Or me.* I try not to think about how many clues I'd missed in the lead-up. Not a natural sleuth.

'We'll still honour our guarantee to her,' Anwar says.

I look at him beside me on the couch, freshly showered and wrapped in a borrowed dressing gown. Leaving the paint factory, Marlene had refused point-blank to ride with a dead body, so he'd driven her home in his van. Now she's going to be rewarded for her services with a regular supply of hormones, gratis. But how, exactly, did she help us? A single phone call to Doug made under guard at the Shangri-La.

'My mistake,' Gail says quietly, 'was not seeing beyond Marlene's narcissistic baby obsession to her involvement in the bigger game. Jilted, she's a spiteful creature, and once Doug's plan was under way, she couldn't resist feeding me the story about a new player at Fishermans Bend, even if it risked them being discovered. She wanted to see me rattled — but even more, she wanted to do the rattling.'

'Why did you believe her?'

'There was no reason not to. She gets to hear a lot of things at the Glory Hole. This one had the ring of truth.'

So Gail's 'little birdie' informant was actually a big glittery bird. Who hadn't Marlene betrayed? I wonder how much was intended retaliation, her going to the Neighbourly Arms and hooking up with Doug, and how much was simply the compulsion to salve rejection with more sex.

My thoughts swing to someone else whose motives I haven't entirely got a handle on. 'Mojo Meg sided with us at the speakeasy when she didn't have to. If she was prepared to do that, I don't get why she hung you out to dry till then.'

'Meg has no respect for those she thinks show weakness in their business dealings,' Gail answers. 'That I would let EHg and my own company be compromised like that was a sign of weakness to her. Her move to try and get C&C's buyers list first, through you, was a pragmatic one — but everything changed once she realised it was Doug, an *outsider*, trying to muscle in on the Ethical network.'

'I would never have given away anyone on the list,' I say, dismayed.

'I know that,' Gail responds. 'I *counted* on it. Don't blame Meg for the recruitment drive; you're too good a courier not to try to steal.'

Another thing occurs to me. 'Marlene said Doug was going to "sort" his farm contact, but now we'll never know who that was.'

She looks at me. 'He did sort the guy; and then told me in some detail how …' She rubs her wrists. 'Remember the Rohypnol incident logged with Drugs Watch? It turns out that dairy worker was Doug's supplier.'

An alarm starts in my head.

'He was the caretaker of the dairy, and had access to all areas,' she continues. 'Apparently, when he realised he'd been drugged by on APV cell, he saw a way to get his revenge. The farm does a sideline in growth-hormone extracts got from the foals they send to the knackery. He'd been siphoning off some of the stuff and delivering it to Doug at Fishermans Bend for a cash dividend from Gateway Enterprises. The batch he'd put aside for his usual Sunday delivery was in the distillery room. He knew the EHg brand name was being used as the Trojan horse, and in his mind it's people like those in the APV who buy that non-animal-cruelty stuff. He thought by spiking the batch he was poisoning his enemies.'

The alarm has cut out, replaced by a sickening realisation. *We'd* Rohypnoled Doug's inside man. Our last horse rescue had set the wheels in motion for an angry act of retaliation, and subsequently caused Albee's brush with death. He — and unknown others — had gone through what they had because of us.

I feel completely winded. I put my head in my hands.

'Salisbury?' Gail's voice is sharp with concern.

I can't drag my eyes from the floorboards. 'That was our raid,' I say weakly. 'A joint operation with another cell.'

'I know,' she replies sympathetically. 'Don't beat yourself up over this. You couldn't have foreseen Doug's scheme colliding with an APV rescue, or that Greengate's caretaker would exact retribution in the way he did.'

Kind words, but I don't feel any better. Our actions have rippled into a widening pool of disastrous consequences.

Belatedly, I realise why the snoop trips to Fishermans Bend and surveillance at Ferguson's had been a failure. Sundays were delivery day. That first Sunday, I'd seen the marker but mistaken the clues; the next — just after the horse rustling — Geeta had been attacked and Anwar lost his tyres, neither of us anywhere near the paint factory when Doug would have been heat-stamping the polystyrene shells containing the OP-spiked kit. Two nights later, Marlene would have told him she'd accidentally poisoned Albee: end of Plan A.

I groan. The bitter irony is if I'd let Lydia loose in the distillery to do the damage she'd so wanted to, Doug's guy wouldn't have had the opportunity to spike anything.

'Salisbury.' Gail commands my attention, and I obey.

She leans forward. 'I know what you're thinking, but the alternative is inaction. For fighters like you, that isn't a choice. It's why the people around you trust you and look out for you' — she throws a glance at Anwar — 'even if you don't know it most of the time. It's why you're here now, sitting on that couch drinking tea. Never doubt that. I don't.'

She sits back. In the ensuing silence the images of my life reel like film: twenty-nine years, and a catalogue of struggle. Under Nation First, things will only get worse for transgressives, but this is about the animals in the hormone farms, and turning a blind eye to the atrocities means abandoning them to an unbearable fate.

I check sideways at Anwar, and remember him wielding the crowbar in Gail's defence, no doubt in my mind as to whether he would use it. Doug underestimated all of us, not just Marlene.

My thoughts return to Ferguson's and the two NVB lackeys left to sleep off their sedative jabs. They'll be waking soon with sore bones and gaps in their memories. The factory space devoid of clues, they'll try to put the pieces together with the others who escaped, but they'll never find their self-serving captain. I can't help thinking one day there'll be a reckoning: the five secretly nursing their injured pride until it rises into retaliatory action like a gas bubble bursting from a bog. I just hope we'll be ready when that happens.

Gail tips back the dregs of her tea. 'Come see the garden,' she says.

31

Walking isn't so bad, especially on a day like this, the city washed with a sudden shower then swept through by an invigorating southerly. Sun slices down between the clouds, steam rising off the pavement. It makes me feel restless and excited, as if this small part of the world has been imbued with fresh hope, the possibility of change.

Rosie greets me at the speakeasy's door with a broad grin. 'Mate — that was a wicked night. You come out of it okay?' She stands back to inspect me.

'Yeah, I'm fine,' I tell her, hoping she won't ask about Doug. 'Gail's back with us.'

She punches her fist in the air. 'You can't keep a good transgressive down,' she says, all fired up.

No, you can't. But some people can do a damn good job of trying.

I glance into the unattended cloakroom: Gabe's day off and no replacement for Marlene yet. As if there ever could

313

be. Her dislike of me made plain, I'm wondering if I'll be haunted by her sequinned spectre from now on. Doug may have been the mastermind of their scheme, but out of the two of them I think of her as the more devious. And now Doug is dead, while she's who-knows-where …

I descend the stairs. The lunchtime crowd is in and upbeat, a din emanating from the bar area. I glance to where Sandy and Merlyn are maintaining their usual vigil outside Meg's alcove, the boss's curtains open behind them.

Meg nods to me from her table then speaks to Merlyn, who leaves her post and comes towards me. Instinctively, I step back, but she's holding out the jacket hauled off me in the Rob Roy. I take it gratefully. It's my favourite.

Sandy joins us. I brace for the backslap, delivered today with extra enthusiasm.

'You still on the lemonade wagon?' she asks. 'Whaddya say to a soft drink sometime with me and Merl? Your shout.'

She laughs, and I get a reprise image of her downing schooners of ale like water. I make some noises of agreement then watch them trek back to their stations. If my stint at Prestige Couriers has shown me nothing else, it's that there's hope yet for Meg's universally disliked minders.

Something sparkles in the air. Trin is flipping glasses for a row of worshippers at the bar. Who could resist those well-toned arms in their muscle shirt?

My mobile burrs in my hand. It's Max. 'Welcome back,' he says. 'We missed you.'

News travels fast. At least this time it's good news.

'By the way,' he adds, 'I've saved you a place in the chicken rescue van.'

'Glad to hear it. I'll swing by for my instructions.'

I pocket the mobile and scan for Tallis.

The call from SANE's emergency coordinator had come while I was in Gail's garden, Gail relaying her request to see me. I'd leapt at the opportunity to visit her again in her peaceful enclave, but she'd suggested a change of scenery.

I see her standing by an alcove and go over.

She shepherds me in. 'Savannah and I were just comparing notes on a mutual acquaintance,' she says, one hand on my arm, the other signalling to the bar staff for coffee.

Her companion rises with a catlike grace. She's clad in slim-fit jeans and a sky-blue chambray shirt. Why is it I always feel so awed by her presence? Here are two of the most impressive — and contrasting — women I know. Add Gail to the mix and you have a formidable team.

All of us seated, Tallis starts proceedings by saying, 'Roshani's café friend was no SADA worker.'

Even here, Geeta gets to keep her work alias.

'The name she gave, Angela Morgan, didn't correspond to any of our workers, past or present,' Tallis continues, 'so Savannah suggested we use the brokers' lists to look at the *applicants* for the Ovum Recipient Program across the last couple of years. That's when we noticed something odd. Several who'd been rejected pre-interview as emotionally unsuitable to enter into an embryo-transfer agreement, had

315

all requested precisely the same attributes for their desired ovum donor. No prizes for guessing whose.'

I have to think. 'Marlene, under various aliases, was trying to engineer a "perfect match" with Gail?'

'Right,' Tallis replies. 'Egg donors can use more than one broker if they choose. Miss Bott, not being privileged with that information, applied to them all.'

'Rejection doesn't faze her then,' I say, and Tallis concurs wryly.

Our attention is momentarily diverted by three coffees arriving on a tray. I sip. The brew is good — but not as good as Frank's.

Savannah takes up the thread. 'Brokers don't usually compare rejections, so it took a bit of digging to put the pieces together. None of those failed candidates checked out as being real. As for Marlene, she may have created a new identity on paper each time, but she couldn't pass the psych evaluations. She began to woo Gail directly, and somehow figured out her arrangement was with me and the fertility centre in Cutters Lane. That's when things got dangerous.'

It occurs to me that Marlene might have been behind the prayer group's midnight attack in the Red Quarter if she was desperate enough for what was in my courier's bag.

'In the course of applying for and being rejected from the OR Program, Marlene befriended Roshani,' Tallis inserts. 'She must have marked the poor girl soon after she moved into the sponsored accommodation. She told her she worked for SADA and suggested they meet regularly.

Roshani didn't have any reason to disbelieve her, but apparently "Angela" got spooky and intense at their café tête-è-têtes.'

'What was she after?' I ask.

'Insider information ... a vicarious experience of pregnancy ... We don't really know. Eventually Roshani said she couldn't meet her any more and that's when we think Marlene, miffed, did what she does best. She retaliated by setting the dogs on her new friend. Probably an anonymous tip to one of the vigilante squads who go about the city doing "God's work".' Tallis rubs a hand across her temple. 'Roshani was attacked and lost the baby because of Marlene's spite.'

I glance at Savannah, who looks grim, and silently apologise to the Nancarrows at the Tea House for thinking they might have had anything to do with this. It's far too easy in a climate of restriction and fear to suspect everyone and their aunty of being a potential NF card-carrier or Neighbourly Watch stooge. They're probably just your run-of-the-mill busybodies.

My thoughts turn to Helen. If she were ever to find out who was responsible for the miscarriage, it wouldn't be just Michael after Doug, it'd be her after Marlene. Those two in confrontation is not a happy thought.

'So Marlene didn't know whose baby Roshani was carrying?' I'm careful not to divulge names.

'She couldn't have,' Tallis responds. 'She knew enough about the donor and surrogacy system to fool Roshani, but she never got inside SADA, and Roshani couldn't have told her who her recipients were because she didn't know.'

I finish the dregs of my coffee. 'How's Roshani now?'

'Contemplating a rosy future. She's been rehoused and is working as an admin assistant for us at SANE. Weekends, she's with Braheem at the markets.'

'I was thinking of dropping in there sometime,' I say, too embarrassed to add that being in their company last Friday gave me back some hope for sibling relationships everywhere. As for mine with Helen, I don't know. To keep her world order from tipping into chaos, she'd provided me with the means to rescue Gail, but will that change anything between us?

'I'm sure they'd both love to see you.' Tallis rises from her seat, and I follow suit.

She hugs me warmly. 'And that's the end of it, as far as Marlene goes. We hope.'

My heart is singing hallelujah choruses. Albee's out of his coma and about to be discharged, and Gail has escaped Doug's ministrations at Ferguson's unharmed. I've been home and told the cat; now, scrubbed and combed and in fresh clothes, I'm too impatient for the hospital lifts. I take the fire stairs in exultant pairs and triples, then push on the door to the medical wards.

I stride the corridor and launch into Albee's room — and stop. Inez is sitting in the armchair on the far side of his bed.

My heart rams into my throat and cuts off my breath. Someone get me the oxygen mask.

Ellie enters the room behind me, a takeaway coffee in each hand.

'At last!' she exclaims, and kisses my cheek. 'We'd decided Meg had kidnapped you, and were planning to send in a Red Quarter protection team to get you back.'

Not as far from the truth as she might think. My eyes go to Inez then Albee propped up on pillows.

'Salisbury,' he says, his face one big smile.

'By the way,' Ellie whispers in my ear, 'Albee and I decided it was time Inez came for a visit. Then, of course, you made yourself scarce. You're a hard one to keep tabs on.' She gives me a little nudge forward then hands Inez her coffee.

I stop at the foot of the bed, feeling gawky and shy. The past week has been a nightmare of fast-emerging fears: some realised — Marlene and Doug's collusion to bring Gail down; and some vanquished — the news of Gail's OD, and Albee's near-death experience; but I truly thought I'd lost Inez, and now I very badly want the chance to change the ending.

I lift my gaze to her and she smiles crookedly.

'Hey,' she says.

The touchpaper of hope. A flame flickers in my hurting heart and the awkwardness eases a little.

As I move around the bed, Inez reaches out her hand. Tentatively I take it, and feel that warm, capable grip, so missed and so longed for, again in mine.

Albee grins at us like a naughty schoolboy.

'You …' I say to him. 'You're a bucket-load of trouble, matey.' But *acceptance* is what I'm really thinking: the gift of loving friends.

Inez drives me to a park east of the city grid, and arm in arm we walk the shadowed paths below moulting elms, the sparrows clustered in the bunya pines noisily chirruping in the dusk. The Fidelity Gardens conservatory is one of her favourite places. She has a whole bunch of them she likes to visit — secret nooks in various inner-city locations discovered over the short time she's lived here — and I want to be the only one she shows them to.

The building is Spanish Mission style, its pillars and archways flanked all sides by bleached brownlands that used to be grass. At the northern entrance, a magpie is jackhammering for worms under a giant date palm. With so little beneath the surface of such dry ground, even the battle-hardened ruffians of suburbia are doing it tough.

We open the glass door, its loose panes rattling, and are immediately enveloped by a thick humidity of light-suffused green. We follow the walkway over a bridge to a bench seat set amid a profusion of broad, rubbery leaves. Above us delicately beaded stems trail flowers; beside, a channel trickles water into a pond, the ferns in the rock crevices unfurling pristine new fronds and the bromeliads displaying their exotic wet interiors.

'No one comes in here mid-week,' Inez whispers, her breath tickling my ear.

Our bodies move close and we kiss standing, mouth hungrily on mouth, the scents that slough off our skin mingling with the lush perfume of the plants.

I lower onto the seat, drawing her down to face me, her knees astride my lap. A trickle of sweat glistens on her neck. It reaches her collarbone and is held there, glittering in the scoop of bone, a perfect teardrop. I watch, fascinated; I want to press my lips to her hot brown skin and lap like a kitten.

The glass door rattles and three people enter. Inez laughs softly and rolls off my lap. Today we don't care that we are perverts and miscreants and could be arrested for our public display. They move through the greenhouse, not really looking, and exit via the door at the opposite end. They must have picked up the transgressor vibe.

Cuddled together on the bench, we talk awhile, filling in the gaps of the last few days for each other. No one else arrives through the door, the building's subtropical interior a private wonderland kept just for us.

My unhappy girlfriend had buried herself in work, one of her jobs being for Savannah, who'd quickly winkled out the cause of her barriers-up demeanour. Savannah knows Ellie, and Ellie talked to Albee when he woke … Inez smiles and shrugs, the rest known.

'Sal.' She faces me, all levity aside. 'I'm sorry about my behaviour in the speakeasy, but the last person I committed to, heart and soul, cheated on me with her Pilates teacher. The affair went on for months until I found out: a sex text from her to him, sent to me by accident. I was shattered. It's the main reason I relocated to Melbourne. I felt so betrayed, I couldn't stay in the same city as her.'

She looks away. I reach for her hand and enclose it in mine.

'So when you said you were ditching Gail to go work for Meg — the *enemy*, in my book — I overreacted, as if it was happening all over again: someone I thought I knew, and was beginning to trust, doing something that revealed them to be the opposite. Then, when I realised it was Gail putting you at risk, I felt really angry. I was afraid of what you were getting yourself into, and what all that secrecy and subterfuge would do to us.' She pauses. 'It was Savannah who put me right — not by giving away any confidences, but by giving me *context*. She made me realise I should trust you, and hang in there like you wanted me to. It was hard not seeing you after the news of Gail's OD, but Savannah asked me to sit tight while things played out. She had her eye on the bigger picture.' A smile emerges. 'I wish I'd seen her flexing her professional muscles on Marlene.'

'It was an experience to treasure,' I reply.

I bring my arm around her and she gets a pained expression. 'What?' I draw back, worried I've done something.

She laughs. 'I was imagining Savannah giving Marlene a *real* lashing, and I bit the inside of my lip.'

My tongue searches for the wound. I find it, and taste blood. It's unbearably sexy. We breathe into each other as we kiss, and the myriad sensations coalesce, become an emotional cascade. Inez strokes up inside my thigh and every muscle in me aches with want: to fuck right here among the ruby-throated flowers and light-splecked leaves; to fuck and hold her till we're both drenched in sweat and weeping.

32

Albee's in his workshop the next afternoon when I arrive at Bike Heaven, the OPEN sign affixed to new glass. I call out, then on his reply stroll down an aisle of shelving to where he's seated at the workbench, oiling the chain and working the gear changes on a mountain bike that's seen better days.

'Hey, Mr Wainwright,' I say, handing him his car keys.

He shrugs out of his vinyl work apron and stands up shakily, using the bench as a prop. We hug. It's apparent how much weight he's lost. I'm careful not to squeeze too hard.

Underneath the apron he's spruce in jeans, a pressed shirt and thin black tie.

'You look nice.'

'I'm going back to the hospital later,' he says casually.

I look at him in surprise. 'What for?'

'A few things to do.'

I spy the roses wrapped and ribboned atop the bar fridge. 'Any of them with flowers?'

He looks bashful. 'They're a thank you for Sarah.'

'Albee, you wouldn't happen to be carrying a torch for your nice ICU nurse, would you?' I tease, and he blushes furiously.

I lean on the bench and smile up at him. 'She's one very cool RN.'

A gleam comes into his eye. 'I've got something for you.'

He goes slowly down the aisle that leads to the door of his flat, then disappears and comes out again wheeling a bike. It's an electric-blue racer with black cranks and handlebars. A thing of beauty; a thing of joy.

'I was very sorry to hear what happened to your old treadly,' he says, 'but it's time you upgraded. This one's a rocket — smooth as ...'

I'm only half listening as he gives a loving rundown of components.

'Albee.' Tears prick. Words fail me.

He gestures me to take it.

I test its weight. Lighter than my old one. Setting it back down, I fit my hands to the bars and squeeze the brakes. Already I can tell the angles and distances have been tailored to me, and I feel a flush of excitement at the thought of riding it.

'What do I owe you?'

'Nothing.'

'But I need to pay you something. This is an expensive build, and you're about to get a swag of hospital bills.'

'Rubbish,' he says. 'It's a gift. I had it all ready to go, before ...'

He's teared up, and I'm in no better state. We've weathered a lot together — some pretty dramatic changes across the years — and are both still here.

A wave of regret rushes in on me. 'I have to tell you about the last few weeks.'

He looks at me candidly, then goes to the bar fridge and opens the door wide. Bottles glint green, labels out: Tasmanian tigers all in a row. 'These will be waiting for the moment,' he says. 'Until then, I don't care about the details. Now go, my friend, and ride your new bike.'

I'm spinning along the cycle tracks from South Melbourne to the city, exhilarated by the kinaesthetic sync of parts, body with machine. It's like being a kid again on my revelatory first ride.

I cross the Port Melbourne tramway and dip under a low-level bridge, monitoring how the bike reacts with my shifting weight and adjusting to its subtle differences in gearing. I can't fault the mechanism — it's as smooth as silk; there's even a new pair of my favourite soft-cage strap-ons fitted to the pedals.

The cityscape slides by, other cyclists whizzing past. But I'm in no hurry, having given over completely to the pleasure of the ride, and the relief of knowing that tomorrow I will be couriering again for Gail.

Earlier in the day, I'd dodged the cyclists scurrying in and out of the roller entrance on Banana Alley to give back

Meg's envelope of cash. She'd refused it. 'Call it a shift's pay,' she'd said from behind her oversized desk. 'If you ever want to do some more work for Prestige Couriers, you know where we are.'

I'd left with the money, but it didn't feel right. So now I have a delivery to make.

I head north along the wide city avenues into Carlton, zigzagging through the suburb until I get to a small acacia-lined street. Halfway along, I ride up onto the pavement and dismount.

The Carlton Animal Shelter is grey and featureless from the front, the barred windows making it look like a remand centre and belying the atmosphere of kindness that flourishes inside. Its warren of partitioned spaces includes a vet clinic and small operating theatre, several rooms of comfy cages and a corridor of aquaria leading to a sprawling backyard populated with hutches, kennels and runs, all bounded by some very high fences set with security cameras.

This is the shelter I got Nitro from eight years ago.

It's after hours now, the office closed. I walk in the gate and the security lights trigger, illuminating my way to the door.

I could ring the bell and bring out the night vet, but instead I lift the steel mail flap in the wall and pop my envelope through the slot. It lands with a satisfying thud on the floor behind.

Knock & drop.

The gate clicks shut. I swing a leg over my beautiful new bike, and ride on.

Acknowledgements

Big thanks to Stephanie and all the folk at HarperCollins, and to Nicola, editor extraordinaire: a second book! Also to Ruth, Brenda, Jake, Rob, my trusty readers and expert advisors, for their huge generosity and enthusiasm. Technical help came from many quarters. Thanks go to Jenny Rochow, nurse unit manager of the ICU at Canberra Hospital, Colette Needham, Emma Whyte, Dr Elizabeth Minchin, Danielle Tassius, PPG Coatings, and to Don, Lisa, and Anne for some timely first aid. Special thanks to Miriana, Jamie, the lovely Josh, and all the wonderful staff at Milk&Honey for my treasured corner in their café house, and to Greer for her perfect image of Salisbury's bike on my website. Also to Beth, Mary-Lou, Alan, Patrick, and the people close in my heart who've helped me these past two years to find the shining space between dark and dark*. This story pays homage the many groups that work against the cruelty of the bile and factory farming industries, including those tireless champions of the animals, the Voiceless team, and Animals Asia. This story is also for gender explorers everywhere: *not* fantasy. Not science fiction.

*Jeanette Winterson (*The Guardian* interview 2010) from a Robert Graves poem